Deadly Quiet

The Eliza Fox Files

DEADLY QUIET

The Eliza Fox Files

CATHLEEN WATKINS

Torchflame Books

Vista, CA

ISBN: 978-1-61153-386-6 (paperback)
ISBN: 978-1-61153-396-5 (ebook)

Library of Congress Control Number: 2024905507

Deadly Quiet is published by: Torchflame Books, an imprint of Top Reads Publishing, LLC, USA

For information about special discounts for bulk purchases, please direct emails to: publisher@torchflamebooks.com

Cover design: Jori Hanna
Book interior layout: Teri Rider

Printed in the United States of America

Cover images: Adobe Stock

Dedication

Remembering Ettore and Lucia, who taught me so much.

Consider your origin.
You were not formed to live like brutes, but to follow
virtue and knowledge.

Dante Alighieri, *The Divine Comedy*

CHAPTER 1

Tuesday, May 7

Kendra closed her laptop and picked up her phone. Again. Maybe she'd missed Martina's text. She and her roommate, Martina Noto, had agreed to meet on campus around 11 a.m. for a late breakfast, and Martina was supposed to text when she left Carter House. It was 11:20 a.m., and still no message.

Kendra was more hungry than worried. Martina had left the condo around 8:30 a.m. for the practice rooms at Carter. She had wanted to get to the piano early before those officially enrolled as music students arrived. Although she was a computer science major, Martina had a love affair with Debussy and was polishing a piece for a fast-approaching recital.

Kendra had texted and called Martina repeatedly that morning, but no response. Because Kendra was a worrier, she checked the Find My Friends app, confirming that Martina's phone was at Carter. Kendra knew how absorbed Martina could be when she was practicing and figured she'd give her another five minutes. Then she'd walk to the practice rooms and physically pull her away from the piano. The girl had to eat.

Kendra and Martina first met the previous August, just before the fall semester started. Martina, a student at University of Bologna, was beginning a one-year study abroad program at Wexford College. At the time, Kendra needed a roommate to share her off-campus condo. The housing office put them in touch.

Kendra sometimes felt inferior to Martina, cast as the tugboat guiding the glamorous ocean liner on foreign waters. Martina was unlike most of the students at Wexford, and Kendra found her mesmerizing. Having grown up in Rome, Martina was more.... What word did Kendra want? It was obvious that she was more global than her American counterparts, especially since she spoke three languages fluently. But there was something about Martina's composure. She was less needy than Kendra's peers, more self-contained.

Kendra attributed this largely to Martina's appearance. She was beautiful in a no-need-for-make-up way. Without any effort on Martina's part, men openly ogled her as she passed, eyeing her long legs and curvy torso. Martina could throw on a bulky sweater and some leggings, her chestnut waves gathered loosely in a clip at the top of her head, and look terrific.

Kendra envied how confident her roommate was, but she knew some of their classmates saw Martina as aloof. Kendra overheard the comments -- the Italian girl was "stuck up," "privileged," or "a snobby rich kid who was too good to chill."

Wexford had seemed an odd choice, given that Martina could have gone anywhere to study. Wexford was a small college embedded in San Vicente, a suburb hugging the foothills north of Los Angeles. Kendra, herself, had picked it because it was close enough to the beach and her hometown of Encinitas, just north of San Diego. The locale allowed Kendra to surf when she wanted or make a quick trip home if she felt disconnected. Martina told Kendra that she chose Wexford because she was a computer geek—part of the Girls Who Code group—and Wexford had a strong computer science program.

Whatever. Martina was a very good roommate who paid her rent and washed up her dishes. Kendra didn't need more than that.

She looked at her phone again and then got moving. Kendra vowed to hit the library that afternoon as she slipped her bio notebook and laptop into her backpack, aware that she needed some serious study hours before the rapidly approaching final exam.

Kendra began the steep climb to Carter House. The clouds were burning off, and it was going to be a nice LA afternoon. Her thoughts drifting to the beach, Kendra wondered if the Tuesday traffic would allow her to slip in a sunset surfing session at Hermosa Beach. It seemed unlikely if she was going to keep her pledge to study all afternoon.

About a ten-minute walk from the condo, Carter House was situated just outside the main entrance to campus in a large craftsman built at the turn of the previous century. The Carter family had gifted the house and the surrounding acreage to Wexford in the 1980s, with instructions that it be used for the arts. The college also had to maintain the park-like grounds around the house. The upper floor, which was bathed in natural light, was dedicated to the visual art students, mostly painters and sculptors, while the basement had been converted to a maze of tiny practice closets, each with a small piano. The main level housed a small theater for live performance and films. One of Carter's rules, strictly enforced, was no food, so Kendra knew Martina would be starving, especially if she had been practicing for three hours.

Kendra crossed the wide green lawn in front of Carter and climbed the stone porch steps. She swiped her keycard, waiting for the door to unlock. Once inside, Kendra found the staircase to the lower level and skipped lightly down. She could hear the flutes, the violins, and the voice majors, all contributing to the clamor.

Kendra listened for a piano but could only make out a jazz melody coming from a room near the staircase. She doubted Martina was playing jazz, and it was unlikely she would have chosen a room so near the stairs. Martina preferred the practice room at the east end of the hall because of its large window.

Kendra pulled out her phone again to see if Martina had texted in the past ten minutes. Nothing, so she headed toward the eastside rooms and dialed Martina's phone, its ring tone meant to resemble a vintage phone from the 1960s. Kendra strained to hear it, then smiled as she stood outside of Martina's favorite practice room and discerned the familiar sound of her friend's phone. But instead of Martina's usual *salve* when she answered, the call went to voicemail. Kendra knocked loudly on the door, incredulous that Martina was ignoring her.

"Hey, I'm starving. And you're late. Let's go," Kendra barked, turning the doorknob and pushing on the heavy, old door, surprised when it only opened about a foot.

"Martina, open the door."

Impatient and truly worried now, Kendra put her shoulder to the door and put some force into it, pushing it wide enough to squeeze her head inside. Martina was lying on the floor on her side, the piano bench upturned and preventing Kendra from entering easily.

"What are you doing?" Kendra demanded, at first not making sense of what she saw.

And then Kendra recognized the scene for the devastating thing that it was. She pushed the door open a few more inches and managed to wiggle into the room. Navigating around the piano bench, she turned Martina onto her back. Kendra looked at her friend's frozen gaze, confirming the lifelessness in Martina's dark brown eyes. With a scream climbing from deep in her gut, Kendra jumped back from the body and collapsed on the dirty, thin carpet. In a panic, Kendra turned and maneuvered out of the airless room. The quizzical voices of the other students wafted from the adjacent practice rooms as Kendra sprinted toward the nearest bathroom, vomiting into the first trashcan she found.

Even as she wretched, Kendra continued to hear the even beat of Martina's metronome. *Click. Click. Click.*

CHAPTER TWO

Tuesday, May 7—Midday

Eliza Fox was standing outside when the first helicopter passed over her house. She had been tending plants in the backyard of her small, rented home while Lucas, her four-year-old son, kicked a ball nearby. She pulled the garden gloves from her hands and ran her fingers through her chin-length brown waves as she looked skyward. Eliza had been about to head inside to make lunch for Lucas, when he loudly yelled, "Ambulance!" delighted at the sound of the distant sirens. Then another helicopter, a police copter, flew overhead. Eliza assumed the commotion was in response to a bad accident on the freeway that ribboned the foothills just north of their neighborhood in San Vicente.

Lucas was enthralled by all types of emergency vehicles and aircraft. While he settled on the grass to monitor the skies, Eliza went inside to find her phone. Maybe she could pick up a news bulletin about whatever was going on.

As a thirty-three-year-old single mom, Eliza loved living in the normally quiet city of San Vicente. It had the benefit of being close enough to LA to enjoy great restaurants, live music, and a vibrant arts scene. At the same time, she could hike in the local mountains, go for a run in her neighborhood, or ride her bike to the grocery store. She had the advantage of living in a community where she knew most of her neighbors and could turn to one of them if she needed a favor.

She felt safe, and that mattered to her as a parent who lived alone with a young child.

To blend in some excitement, Eliza's job in downtown LA at a boutique law firm was never boring, and she appreciated that this was a rare gift. As part of its caseload, Fowler & Haverford handled numerous class actions, and the attorneys relied on her skills as an investigator and paralegal to locate potential victims of whatever matter they were pursuing. She also did background investigations and property research, all in civil cases. Eliza was especially happy when one of the partners, a former prosecutor, brought in a criminal case. These often involved an elected official accused of malfeasance or a sports celebrity in legal trouble over domestic violence charges or a serious driving offense. When these cases were active, Eliza's workday was different; the media was underfoot and their cases made headlines. Mostly Eliza enjoyed putting the puzzle pieces together, finding information that would help the attorneys build their case.

As a girl, she wanted to be a lawyer, and maybe she'd get there when Lucas was older. For now, she needed the salary the law firm paid her, acknowledging that she presently lacked the capacity to be a part-time law student. Raising a child alone had not been part of Eliza's life plan, but when was solo parenting ever in anyone's plan? She was grateful that her boss let her work from home a couple days each week, which was why she happened to be home with Lucas midday on a Tuesday.

Eliza felt badly that David, her ex-husband, was married to someone else now and had little interest in Lucas, but she couldn't fix every problem. Thankfully, his job as a lawyer paid him very well, and he reliably sent a monthly childcare check.

"È disgustoso," Eliza muttered under her breath, quoting her mother's favorite Italian one-line insult about David. While she fully agreed with this assessment, Eliza was deeply contented to be Lucas's mama.

As she waited for the water for her son's pasta to boil, she scanned the news to see what was causing the commotion. Traffic apps showed that the freeway was clear in both directions, meaning her idea about a bad accident was wrong. Eliza opened the back door and stood on the small landing at the top of the steps to look for Lucas. He was still in the same spot looking skyward.

"What do you see?" she asked.

"Choppers," he said. Eliza tilted her gaze upward as another helicopter circled over her neighborhood. It was part of the San Vicente Police Department.

"I wonder if something happened at the college," Eliza said, mostly to herself.

Remembering the water on the stove, she went back to the kitchen, calling Lucas in for his favorite lunch of angel hair with parmesan. Eliza also sat down at the small kitchen table while Lucas ate, continuing to scroll through her phone. She knew she was breaking her rule about no devices during meals, but her curiosity was piqued and overrode her usual "good mom" mode. Eliza mindlessly ate the apple slices she had set out for Lucas as she texted her friend Travis, a reporter at KCSV, the local TV news station.

> Eliza: Police choppers over campus, whatup?
> Travis: Dead student
> Eliza: Yikes. Details?
> Travis: Female idk more
> Eliza: Send word when yk

Eliza put her phone down, contemplating what this meant. Overdose? Suicide? Murder? Rape and murder? In the dorms? In a car? A classroom? Was there an immediate threat in San Vicente? A sexual predator? Serial killer? Rapist serial killer?

"Mommy," Lucas said.

"Mama!" now louder and more demanding.

"Liza!!" Lucas then barked, poking Eliza's arm. "More cheese. Please."

"Lucas, please no yelling," Eliza finally replied as she stood up from the table. "And don't call me Liza. You know I don't like it."

Eliza's phone chirped, announcing that her own mother, Francesca, was calling. She grabbed the parmesan from the fridge and her iPad from a nearby counter and handed both to Lucas.

"*Nonna* is calling, and I need to talk to her. You can play your game on my iPad."

Now she had truly broken protocol by letting Lucas play a computer game during a meal. She and her son would have to designate a technology-free day soon to make up for it. But Eliza sensed that something very unsettling was unfolding in San Vicente, and she needed to connect with Francesca, who probably had information about what was going on.

∿

Francesca Noto-Fox had reduced her teaching load about three years ago and now mostly served as an advisor on senior projects and graduate theses. Francesca had loved—still loved—her work as an art history professor. But she also adored her grandson and devoted several hours every week to caring for Lucas while Eliza worked.

Francesca had been a member of the Wexford community for nearly twenty years. She and her husband, Colin Fox, had both joined the faculty at the same time, he in the English department and she in art history. Francesca knew when they were being recruited Colin was the star the campus wanted and she was the lesser half of the package deal. But in the ensuing years, Francesca had shown her value. She served on faculty committees without complaint, earned high ratings from her students, and gave popular lectures on Renaissance art to alumni and donors at college fundraisers. When Colin had died suddenly three years ago, the Wexford community had embraced and supported her. Without noticing it, Francesca had forged deep connections in San Vicente over the years, and now this terrible news was hitting her like a gut-punch.

Francesca surveyed her garden from the kitchen window as she waited for Eliza to answer her phone. Seeing the plum tree Colin had planted, she was reminded to cover it before the birds picked at all the fruit. After four rings, Francesca half-expected the call to go to voicemail. Then she heard Eliza's voice.

"Mama," she said. "What's happening?"

A few minutes earlier, Francesca had received a campus-wide text message, and she read it to her daughter:

Dear Wexford Community,

With a heavy heart, I must sadly inform you of the death of one of our students this morning near the north quadrant of the campus. Classes have been canceled for today, and possibly tomorrow, while the police investigate. Please avoid this area and watch for further bulletins as more information develops. If you have any knowledge about this matter, you are urged to bring it to the attention of our campus law enforcement. Also use extreme caution as you navigate the campus today. This is a developing situation. Please support each other in this crisis.

President Carole Gardener

Eliza asked her mother to forward the text so she could look more carefully at the message's phrasing and content while they talked. But the message didn't reveal much. The north quadrant of the campus included dorms, classrooms, labs, and athletic fields. This incident could have occurred in any number of places. Eliza already knew from Travis that the victim was female, which was more than President Gardener had shared.

"The parts about 'a developing situation' and to 'use extreme caution' are ominous, don't you think?" Eliza said.

"What do you think they mean?"

"That the police are looking at a homicide. If it was a suicide or accidental death, the president's message would have been about offering counseling to the friends of the victim and scheduling a candlelight service and less about staying safe."

"Right," Francesca agreed. "Now you're scaring me. Do we have a killer in the area? Where's Lucas? Go lock your doors."

"Lucas is eating pasta in the kitchen. He's fine."

"Okay but lock the doors. And the windows. I'm going to make some calls, and also try to reach Martina. I haven't heard from her in a couple of weeks. I wanted to invite her to dinner anyway. Can you and Lucas come this Saturday for dinner with Martina?"

"Yeah, that's fine. We'll probably see you before then. But Saturday evening for sure. And you lock your doors, too. *Ciao,* Mama."

"*Ciao, mia figlia bella.*"

MARTINA'S JOURNAL

September 19 (Eight months earlier)

I love California, but LA is the best part. It's the openness of the place. The food's a metaphor for the whole Cali lifestyle.

Last Saturday, I started the day in the neighborhood called Highland Park with excellent breakfast tacos alongside a bottomless cup of American-style coffee (not two swallows of espresso). Around mid-afternoon I followed up with an In-N-Out burger in Pasadena, and finally spent some $$$ on a sushi dinner in the Arts District in downtown LA.

That was my "three square" as the frat boys say. Many kids party all night with whatever intoxicants suit them—tequila, designer cocktails, mocktails for my sober *amici*, California wines, edibles, other drugs. All of this while your favorite playlist provides the soundtrack. A girl could get addicted to California. Except for the avocados, which make no sense, but are everywhere, even in the sushi. Avocados are the one California thing I hate.

As a little girl growing up in Rome, I found LA enthralling. I soaked up the movies and TV, staring at the images of gritty Los Angeles, the San Francisco skyline, Beverly Hills rich kids, Santa Monica beach, even the Berkeley campus. I had to figure out a way to get here, and now I'm spending a year studying abroad at Wexford College in San Vicente. When I'm older, I want to remember my year here—all the things I loved, or maybe I found weird, or that I hated. My idea was to collect my memories in this journal. It'll be fun to read some day. I'll also practice my English as I write.

First, how did I get here? It was unimaginable that my over-protective parents were going to let me out of their control for four years to attend university in Southern California. But with Dr. Francesca Noto-Fox on the faculty at Wexford, I had a chance of their approval. Roberto, my papa, and Francesca are first cousins, a family connection that I—what do the Americans say—that I milked (???) to spend two semesters abroad at Wexford.

I began college at University of Bologna, a few hours by train from Roma, intending to spend my junior year at Wexford in San Vicente. I majored in computer science, which dovetailed nicely with my plans to study at Wexford, where they offer excellent high-tech programs and access to Silicon Valley. I bored my friends in Bologna with incessant talk about California, and they were envious, of course. Who wouldn't be?

But now that I'm away from them, perhaps I undervalued those Bologna *ragazzi.* They were real people, who I could talk to. I've been texting and facetiming with them. I have to admit I've been a little lonely and homesick. Of course, I was lucky to find Kendra and her condo. She is terrific, and her flat is close to campus. That's all *molto bene.* But the other Wexford kids—mostly the girls—have not been so nice. To be honest, they've been ugly to me.

I sense they're talking behind my back, which makes me question whether I'm speaking the right dialect of Cali English. Am I losing some nuance in the translation? The mean ones run in a pack, like she-wolves: Dahlia, Chelsea, Li-Ann, and a couple of others. I don't remember their weird American names. But Wexford is a small campus, so these kids have a wide reach. Maybe I'm exaggerating and I should give it some time. Girl friendships can be tricky. The guys are attentive to me, especially the computer geeks, but I don't want any boyfriends right now. Mostly, I spend time with Kendra, or by myself, except for dinners at my cousin Francesca's house. Eliza, Francesca's daughter, has been at dinner sometimes. We're second cousins, and I haven't spent any real time with her until now. While I was growing up in Roma, Eliza's parents were already teaching at Wexford. Our families didn't get together too often, maybe every three or four years at Christmas, when the Foxes returned to Italy to visit.

I'm impressed by Eliza and how patient she is with Lucas. While her kid is cute, he's a reminder to keep my birth control current and always have condoms handy. No *bambini*!

CHAPTER THREE

Tuesday, May 7—Still Midday

Knowing that campus police had reached Carter House ahead of him, in addition to several uniformed officers from San Vicente Police Department (SVPD), Detective Byron Comstock was worried. He was willing to bet his daughter's dachshund that the Wexford cops had contaminated the crime scene. While they were experienced with alcohol poisoning, drug offenses, stolen laptops, and maybe a rare stalking case, campus police encountered very few dead bodies and fewer murder victims, assuming a homicide had truly taken place at Carter.

Now Byron was headed for a turf war with his old mentor, Chief Gilbert Mendoza, head of Wexford's campus safety division. Undoubtedly, that unctuous people-pleaser President Gardener was going to be in the mix. While the college controlled the use of Carter House and maintained the park-like grounds, Byron was confident that policing the property fell within SVPD's jurisdiction, since the building was situated outside the campus property line.

Byron felt a familiar twinge in his gut as he remembered his troubled departure from his job at Wexford, even though eight years had passed. He had been young and naïve then, with no understanding of the power that rich donors held over college presidents. In retrospect, a tiny incident had mushroomed, as can happen with a toxic mix of money and college sports.

Byron, who had been on the campus safety squad, was working security at an important Wexford home game, the men's basketball finals, when an elderly, drunk donor got handsy with a Wexford cheerleader. Later, the consensus was that Byron had needlessly manhandled the beloved Wexy, a gentleman who had graduated from the college in the 1960s and given generously to his alma mater ever since. To complicate the story, this alumnus had not missed a Wexford Rockets home game in forty years. The video from several cell phones gave the impression that Byron was a barroom bouncer removing a belligerent drunk, which was indeed a close approximation of what had taken place.

Unfortunately, President Gardener opined later that Byron should have taken a less forceful stance. She would have preferred him to assume more of a counseling role, explaining to Mr. Millionaire that the cheerleaders were in the "do not touch" category. As if this needed to be spelled out. In the end, his boss, Chief Mendoza, negotiated a resolution that required Byron to write an apology letter and quietly end his campus employment, receiving satisfactory job references. Byron's departure was in exchange for Mr. Millionaire's agreement not to sue Wexford, or Byron personally, for assault.

In the ensuing years, campus culture had further devolved in Byron's view. Aside from the pampered alumni, the Wexford community was awash with young adults who were treated like incubator babies. Byron rolled his eyes thinking about it, fully aware that he was engaging in micro-aggressions. To her credit, President Gardener did a pretty good job of catering to all of them and keeping everyone appeased.

But now this delicately balanced equilibrium was going to be upended with the possibility that a Wexford coed was murdered in Carter House.

∿

Byron arrived on the lower level of Carter House around 1:30 p.m. in time to talk to Sonia Cadena, the coroner's investigator. The medical examiner would provide the official autopsy report later, but Byron wanted Sonia's initial assessment before he talked to the student who found the body. Sonia was new to the job, but Byron had heard from cop talk that she was sharp and focused.

He caught her attention and motioned to an empty practice room where they could have a quick word. Byron had not worked with Sonia previously, so he introduced himself, then got to the point.

"What's her name?" he asked.

"The victim is Martina Noto," Sonia responded. "An Italian citizen, according to the information in her wallet. She's twenty-one, an exchange student."

Byron took a beat to consider this. He had not anticipated an international incident.

"Your initial impression?" he asked.

"Too soon to say, sir, other than I think she's too young to be dead," she quipped.

"I got that. Any theory on how she died, or why?"

"At first glance, it looks like blunt force trauma, but that's unconfirmed. She hit the side of her head pretty hard."

"Are we sure this is a homicide and not some crazy slip and fall? I'd appreciate your thoughts on this."

Sonia considered her answer before responding.

"The decedent has broken skin and matted blood on the left side of her head above her ear and near her temple, but she doesn't present with any obvious defensive wounds. It's likely that the student who found her turned her onto her back, and she didn't land as she is now."

"Okay. Any signs of sexual assault?"

"No, at least nothing definitive. Her dress was up around her hips, but her underwear appears to be in place, undisturbed. I don't know. Maybe her dress edged up when she fell from the piano bench. She had on a loose dress, not a tight one."

"Do you think she was pushed and hit her head when she landed, or was she struck with something hard that caused the contusion?"

"Sorry, not ready to offer a definite opinion on that. If I had to offer a theory, by the position of the piano bench and generally where her body is laying, it's very possible someone pushed her and she hit the side of her head."

"So, homicide then," Byron said. Sonia's failure to offer a counter theory was enough for Byron for now. He'd move forward with a murder investigation.

Sonia then confirmed that based on body temperature, the victim had died that morning, rather than the night before. Beyond that, she advised Byron that more information would be available once the medical examiner's work was done.

Sonia needed a few more minutes to finish up, and the crime scene photographer was still taking some shots. Byron waited in the hallway while they worked, but before they removed the body, he stepped into the little room where Martina lay. Her static form was surrounded on three sides by the exterior wall, the piano, and upturned piano bench. Byron assessed the overall scene, including how her clothing and limbs were situated. Martina's blue-and-white print dress was pushed up toward her hips, revealing her long, shapely legs and a glimpse of her black underwear. Lying on her back, she looked as if she was taking a brief rest. Her right leg was bent in the shape of an inverted "V" with her knee pointed toward the door, her left leg extended straight. Her arms were relaxed at her sides, her hands resting near her hips. Byron used his pen to lift the rounded neckline of Martina's dress, and he noted that her bra was still hooked in place.

With the practice rooms located on the lower level of Carter House, the building's original foundation was visible in many of the little rooms. The old structure had been built on large river rocks, a common practice for buildings in the area constructed in the early twentieth century. Although the foundation had been shored up and the structure made seismically safe over the years, many of these boulders stood firmly in place and protruded at various points along the floor line. Byron saw several gray stones embedded under the window, close to Martina's head. It was possible she had fallen sideways with some force, causing her skull to collide with the immoveable stones.

Seeing the lifeless visage, Byron fixated on how shocking it was for a campus murder to occur, especially in suburban San Vicente. There would inevitably be demands for a quick resolution to the case. He also thought more about the victim's name—Martina Noto. Byron wondered if she was related to the art professor at Wexford with a similar name. Was it hyphenated? Noto-Cox? Noto-Sox? Then it clicked: Noto-Fox. Professor Noto-Fox, who was from Italy.

"Dammit," Byron said to himself, realizing that the student lying in front of him was very likely a relative of a tenured member of the Wexford faculty. "This is going to be a mess."

Rays of sunlight from the large cathedral window illuminated Martina's stunning features, and he looked more closely at the elegant window on the back wall. It made the room brighter and more cheerful than the other tiny rooms lining the hallway. It was obvious why someone would pick this particular room, especially if she planned to woodshed for several hours.

Because it was set close to ground level, the window, which swung outward, offered an easy exit. Byron was not surprised when he found it was unlocked and slightly ajar. He considered that Martina had died in a common space used by multiple students, doubting the window frame or its hardware would yield any useful fingerprints.

The techs working the crime scene had set up a perimeter around the building, and Byron intended to go outside soon to see if they found anything. Before leaving the practice room, he pulled his iPhone from his pocket and took some quick photos.

Byron next went outside and around the backside of Carter House. The ground was hard and dry, given the dearth of rain, and there was no evidence of footprints or disturbed foliage. Hopefully, more information would be gleaned as the exterior was more closely examined. "Criminals are mostly stupid," Byron repeated his mantra, "which is why they are mostly caught."

His phone chimed with a text from his partner, who was walking onto campus. It was time for a first interview with Kendra Reid, who was waiting at the student clinic while she recovered from the shock of finding the body. Byron replied that he would meet Jessica at the clinic in ten minutes, and he began to cross the familiar Wexford campus.

As he walked, Byron called Chief Mendoza. He wanted to work out how the two agencies would approach the growing list of things that needed doing. While it was clear that SVPD would lead the homicide investigation, Chief Mendoza and his team had a softer touch and would be better at handling inquiries from students and their nervous parents. Mendoza's team, composed of cops who were already working on campus, could monitor the area around Carter House and step up patrols. Managing the media would be a nightmare, requiring carefully coordinated messaging from both the campus and SVPD.

Gil Mendoza, always an affable fellow, agreed to the basic division of labor that Byron sketched out and was already working with President Gardener's office on the campus response and coordinating with the media relations office. A campus-wide advisory from President Gardener had already been issued. Byron learned that a press conference was scheduled for 11 a.m. the next morning to be held on the quad. Check and check.

Before ending the call, Byron made sure to ask Mendoza about the victim's phone, laptop, and other devices. The chief's early information was that no laptop was found at the scene. The victim's phone, purse, credit cards, a few dollars and euros, an old metronome, and piano music were all being collected from the practice room, but if she had a backpack and laptop with her, they were gone. Byron made a mental note; the credit cards and cash found at the scene suggested a motive other than robbery.

∿

Jessica Fonseca was already waiting for Byron in front of the campus clinic. She was of medium build, her long, dark hair twisted into a loose chignon. She looked strong and muscular, and Byron was glad to partner with her. Jessica's demeanor was mostly even-keeled and quiet, which Byron appreciated. He saw that people trusted her and responded to her, and they easily fell into calling her "Jess" or "Jessie."

She gave Byron a small wave when she saw him, and in reply, he motioned toward a nearby bench where they could confer before heading into the clinic. Byron wanted to tell her what he saw at Carter House. He also wanted her to take the lead in the interview with Kendra Reid. Byron knew that Kendra would be rattled, and his height and bulky frame sometimes intimidated people. During the interview, he planned to have Jessica sit closer to Kendra than he did. Byron would also slump and fold forward to make his big body appear smaller, compressing himself into a human origami. Detective Fonseca was very capable and could pose questions to Kendra.

She agreed, happy to take the lead. Together they entered the clinic and looked for someone to show them where Kendra was waiting.

CHAPTER FOUR

Tuesday, May 7—Midday Continues

Kendra was hungry and anxious. Full of nervous energy, she rummaged through the drawers and cupboards of the vacant office where she had been sent to wait, looking for forgotten snacks, maybe some peanuts or dried apricots. Her body craved something more substantial to eat than the orange juice and granola bar the clinic provided. She thought of Martina and the breakfast they would never have. It seemed like a trivial thing to think of, and Kendra tried to channel her thoughts elsewhere. But her mind was displaying images of Martina on a continuous loop, and she was relieved to hear a knock on the door.

Before Kendra could respond, the door opened a few inches and a woman's head popped in. She appeared to be in her forties, her long, brown hair pulled into a knot at the top of her head. Kendra could see the collar of a white blouse laying against a gray blazer.

"Kendra? I'm Detective Jessica Fonseca. Can we talk? I'm here with my partner, Detective Byron Comstock. We're from San Vicente PD. Can we come in?"

Kendra nodded and the two detectives were immediately in the room, finding chairs, asking Kendra if she was okay, fetching her a cup of tea, pressing their business cards on her. Kendra was relieved that the woman cop—"Call me Jess"—seemed to be in charge, while the guy—was he called Comstock?—sat in the corner with a notepad and pen. He was tall, at least a head taller than his female partner, and Kendra saw that he slouched. Kendra knew something about slouching. She was five-foot-ten, and her mother's voice reverberated in her head almost daily: "Stand tall, sweetpea. Lots of kids would envy your inches." His slouching somehow made her feel less scared.

Kendra did her best to answer Jess's questions. She had watched a lot of *CSI* and other crime shows, so she knew what to expect, but it was still very weird to be questioned by cops and doubly weird to be talking about Martina in the past tense. Jess asked how Kendra and Martina met and background about Martina's family. Then Jess seemed to be developing a timeline of Martina's usual routine and what had happened that morning. Did Kendra see Martina that morning? What time did Martina leave the condo? How often did she go to Carter House to practice? Was it always in the morning? Kendra thought carefully before answering.

With the detective's questions forcing her to think about what had transpired that morning, Kendra realized she had not actually laid eyes on Martina that day—until seeing her body in the practice room. Rather, she had heard her, padding around the condo and then taking a shower.

Kendra told the female detective this, and she seemed to note it down. Jess then asked again about Martina's practice sessions at Carter House.

"She liked the practice room with the window," Kendra said, "so she tried to get there ahead of the other music kids. Martina isn't—wasn't—a music major, but she liked to play. She had studied piano since she was a little girl and has an electronic keyboard at the condo, but she preferred to play on a real piano."

The male detective took out his phone and asked if Kendra was strong enough to look at some photos. He wanted to know if she had moved Martina's body. Kendra glanced at the images of the crime scene and felt another wave of nausea. She quickly turned away. Honestly, it was hard to remember what she had seen in the practice room. Even though the events had happened only a few hours earlier, her memories were fractured, more like snapshots than a fully realized video. It was possible she had moved the body, and she told the detectives this. But she had no independent recollection of it.

Eventually, Jess got to the question Kendra herself had been considering since her shocking discovery at Carter House. If Martina *was* murdered, who would want to harm her?

Kendra was at a loss to answer, and Jess offered some suggestions. Jealous boyfriend? Other enemies? Frenemies? Had anyone been bothering Martina? Stalking her?

"No, no one," Kendra said. "No one that I took seriously as a threat."

Kendra saw the two detectives make eye contact, and Byron leaned into the conversation.

"What do you mean, Kendra?" he asked. "Did someone threaten Martina?"

Kendra paused a long time before answering, aware that her answer would forever damage her social standing at Wexford.

"Martina was not well liked by some of the kids here, mostly a clique of popular girls. They fixated on her in a hateful way. I assumed they were jealous of her, with her beautiful face and Italian upbringing, but I didn't think they'd ever hurt her."

"Names," both cops said simultaneously.

Kendra identified Chelsea Miller, Li-Ann Wong, and Dahlia Moreno, all members of the same sorority. She also offered the names Molly and Olivia, but Kendra didn't know their surnames.

"They're the main ones who talk shit about Martina and mimic her with their fake 'ciao bellas' behind her back."

At that moment, Kendra wanted the interview to be over. She felt her shoulders drop and her head become heavy. She wanted to see and smell the ocean. She wanted the sand and waves and the tides. She wanted their rhythms and constancy and permanence. Kendra wanted her mom and mac and cheese. She faintly heard Jess tell her calmly and directly:

"Kendra, I know you've had a rough morning, and we're so sorry that you've lost someone close to you, but we need you to focus for another minute. Are you sure Martina didn't have any romantic partners? Or sex partners? Friends with benefits?"

Kendra then remembered Jason. "You should talk to Jason Chang. He's a student here. Martina and Jason hung out together for about six or eight weeks earlier in the semester. She broke it off with him, and he seemed upset about it for a while. He'll be devastated to hear about Martina."

The detectives closed their notebooks and stood up to leave. At this point, Byron asked Kendra if she remembered seeing Martina's laptop or backpack that morning in the condo. When Kendra responded that she wasn't sure, he asked her gently to look for them as soon as she got back to the condo and to let them know if she found either. He stressed how important these items were. The detectives also told Kendra to stay close to campus while the investigation was underway. Kendra realized she was an important witness, which made it unlikely she would be mollifying her heavy heart with the comforts of home. Maybe her mom would drive up and bring some homemade mac and cheese.

∿

The two detectives returned to the table outside the student clinic to confer. Obviously, they had witnesses to pursue. Byron would track down Jason, and Jessica would round up the mean girls.

They also needed to talk with Campus PD about contacting the other students in the basement at Carter House that morning and the staff who were working the front desk. Byron and Jessica agreed to delegate this group of witnesses to Chief Mendoza's officers. Since SVPD was short staffed due to recent budget cuts, Byron was confident that his own captain wouldn't mind sharing the workload with their campus counterparts. Byron and Jessica could always circle back to these witnesses if they needed more information.

Byron also had a nagging idea that Martina could have caught the attention of someone in the surrounding neighborhood, maybe a sex offender who became obsessed with her and turned lethal when she rebuffed him. This could be a case of stranger danger, an attempted rape that ended in a homicide. Byron told Jessica that he intended to follow this angle, too. He was beginning to think that Martina was the kind of young woman men fantasized about, and such fantasies sometimes ended in very dark places.

CHAPTER FIVE

Tuesday, May 7—Late Afternoon

*E*liza left Lucas with a neighbor and rushed to Francesca's house. It was a shock. She found some brandy in the back of a cupboard in her mother's kitchen and poured a couple of ounces into an espresso cup. She pushed the small cup toward her mom, who looked puzzled at first and then got a whiff of the alcohol. Francesca took a sip and then another. Together, they tried to absorb the news that Martina was the dead student at Wexford. It was horrific and unimaginable. Soon the news about Martina would be widely released, and her cousin would be the focus of countless tweets, news clips, and overall media attention.

A few hours earlier, Chief Mendoza had driven to Francesca's house to tell her about Martina, and he waited while Francesca contacted Martina's parents by video call. He had wanted to be present for the call to assure the Notos that the campus and the City of San Vicente would do everything in their power to find out what had happened to their daughter. Roberto and Laura Noto planned to catch the first flight out of Rome. If the timing worked in their favor, they would land at LAX tomorrow around mid-day. Francesca had volunteered Eliza as their driver. She would intercept them as they exited the terminal and bring them to Francesca's house where they would stay until.... Until what? Until the coroner released Martina's body? Until the perpetrator was found? Eliza could not imagine how Roberto and Laura would recover from this.

Eliza remained with her mother for a couple of hours, although they talked little. Both repeatedly refreshed their phones and laptops, absorbing whatever tidbits they could discern from their contacts on campus and in the community.

What had happened to Martina?

～

Wednesday, May 8—Morning

The next morning, Eliza dropped Lucas at his preschool, with a backpack stuffed with his dinosaur pajamas, a toothbrush, a change of clothes, and a favorite toy. She had arranged for him to go home from school that day with Liam, his best friend and schoolmate. Ivy, Liam's mom, would take the boys to her house after school with a loose plan for Lucas to have a sleepover at Liam's. Eliza had no idea how the day would unfold, and she was glad to have a trusted place for Lucas to stay for the next twenty-four hours.

Then Eliza headed to Lulu's, a local coffeehouse. Although she knew she needed food to fuel the day ahead, she was too unhinged to eat much. She had slept poorly, unable to stop thinking about Martina. She wanted to sit undisturbed at Lulu's and get a few things done before driving to LAX. As soon as her almond milk latte arrived, Eliza called Marty, her boss, to tell him she had to take some time off because of a death in the family. She offered to use the vacation days the firm owed her. Eliza found herself being purposefully vague with Marty about who had died, maybe to avoid the big reaction he'd likely have. She didn't want him to know she was related to Martina, at least not yet.

Apologizing for the short notice about her leave, she assured Marty she would hand off her pending work to another paralegal in the firm. Marty's initial reaction was testy, mostly because he was caught off guard by her call, but he calmed down when he heard "death in the family" and "someone close to my mother." Marty had met Francesca a few times and knew she was a widow—an attractive and available one. Marty had a soft spot for Eliza's mom, a card that Eliza played shamelessly.

Next she scanned the local news for updates on Martina or new developments on campus. The media seemed to be rehashing the same footage, which meant they had not come up with any new angles yet. She double-checked that her notifications were set to alert her to news stories about Wexford.

After sending a few more work-related emails, Eliza set an outgoing email message notifying people that she'd be away from work and only checking emails sporadically for the next ten days. Eliza realized that ten days would not be enough time to sort out all the troubles swirling around her family, but it was a start. "*Dio piacendo*," she muttered under her breath, repeating one of her mother's go-to phrases.

Eliza checked the flight times again to make sure the Notos' flight to LA would arrive on time. The flight schedule had worked out for Martina's parents. They'd texted earlier to say they had cleared customs in New York and were getting on their connecting flight. At least the air travel gods were cooperating.

Before leaving Lulu's, Eliza packed up her laptop and stopped at the counter to buy a few bottles of water for herself and extras to offer Roberto and Laura as soon as they got in her car. They would be fatigued to the point of cracking. She couldn't imagine their pain. The idea of losing a child—in her case, Lucas—was incomprehensible.

∿

Eliza arrived at the airport early, but she wasn't interested in circling the airport loop along with the hundreds of other drivers waiting for arriving passengers. Instead, she pulled into a large hotel parking lot that faced Century Boulevard and dozed for a few minutes inside her car. Finally, Roberto sent a message that they were in baggage claim, and Eliza inched into the traffic approaching the airport. She had not seen Martina's parents for several years, but she was confident she would recognize them.

Edging her car along the curb outside of the designated terminal, Eliza scanned the crowd of waiting passengers. People of all ages, ethnic backgrounds, and income levels crowded the sidewalk. Some travelers only had backpacks. One group included about twenty high-school-aged boys, probably a traveling soccer team based on their clothing and sports bags. Eliza continued to scan the crowd and eventually spotted her relatives just as they exited baggage claim, their luggage stacked precariously on a cart. Eliza eyed Roberto's tangle of gray curls and his European glasses, noting that he looked only slightly older than when she last saw him four years before. Then she glimpsed Laura, whose appearance caused Eliza to gasp audibly. Eliza's memories of Martina's mother were of a slim, middle-aged woman who radiated energy. Today, Laura was dressed in black slacks and a long dark gray tunic. Her usual sparkle was missing, except for the lime green, low-heeled sandals on her feet. Eliza assumed that in the haste to pack, Laura couldn't find any shoes in her closet that matched her somber demeanor.

"Roberto, Laura!" Eliza shouted, waving vigorously to get their attention, but her voice was lost amid the cacophony of street noise and human sounds.

Eliza pulled out her phone and texted Roberto: *Look left to the curb. White Volvo station wagon.*

She watched as he took his phone from his pocket, digested her text, squeezed his wife's shoulder, and then turned in her direction to wave. Within a few minutes, they had loaded the baggage into the rear of the car and were en route to Francesca's house.

Sipping from the water bottles Eliza had pressed on them, Roberto and Laura were grateful she had picked them up and acknowledged that they would have wilted under the burden of securing a ride from LAX to San Vicente. They asked her about Lucas and about her job, making small talk to postpone the Möbius strip of conversations they faced about their daughter. Eliza followed their lead, avoiding the topic of Martina. She eventually found some music on her iPhone, a string quartet to carry them on their journey.

∿

They arrived at Francesca's around 2 p.m., where sandwiches and a salad awaited. Eliza made a quick call to check on Lucas, who was happily playing with his buddy. He wanted to spend the night at Liam's, and Eliza agreed after briefly checking that this was still okay with Liam's mom.

Although the Notos were both exhausted from the flight, they wanted to go to the county coroner's office near downtown Los Angeles as soon as possible. Eliza pulled out her phone to set the arrangements in motion, but her mother interceded. Francesca told Eliza that she had already helped enormously by making the drive across LA to the airport. Francesca would handle the next part, fulfilling Roberto and Laura's pressing need to see Martina.

Although Eliza felt she should push back on Francesca's directive, she was grateful to let her mother handle the next steps. Hugging her daughter tightly, Francesca told Eliza to go home and get some rest, especially while Lucas was occupied and didn't need her attention.

Eliza followed her mother's instructions and drove toward her house, making a small detour to her favorite Mexican restaurant for some takeout *caldo de pollo*. After a much-needed nap, Eliza was planning a quiet night of chicken soup and a mindless movie.

The next morning, she woke up early but forced herself to wait until 7 a.m. before calling Ivy to check in with Lucas. The kids were eating breakfast when she called. Eliza told her son she'd pick him up that afternoon when school was over.

Just as she ended that call, her phone rang again, sounding the familiar tune that indicated Francesca was calling. But when Eliza answered with, "Hey, Mama," the voice was Roberto's. He had borrowed her mother's phone to avoid the international calling charges on his Italian cellphone plan.

He apologized for calling so early. He and Laura had been up for hours, unable to sleep thanks to a sorry combination of jet lag and shattered nerves, which were made worse at the coroner's office. They had confirmed that Martina was unquestionably the victim.

Eliza couldn't think of much to say, except for how sorry she was, which seemed wholly inadequate. Roberto then caught Eliza off guard with a request.

"We want you to figure out who killed Martina," he said. "Will you help us? This is your type of work, no? You investigate things."

Eliza stammered, "I'm, I'm not a police detective, Roberto. I have a private investigator's license, but I don't have experience in this area. Besides, both the campus police and the San Vicente PD are already working on the case. What more could I do?"

"You would bring your care and attention. You are Martina's *cugina.* You have a personal connection to what happened. Laura and I don't trust the police to give our daughter's case the time it deserves. Those cops will get distracted by other things. We are afraid the case will grow—how do they say—it will grow icy."

Eliza smiled to herself. "You mean cold. You're worried it won't get solved quickly and will become a cold case."

"Yes, this is a worry for us. If you do your own investigation, we will feel better. Will you do this for us, Eliza? We will pay you, of course, and your mother, Laura and I will share babysitting for Lucas while you work."

Eliza could not imagine taking money from Roberto and Laura to investigate Martina's death. She also didn't see how she could refuse their request.

"Okay. Let's do this: I'll look into the case over the next couple of weeks and see what I can find. Then, if nothing is resolved, we can reassess and decide whether this is a good idea. But we all have to agree to one thing: I will only ask for reimbursement for my expenses. I have some paid vacation time coming, so I won't be behind financially. Agreed?"

Roberto emitted a large sigh and paused. Eliza imagined his effort to hold back tears. "*Sì, grazie.* We agree. *Grazie mille,* Eliza."

"Good. Let's meet in a few hours. I have some questions I want to ask you. I'll see you at my mom's house around 11:30 a.m. Okay?"

"Okay, *ciao,* Eliza. See you then."

Eliza took a minute to internalize what she'd agreed to. Within forty-eight hours, her life had taken an unimaginable turn, and she needed to prepare for what was ahead, both literally and emotionally. She used the time before her meeting with Roberto and Laura to get groceries, pay bills, make a dental appointment, and otherwise attend to personal business. She knew the next couple weeks would be all-consuming, and the more organized she was in the rest of her life, the better.

Eliza hadn't always leaned into organization and structure. Francesca sometimes chuckled when her daughter, who as a teen had performed ballerina-style leaps over the heaps of dirty laundry around her bed, insisted that Lucas pick up his toys and tidy his room each day. Being a single parent was exhausting and often chaotic. It was hard for Eliza to be the only one who did dishes and laundry, the only one who insisted Lucas eat his broccoli, the only one who comforted him when he had night terrors or an illogical fear of spiders. Focusing on the things she could control, like paying her bills on time or keeping her linen closet organized, made Eliza feel safer. She knew at her core that this was fanciful thinking. No matter how much structure one imposed, the unexpected always hovered nearby, just out of range and ready to disrupt the equilibrium. Eliza was also fully aware that her daily struggles were minimal compared to what Martina's parents were suffering now.

Satisfied that she'd done as much prep as she could, she grabbed her keys and left to meet Roberto and Laura.

Pavo, her mother's rescue pup, was yapping as Eliza walked up the path and slipped her key in Francesca's front door. "Mama, I'm here," she called after patting Pavo's head. When Eliza didn't hear a reply, she followed the strong waft of espresso to the kitchen. Through the French doors, she could see Francesca, Roberto, and Laura sitting at the back of the garden around a square table. The late morning sun was slipping through the jacaranda tree canopied above them, leaving streaks of light across their heads and faces. The tree's purple blooms lay scattered across the grass.

Eliza opened the French doors and let Pavo out to join her mother, a signal that she had arrived. Before going outside, she warmed a mug of milk in the microwave and then married it with the remaining espresso in the pot on the stove, creating a makeshift latte. Then, finding some biscotti in the cupboard, she put half a dozen cookies on a plate to replenish the food outside. Eliza intended to ask Martina's parents some difficult questions. Knowing that almost everyone responded to small kindnesses, Eliza hoped the biscotti would be a tiny step toward easing the conversation.

As Eliza approached the table, Francesca stood up, motioning that Eliza should take her seat. "I have work to do, and you have things to talk about," Francesca said. "Will you be comfortable talking outside here? Or do you want to use the den?"

"No, Mama, this is fine," Eliza said. After quick kisses of greeting to everyone, she settled into the cushions, still warm from her mother's presence, and opened her laptop. Roberto and Laura each grabbed a cookie from the fresh supply.

Eliza first collected basic information about Martina, trying to find out what the Notos knew about their daughter's life at Wexford. What projects was she involved in? What friends had she told them about? What were her immediate plans? Had Martina planned to return to school in Bologna the following semester since her year at Wexford was near its end?

Not surprisingly, neither Roberto nor Laura knew many details about Martina's life in California. Eliza was aware of how easy it was to keep secrets from parents, especially when Facetime was the only means of communicating with them. The time difference between

Italy and California was also a factor, likely restricting most of their calls to the weekends.

Eliza had gone to college in Southern California. While she lived on campus, she was still in the same city as her parents. But Martina, being so far from home, would have been like most of Eliza's college friends who only saw their families at Christmas break. Being on another continent, Martina wouldn't have experienced unexpected visits from Dad on Saturday mornings, or pressure from Mom that she show up for Sunday dinner. Francesca had tried to fill in as a substitute mother for Martina while she was at Wexford, but that job had proved difficult. Francesca had complained sometimes that she seemed not to be doing enough with Martina. To Eliza, Martina appeared polite but reserved. She had not given much thought to her cousin's interactions with Francesca. In hindsight, Eliza wished she had paid much closer attention to her cousin.

In response to Eliza's questions, Roberto and Laura talked about Kendra, saying they planned to go to Kendra's condo the following day. Roberto also talked wistfully about Martina's plan to perform in a piano recital in early June. He shared that she had been excited about her computer classes at Wexford and told her parents she was working on an interesting project, something to help the disabled. When asked for details, Roberto couldn't elaborate.

With the small tidbits she was gathering, Eliza began building her witness list. She would talk to Kendra obviously and also to Martina's faculty advisor in the computer science department to learn more about her project.

When Roberto and Laura ran out of things to share, Eliza prompted them: Was Martina involved in any sports at Wexford? Or at the university in Bologna? Did she swim, play tennis, or go to pick-up soccer games? Did she talk about any online activities, like video games, online chess, or apps for making friends? Knowing how common it was for young people to use online apps for dating and sexual connections, Eliza tried to navigate the questions about Martina's computer use carefully. But information about whether

Martina would use online programs to look for potential sexual partners was important. Could a spurned sexual connection have been angry enough to hurt her? Eliza doubted that Roberto or Laura would have any solid information about their daughter's dating life, but a few questions might turn up a lead.

When it seemed that Eliza had mined all she could from Roberto and Laura—at least for the moment—she closed her laptop and started packing up. It was almost time to pick up Lucas from school, and Eliza was missing her son.

But as Eliza stood up, Laura seemed to pull up a memory, blurting, "What about Jason?"

"Who?" Eliza asked, while Roberto chimed in, "Yes. Jason. Good thinking, *amore mio.*"

Laura recalled that Jason seemed to be Martina's boyfriend for a few months, but they had broken up in late February or March. Eliza hadn't known that Martina had been seriously involved with anyone at Wexford, so she asked Laura how she knew about Jason.

She explained that one time when she called Martina on Facetime, a young man had answered Martina's phone. He was standing in the kitchen of the condo Martina and Kendra shared. He had introduced himself as Martina's friend and said that Martina had stepped out to get the mail. Laura was always pleased to talk with any friends of her daughter's. They spoke for a few minutes until Martina returned and took the phone.

Jason knew a few words of Italian, and Laura found him entertaining, even if the call was brief. Martina told her mother that Jason went to school at Wexford. Although Martina had not described Jason as a boyfriend, Laura assumed he was, given that he was comfortable enough to answer Martina's phone. This was especially true since it was clear that a parent was calling via video chat. "What boy would do that if he was not a boyfriend?" Laura asked.

"Yes, what boy would answer such a call?" Eliza wondered.

CHAPTER SIX

Wednesday, May 8—Morning at Wexford

With help from the dean of students, Detectives Comstock and Fonseca arranged for the so-called mean girls to meet them in a conference room in the provost's office. Byron and Jessica found the three young women, whom Kendra had named, huddled at one end of a long conference table, laptops open, phones in their hands. Even though it was only 9:15 a.m., they were dressed professionally with their hair and make-up camera-ready, as if waiting for job interviews or headed to court. Byron laughed to himself. The trio obviously believed that first impressions truly did matter.

"Good morning, ladies. Thanks for being on time and agreeing to meet so early," Byron said, his voice louder than it needed to be. "I'm sorry you didn't get the message that we'll be staggering your interview times. So, two of you need to wait in the hallway. You can decide among yourselves who wants to go first."

Chelsea Miller, tall and dark-haired with a no-nonsense gaze, spoke first. "We want to talk to you as a group," Chelsea stated in a clear tone.

"That's right," Li-Ann and Dahlia said in chorus, clearly comfortable being cast as Chelsea's back-up singers.

"I appreciate that," Byron replied, holding onto his patience. "But that's not how this is going to work. We need to speak to you individually. Just to be clear, we're not accusing you of anything, and you're under no obligation to talk to us today. We just need some information."

"The dean said we could be interviewed together," Chelsea volleyed back, seeming to believe that the dean's word had standing with San Vicente PD.

"Again, ladies, that may be what you want, and I'm sorry if you were given the wrong impression. But it ain't gonna happen. Now decide which of you will be interviewed first. We need to get started. Detective Fonseca and I are busy trying to figure out what happened to your friend."

This conversation made Byron remember how much he hated the arrogance and superiority of Wexford co-eds—a group he knew well from his time working for Chief Mendoza.

Chelsea then leaned into her defiance and made her best offer: "Detective, one of my leadership roles on campus is to be a support person when my classmates are involved in disciplinary hearings," she said. "I've sat through several investigative interviews when students were accused of theft, cheating, even drug charges."

"What's your point?" Byron said, no longer hiding his irritation.

"You can't force us to be alone for these interviews. We're entitled to have another student with us," Chelsea asserted, with both Li-Ann and Dahlia nodding vigorously in support, as if they were Wexford student bobble heads.

Jessica had been quiet long enough.

"Look, we're sorry if the dean misspoke. Let's reschedule these interviews to take place in a few days at police headquarters. Then you can bring your lawyers with you. Did you tell your parents that we were talking to you today?" Jessica asked. "I'm sure they'll want to be involved in organizing your family lawyers for our next meeting."

"I don't think we have a family lawyer," Dahlia mumbled. "And I don't want to involve my parents. I'll talk to you now, without my friends or an attorney. I want to get this over with."

"Great," Jessica said, her tone now cheerful. "We can interview Dahlia now and talk to Li-Ann and Chelsea another day at the station."

Chelsea stood up and began packing her things. "I'm not comfortable with this. I'm calling my dad," she said, motioning to Li-Ann that it was time to leave.

Li-Ann turned toward the detectives. "I'll meet with you today after Dahlia does," Li-Ann told the group. "Chels, finals are coming up. I need to focus on cramming right now. I don't want to have to think about a police interview."

Byron took this opportunity to regain control. He reached out to shake Chelsea's hand.

"Thank you, Chelsea, for coming today. We'll circle back later to talk with you another time. Dahlia, you'll go first. Li-Ann, let's see if we can find a comfortable place for you to wait and maybe we can find you something to drink."

Complying with social etiquette, Chelsea grasped Byron's hand and shook it tepidly. Stone-faced, she left the conference room without a nod to her friends.

An hour later, Byron and Jessica were done interviewing Dahlia and Li-Ann. The two students had characterized Martina as aloof and presented a picture of her as an outsider who didn't crave the approval of Wexford's sorority sisters. Dahlia and Li-Ann both acknowledged talking trash about Martina with Chelsea and other students, including Aidan Kinaga, Zoey Hacopian, and Olivia Huerta. They were both positive that none of them would murder Martina and were confident that no one truly hated her. It was more like a parlor game to make funny quips about the foreign kid who didn't care about fitting in. Neither Li-Ann nor Dahlia knew anyone named Molly, one of the other names Kendra had provided. It was possible that Kendra had been mistaken and was thinking of Zoey Hacopian, presenting another small tangle for the detectives that would need sorting out.

Byron and Jessica agreed that neither Li-Ann nor Dahlia were actual suspects. Li-Ann seemed to have been more in awe of Martina than envious of her, and Dahlia was too much of a rule-follower to commit a crime. Shoplifting a candy bar seemed outside of Dahlia's wheelhouse. More importantly, they both had alibis. Dahlia had slept at her parents' house that Monday night, going there for a family party to celebrate her grandmother's birthday. She didn't have class until Tuesday afternoon and had returned to Wexford from her parents' house to find the campus abuzz with police activity. Li-Ann was in the pool at swim team practice by 6:30 a.m. and then checked into her job at the campus library by 9:30 a.m. While both alibis needed to be verified, Byron and Jessica agreed they were both straightforward explanations and easy enough to check.

Li-Ann volunteered that Martina had dated Jason Chang, a member of the Wexford soccer team, for a while, and he was pretty broken up after she dumped him. Just before walking out of the conference room, Li-Ann offered the detectives another useful crumb. There was a rumor that Martina had stopped seeing Jason because he'd wanted an exclusive relationship with her, an entanglement Martina didn't want. Li-Ann heard from someone that Martina then started sleeping with a professor, but she didn't know which professor, nor did she remember who told her this. Her information was only that Martina had wanted no strings sex, and she didn't like the randomness of dating apps. An older guy, who was grateful for her company, could provide the attention Martina wanted without complications.

Maybe the most valuable information was that neither Li-Ann nor Dahlia had talked to Chelsea or texted her on Tuesday morning, even though they normally spoke and texted each other several times a day. What was Chelsea doing while Martina was at Carter House?

∾

"Let's grab a snack. Somewhere off campus," Byron suggested as he and Jessica left the provost's office. A few minutes later they were sitting outside a mostly empty café with coffee and muffins and, thankfully, no students sitting close enough to overhear them.

"What's next?" Jessica asked. "We definitely need to figure out exactly who was on our victim's list of lovers and ex-lovers."

Byron agreed. They shouldn't rule out the classics. The killer could be someone who became unbalanced because Martina had rejected him or her. "Or," Byron exclaimed, pausing as he lifted his right arm in the air and pointed his index finger skyward, "our perpetrator could be another type of deviant."

"Explain yourself, Detective. Is this your stranger-danger theory?" Jessica asked, mildly amused by his theatrics.

Byron pointed out that he had checked the sex offenders rolls and found a few men living close to campus. While all these individuals needed to be checked out, Byron wanted Jessica to go with him now to the address of one of these men.

"Why not send the patrol officers to his house first?" she asked. "Or call the guy's parole officer? If there's anything suspicious, then you and I can make a pass by his place. You seem oddly intrigued by this one guy."

"Just a hunch. Do you have anything lined up right now?"

Jessica admitted that she did not. Solving Martina's murder was her full-time focus. They returned to Byron's car and drove toward the home of Abel Trenton. Abel lived with his mother about fifteen blocks from the Wexford campus on a street of modest, older homes.

The white, wood-frame house needed paint, and the lawn looked dry and weedy. But so did many of the area's lawns after multiple years of California drought. Jessica smiled at the large sycamore tree situated near the curb of the Trentons' property with its massive bent branches, peeling bark, and yellow-green leaves. It had survived many years on little water. Jessica pictured neighborhood kids scaling up the trunk, just as she and her sister had climbed the sycamore in their mom's front yard. Now, with Abel publicly listed as a sex offender, it was unlikely that any of the local kids approached the Trentons' house.

The two detectives walked up to the large porch, and Byron gave the front door a powerful knock. This set off a high-pitched bark from within, and a woman's voice yelling, "Quiet down, Biscuit!" After a minute, she opened the door a crack, and Byron quickly identified himself and his partner as police officers, showing the elderly woman his badge.

"What did Abel do?" she asked.

Jessica stepped closer to the door.

"Nothing that we know of, ma'am. Is Abel here? We would like to chat with him for a few minutes."

Abel's mother, who appeared frail with a noticeably bent spine, stepped onto the porch, pointed her cane at the driveway, and started walking toward it.

"Abel's in the garage, probably playing video games. Follow me. I'll let him know you're here."

The two detectives trailed behind her, passing a serviceable truck parked in the driveway. Single file, they walked through a gate that enclosed the yard behind the house. Abel wasn't playing video games; rather, he was seated at a round glass patio table, with an old iPod in his hand attached to headphones. He removed them from his ears when he saw his mother and the two detectives.

Byron and Jessica quickly showed Abel their badges. After Byron thanked Mrs. Trenton for her trouble, she headed back toward the house, leaving them to talk to her son out of her presence. The detectives sat down at the table and sized up the man seated there. Abel was in his late forties, his thinning, blond hair combed back off his forehead. He was of medium height and weight and seemed relatively fit. He wore an old Nirvana T-shirt, jeans with holes at the knees, and flip-flops. Although his face was leathery, probably from too much sun and too many substances, he was recently shaven and looked put together. A fresh mug of coffee was within his reach.

After a brief silence, Abel asked the obvious question:

"Why are you here?"

"It's simple. We want to know where you were from around midnight until noon yesterday. So late Monday night into lunch Tuesday," Byron replied.

"I didn't do anything," Abel answered defensively. "Nothing you'd care about."

"We didn't say that you've done anything wrong," Byron said reassuringly. "Just tell us where you were, and we'll leave you in peace."

"Mostly I'm here in the garage or the yard. You can ask my mom. She'll tell you. I don't go anywhere. I usually play video games all day."

"Did you go to the campus yesterday morning?" Byron suggested. "I know you like to go to the campus, Abel. I've seen your arrest record, the campus police file *and* the SVPD file. Following the girls around, exposing your genitals to them, stealing women's underwear out of the campus laundry rooms—none of those things was a good idea, Abel."

"I don't want to talk to you. Go away," Abel said, his temper rising. "I don't go to the campus anymore."

Jessica decided to jump in at this point and take another tact. "Abel, you and your mom both said that you play video games. What kind of device do you use? Can you show me your set-up? I'm a gamer myself."

Abel eyed her for a beat, deciding whether to comply with Jessica's request. Then he stood up and motioned for her to come with him to the garage. He entered through a side door, and she followed him into his...? What would one call it? A lair? A man-cave? A lounge? Jessica saw an old dirty couch, a mini fridge, and a relatively new game console and flatscreen TV. She reasoned that if Abel was home the previous morning playing video games, there would be computer data to prove it stored on the game he was playing or in the memory of the gaming device itself.

To get a better sense of who she was dealing with, Jessica went to the mini-fridge and asked Abel if she could look inside.

"Suit yourself," he said.

Jessica found multiple diet sodas and sports drinks alongside yogurts, cheese sticks, slices of salami, and small boxes of what appeared to be left-over Chinese food.

"Where's the beer?" Jessica asked.

"No beer," Abel replied. "It messes with my meds."

"I see," she said. "What kind of meds?"

"They keep me from getting too depressed or too jittery and amped up," Abel told her. "I don't know the name."

"Ah," Jessica said, as she headed for the side door. "No one wants mood swings. You're smart to stay away from the alcohol."

Together, she and Abel walked back to the table, and Byron asked again where Abel had been early Tuesday morning.

"You mean when all the helicopters and sirens were around the campus? I was here. I was standing on the front porch watching them circle. Ask the neighbors. They probably saw me standing out there. I was holding Biscuit, my mom's dog, in my arms. He doesn't like sirens."

With that, Byron motioned to Jessica that he was ready to leave. She told Abel not to erase anything on his gaming console; she would send a computer forensics specialist to his house to examine it. He seemed to understand what she had told him, and she made a mental note to tell Mrs. Trenton that someone would be coming to look at the gaming console before they left. As the detectives headed toward the street, Byron stopped and turned back to shout one last directive at Abel.

"Don't leave the immediate area," Byron advised, using his best no-nonsense cop voice. "That means stay close to San Vicente."

After thanking Mrs. Trenton for her help, they made their way to the car to plot out the rest of their day. They needed outstanding pieces of evidence—the medical examiner's report and forensics on Martina's phone, specifically. And where was her backpack? Her laptop? Based on what they could see from the victim's phone, she didn't have any tracking devices on those items. Too bad, Byron thought. It would be very helpful to know where they were stashed, which was an obvious steppingstone to uncovering who was involved.

∾

Wednesday, May 8—Afternoon at Wexford

Chelsea messaged Dahlia and Li-Ann shortly after she left the provost's office, directing them to meet her at noon at the oak grove.

Now, perched tensely on the edge of a wooden bench, she waited for them in a bucolic corner of the campus under the shade of massive coast live oak. In full damage-control mode, Chelsea needed to know exactly what had transpired after she left the detectives. She was mindful that neither of them had messaged her back, giving Chelsea some trepidation that they might not show up. She feared her grasp was slipping.

Pedaling up on their vintage bikes a little after noon, Dahlia and Li-Ann approached the grove as a unit. They were in sync now, Chelsea could see, making her feel isolated and combative. She waited silently as they propped their bikes against a tree and joined her at the bench. Although Chelsea wanted to scream profanities at them, she tamped down this urge, cognizant that a few students were studying nearby. Better not to draw any attention, she reminded herself.

"Don't try to apologize," Chelsea snarled quietly. "I don't want to know why you both chose to deviate so dramatically from our plan. We all agreed not to speak to the detectives individually. Power in numbers, remember! Nothing you can say will fix this, but let's start with what the cops asked you and what you told them."

Li-Ann and Dahlia exchanged glances, then Li-Ann spoke first. "Look, Chels, I did what I had to do, and so did Dahlia. We don't know any lawyers. We don't even have relatives who've been to law school. I can't afford to get kicked out of school. Bottom line, the cops are in control. When they want to talk, a person like me—"

Chelsea raised her hand to stop Li-Ann's explanation. "Whatever. I don't want to hear it. I need to know if you told the detectives about the internet stuff we did. What did you share?"

Dahlia jumped in now, more fired up than Chelsea had ever seen her. "Chelsea, you put that shit on the internet to hurt Martina. Not me. And not Li-Ann. You promised us that you deleted it, which I hope is true. For what it's worth, I didn't tell the cops about any of it, mostly because they didn't ask me directly. I won't lie to the police. That seems like a very bad idea. But I also won't throw you under the bus unless I'm asked a direct question. Fair enough?"

"Lower. Your. Voice." Chelsea hissed and turned back to Li-Ann. "What about you? What's your boundary? Is it also not lying to the cops? It surely wasn't having a big laugh at Martina's expense a few weeks ago. You enjoyed cyberbullying her as much as I did."

"Don't worry, Chelsea," Li-Ann chimed in. "The cops didn't ask me anything about your little plot to embarrass Martina. They didn't seem to know about it. And I didn't say anything to lead them in that direction. It's cool. We good?"

When Chelsea nodded grudgingly, Li-Ann and Dahlia turned in unison and walked back to their bikes. Chelsea watched the two of them pedal away, aware that the social order her life had been organized around had just taken a seismic shift. She found it oddly fitting to be in a lovely oak grove where people came to meditate and recharge. A wry smile on her lips, Chelsea decided to live in the moment, breathing in the chaparral and listening to the birdsong. She'd spend a few minutes meditating on her own meeting with the police. Chelsea could stall the cops for a while, but she knew she'd have to talk to Detectives Comstock and Fonseca eventually.

～

Kennedy Thompson, sitting unobtrusively among the trees, watched the three students from some distance. He specifically remembered the tall, pretty one from earlier that morning; she was coming from the provost's office and passed him in the hallway. Even though it was not yet 10 a.m., she was dressed up with her hair and make-up in place. Her professional outfit belied her lack of composure, however. Kennedy caught a glimpse of her face as she swept by, and she looked on the edge of tears. With the detectives doing interviews there, she must have been questioned for the Noto case. It didn't take Kennedy long to figure out her name. All he had to do was ask a few other cops on the campus security force, and then he did a little googling. She was Chelsea Miller, a sorority sister and daughter of a respected attorney based in nearby Pasadena.

Seeing the three students together now, Kennedy wondered if they were all connected to the Noto case. The two girls who'd ridden up on their bikes to meet Chelsea didn't look happy. There were no warm smiles or friendly greetings. Given that a Wexford student had died yesterday, Kennedy would have expected these young women to embrace or otherwise offer emotional support. From his vantage point, their conversation looked tense, and Kennedy was curious why. He had a special interest in the Noto investigation. He had met Martina Noto about four weeks earlier when her things were stolen from a locker. As a campus cop, he was part of the team working on the burglary, and it was a serious one—lots of valuables had been taken from several lockers in the wellness center. While Kennedy and the other officers had not solved that case yet, he was certain Wexford kids were involved in stealing and then reselling the stolen articles. Although he couldn't prove anything yet, he wanted to find the thieves. Solving that kind of crime would get an officer noticed, which would lead to promotions or, better yet, a job with a more respected police agency. No one wanted to spend their career as a campus cop, not if they had any ambition.

Following the locker break-ins, things had gotten more intense. There was pressure on everyone to solve Martina's murder. Kennedy was aware that information equaled power in the police world. For now, Chelsea and her crew were worth his time and attention.

CHAPTER SEVEN

Thursday, May 9—Early Morning

Even though it was still dark outside, Kendra could smell the coffee brewing downstairs. This meant that her dad was in the kitchen engaged in his morning routine. Kendra could picture him slicing an apple for his oatmeal, feeding Nomad, the family beagle, and opening his laptop at the kitchen table to check the latest news. Around 7:15 a.m., he would get in his car and drive to his job as a manager in an aerospace firm. This would all take place while her mom dozed in bed until half past nine. Dad was the responsible one, Mom, not so much.

Kendra had slipped out of San Vicente late Wednesday evening and headed south toward San Diego and the predictability of home. The only thing she wanted was to don a spring wetsuit and find a way to rebalance herself. Doing that in some choice waves seemed the obvious solution. The shock of seeing Martina's body, the interview with the detectives, and the constant pinging of her phone were more than Kendra could handle. Around 10 p.m., she had phoned her parents—whom Kendra usually referred to by their given names, Bob and Gwen—to say she would be spending a few days at home, so they shouldn't be alarmed when she pulled into the garage around midnight.

As Kendra packed her overnight bag, she knew she was supposed to stay put, just as the detectives had told her. But she couldn't shake the feeling that the walls were closing in, and she was finding it hard to sleep—or even to breathe. She would only be a few hours from San

Vicente. The cops could either Facetime with her or drive a couple of hours south if they really needed to talk to her face to face.

The campus vigil for Martina was scheduled for Sunday evening, and she intended to be back for it. Until then Kendra would spend the weekend at home, wrapping her brain around what had happened to Martina. Now she had a strong desire to reenact a familiar part of her childhood. She pushed off the blankets and galloped down the stairs. Her father calling out, "Hi, baby," was enough to bring tears, and she let his long arms encircle her. Kendra inhaled the musky bar soap he preferred. After a few minutes of soaking up the safe and familiar surroundings, she was able to calm herself.

"Are you okay? Do you want to talk about it?" Bob quietly asked.

"Not even close to okay, but I don't want to talk about it now. Maybe later. Now I need to be in the waves."

Her father held her shoulders at arm's length, looked closely at Kendra's countenance, and made his assessment. He decided not to press her for now.

"Oatmeal, then? A girl needs energy."

"No, Daddy. I'll take a banana and a granola bar instead. And eat with Gwen when I get home."

Kendra was out the door a few minutes later with her Prius pointed west to the D Street surf. The sun was just coming up, and she was already feeling a little better. Two days had passed since Martina had walked out of the condo with plans to meet her for breakfast, and chaos had encircled Kendra since. The campus was the center of police activity and media frenzy, and the student body was afraid and anxious. Faculty and prominent student groups were organizing Martina's vigil. Kendra was wary that it would turn into a political rally with chants about police incompetence and calls to end sexual violence. While this was a true and worthy cause, Kendra knew that no information about how Martina actually died had been publicly released. Was it sexual violence?

Given that she was Martina's roommate, Kendra was being asked to play a prominent role in the vigil, which had led Kendra to take the rare step of turning off her phone. Her stress-level was over the top. She would return to San Vicente on Sunday afternoon in time for the vigil, but she had no plans to make a speech, stand on a platform, or brandish a heavy homemade sign. At best, Kendra could picture herself wearing a hoodie, carrying a small candle, talking quietly with a few people about the brilliant person Martina was, and maybe singing a song in remembrance.

Kendra knew her parents were worried about her, which was another reason she had driven home. It was better than having her mother arrive at the condo unannounced.

Kendra slipped the Prius into an excellent parking spot with easy beach access. She noticed some familiar vans and trucks parked nearby, which told her that the locals were also arriving for an early morning session. Looking out to the waves, Kendra saw several people either in the water or getting ready, including old dudes who had surfed this beach since the 1980s and high school kids who were squeezing in a sesh before school. Kendra grabbed her board and headed toward the rhythmic pounding, her breathing already calmer.

∼

A couple of hours later Kendra was back in her car and tired in a good way. Out of habit, she grabbed her phone and was almost surprised to see that it was off. She turned it on and winced when she saw seventeen missed calls, all from today, with several from the same unfamiliar LA number. Then she clicked on her texts and saw this message:

> Hi Kendra, Vanessa Delaware here from the LA Daily Post. So sorry for your loss. Would love to talk about what happened to Martina plz call me anytime. Sorry to text but your voicemail is full. This is my direct line REALLY CALL ANYTIME

Kendra's immediate reaction was annoyance. She wondered how this reporter had gotten her cellphone number. But it wasn't hard to puzzle out. One of her classmates at Wexford must have shared Kendra's number with the reporter. Thinking about it, Kendra was surprised she didn't have more media calls.

Kendra next read a text from Martina's father, Roberto Noto. Martina's parents wanted to meet with her today. Damn, why wouldn't everyone leave her alone! Kendra replied that she had to leave San Vicente for a few days but would be back on Sunday afternoon. Could she meet with the Notos then?

Detective Jessica Fonseca had also tried to reach her about some follow-up questions. Kendra decided to call her back after she was dry and had some more food in her stomach. As Kendra was about to toss her phone onto the passenger seat, it pinged again. This time the text was from Eliza Fox, Martina's cousin.

> Hey Kendra, met u before at dinner at
> my mom's. Can u call me today? I have
> some questions about everything. Sorry to
> pester you, IK u must feel like crap. We all
> do, hoping you can help. Eliza

Kendra liked Eliza and thought her son, Lucas, was adorable. Kendra sent a text that she'd call Eliza around noon, maybe earlier. She started the familiar drive home, where her mom would be starting to stir. Kendra knew that over breakfast Gwen would expertly weave concern about Kendra's well-being with a mild annoyance that the events in Kendra's life had upset her family's equilibrium. Her mother would somehow turn Martina's death into something significant that had happened to Gwen, rather than simply supporting her daughter. Families were a pain, but unlike the Notos, Kendra and her parents still had time to sort out the complexities of their family circle. As she drove eastward, Kendra had to admit that she was looking forward to a hug from Gwen, who would always be her mother, despite her shifting moods and sharp edges.

MARTINA'S JOURNAL

November 23 (Six months earlier)

Quiet Friday here at Wexford, as it's the day after the big Turkey *festa*. Kendra and the other kids have gone home for Thanksgiving break, and this rare day off has made me think of you, my very neglected journal.

It was a nice day yesterday at Francesca's house, eating and laughing with Eliza, her *figlio* Lucas, and some of Francesca's neighbors. Now I can snack on the turkey, potatoes, and other food that Francesca forced me to take back to the condo. Cranberries are a revelation. So wonderfully tart.

I've been a little lonely the past weeks. It's impossible to make friends with these American kids. The boys drink too much and only want to have sex with me, and the girls are not much different. They also drink too much and some of them want to have sex with me. The girls appear nice at first, but after a while, the connections seem forced and fake. It seems they don't trust me, and I don't know why. Kendra is the exception, but she's too busy on the weekends, always surfing at different beaches.

Okay, enough stressing. As the Americans say, no worries. Ever since Levi approached me last month about the project, I've been busy in the computer lab. Maybe being without friends has its upside. Hopefully, Levi and I can make our idea for a medical device work. It would help so many people. Imagine if you didn't have full use of your hands and fingers because of an injury, an illness, or a birth defect. You couldn't play the piano, use a pencil, type on a keyboard, or button your shirt—any number of things that most people don't think twice about. It was humbling to meet Mr. Willie Ducane, who could really use the device we're developing. He's a veteran of the Iraq war who lost several fingers on his left hand from an explosive device. It's true that Willie is luckier than other soldiers. He survived the war with most of his limbs intact. But imagine how much better his life could be if he had full use of both hands. Anyway, it was helpful for me to see exactly how Levi's prototype would fit Willie's hand.

Levi is a brilliant engineer. Only 24 years old, Levi will have a PhD soon. If we can make prosthetic hands function better, we'll be famous:

"Levi Newcomb and Martina Noto win Nobel with ingenious prosthesis to improve fine-motor function"

OK, maybe that's "pie in the sky" (is that the American expression?), but Levi and I could make a measurable difference. Meanwhile, Levi has insisted on an annoying amount of secrecy around this project, saying that we need to worry about intellectual property theft. I guess he's right. Some people will steal anything, and academics are known to have big fights over their inventions and patents.

Basta with the writing now. This is a perfect day to work. I have to do a lot of research for Levi plus study for the rest of my classes. I'll write soon, dear journal. *Ciao* for now.

MEDIA RELATIONS OFFICE
SAN VICENTE POLICE DEPARTMENT
FOR IMMEDIATE RELEASE

WEXFORD EXCHANGE STUDENT FOUND DEAD AT CARTER HOUSE

Martina Noto, an Italian citizen who has been studying at Wexford College during this academic year, was found dead in a music practice room in the basement of Carter House, an arts center adjacent to the Wexford campus. San Vicente PD is looking for any information about what happened to Ms. Noto. Contact the SVPD Crime Stoppers Tip Line at 999-800-7000. #SVPD #crimestoppers #lawenforcement #investigation

CHAPTER EIGHT

Thursday, May 9—Late Morning

*T*wenty minutes earlier, Eliza had thrown her phone into her oversized purse, and now she was having a hard time finding it amid the detritus. Finally, her fingers felt the familiar buzzing rectangle, and she was able to answer before Kendra's call slipped into the voicemail abyss. Eliza had met Kendra at a few dinners at Francesca's, when Martina had brought her along for a meal. Now Kendra was an important witness, and Eliza wanted to speak with her.

"Hey, Kendra. Thanks for calling. How are you doing? All of this must be rough on you, yeah?" Eliza began the call.

"Hi. Yeah, it was getting to be too much. I left campus for a few days to chill at my parents' house."

"Of course," Eliza commiserated. "I would do the same thing if I could. Look, I assume you'll be back on Sunday for the vigil. We should get together in person to go over stuff. I know Martina's parents want to see you, too. But maybe we could talk for a few minutes now? I'm working on trying to figure out what happened to Martina, and I had a few things I wanted to ask you."

Eliza explained that she was investigating Martina's death at the behest of the family. Even though Kendra had already talked to SVPD, Eliza might have different questions than the police did. Kendra agreed to help, sharing what she had already told the police about some students not liking Martina. Eliza then asked about Martina's phone, laptop, and backpack.

"The police must have the phone," Kendra said. "It was with Martina in the practice room. I remember calling Martina's phone and hearing it ring right before I pushed my way into the room and found her."

Eliza could hear Kendra's voice crack as she said this, a sonic billboard of how raw everything still was. As for the laptop and backpack, Kendra had no idea where they were and told Eliza this. Kendra had looked for them in the condo and figured that Martina had taken them with her that morning when she went to Carter House.

"The laptop was brand new, an expensive one," Kendra recounted. She explained that Martina's old laptop had been stolen out of a locker in the student wellness center. Martina had gone there for a yoga class. During the class, about a dozen lockers were broken into, and people's wallets, tablets, and laptops had been taken.

"The laptop Martina brought to Carter House that day was a new one," Kendra said.

"When did the other computer get taken?" Eliza asked. "Did Martina report the theft to campus police?"

"It was about four weeks ago, I guess. Campus police were definitely involved."

Eliza took note of this information, not sure what it meant. "Tell me about Jason Chang," she asked next. Kendra paused, feeling even more wistful. She had liked Jason and had felt a bit sorry for him when Martina broke off their relationship.

"Have you seen Jason since Martina stopped dating him?" Eliza prodded.

"Yeah, sure. Jason is in my Spanish class. He was pretty gutted for a while after they broke up, but he seemed better lately. Jason's been planning a long camping trip for when the semester ends, so he's looking forward to that."

"When did they stop dating?"

Kendra thought for a few seconds before answering. "Well, the first time they broke up was around spring break, which was the middle of March. But I think Martina kept hooking up with Jason, giving him hope. Then she would decide again she didn't want anything serious with him and end it. There was a shitload of drama for a few weeks, but they finally ended it about four or five weeks ago. At least it outwardly looked like they had ended it, but you know, they could have kept it quiet."

"Okay," Eliza said. "Last thing. Anything weird that was going on with Martina recently? Anyone she was having problems with?"

"I don't think so. Martina didn't have a ton of friends at Wexford, but I don't think anyone would physically hurt her," Kendra replied.

Eliza was about to end the call when she remembered Roberto's comment from the previous day about a project Martina was working on to help people with disabilities. "Kendra, did she mention a special project? Something that was connected to helping people with physical impairments. Does that sound familiar?"

"Oh, yeah," Kendra recalled. "She called it her *auitare le mani* project. I think it means 'helping hands.' Sorry, I'm not good with languages. I don't know the details. She was secretive about it. Maybe you can ask her faculty advisor in the computer department."

"Good idea. Who was her advisor?"

"Professor O'Keefe."

"What can you tell me about him?"

"You haven't heard of him?" Kendra replied incredulously. "The hottie professor, Tim O'Keefe, who made all that money in Silicon and then became a visiting professor at Wexford. He was Martina's advisor."

"No, I somehow missed the story on Professor O'Keefe. Thanks, Kendra. This is great information. Look, let's plan to get together on Monday after the vigil is behind us. I want to know more about Martina's day-to-day schedule: where she went and what she did. While you're away from campus, can you write down what you remember about Martina's activities, both related to her classes and social stuff?"

Kendra agreed, and they ended the call. Fifteen seconds later, Eliza was googling Timothy Patrick O'Keefe, who had developed an early version of the 3D printer and then made serious money when he sold this idea and his fledgling company. After traveling around Asia for a few years, he joined the Wexford faculty as a visiting professor— around the same time that Eliza's father had passed away. It made sense that she had missed the news about his arrival in San Vicente. At that time, she was coping with a baby, a failing marriage, the unexpected loss of her father, and her grieving mother.

Eliza checked her phone and jumped when she saw the time. She had to shop for groceries, collect Lucas from school, and eventually make dinner. After Lucas had settled down for the night, Eliza planned on doing a couple loads of laundry while she thought more about Martina and all the connections she had forged at Wexford, both good and bad. Eliza needed to consider the best ways to approach Jason Chang and Timothy O'Keefe for interviews.

CHAPTER NINE

Friday, May 10—Morning

Eliza slept poorly Thursday night, as she obsessed over each sliver of information she had collected. But despite her fitful night, she woke up optimistic. She was determined to follow the clues she had. After dropping Lucas at school, Eliza planned to slide into work mode for the rest of the day. Her mom was scheduled to pick Lucas up from school and take care of him until Eliza collected him later that night. Lucas was very close to his grandmother, who went out of her way to keep him engaged. She imagined that her mother and her son would get an ice cream after school and then take Pavo to the dog park, so that both Lucas and the dog could expend some physical energy. Then Francesca would cook something wonderful for dinner, while Lucas watched one of his favorite movies or played with Legos. As a single mom, Eliza was grateful to be close to her own mom and felt supported having her nearby. Eliza also appreciated that they all shared the same intense focus to find Martina's killer, despite how wrecked they all felt individually about what had happened.

With her mind on her family, Eliza found it oddly fitting when her phone rang and she saw that it was her ex-husband calling.

"David. Hi. Everything all right?" Eliza said, grabbing her phone from the nightstand.

"Eliza, are you on vacation? I just emailed you and got an autoreply that you were away from work for a couple of weeks."

"Oh, sorry, No. I mean, it's true that I'm not working for Marty for a couple weeks. I'm taking some time off. I should have called you. Did you hear that the body they found on campus was Martina, my cousin? I'm sorry I didn't text or tell you anything about it. So much has been going on."

"What? Oh, my God. That's crazy. I'm so sorry. How are you doing? How's your mom?"

"We're okay. Coping as best we can. Martina's parents arrived from Italy a couple of days ago. They asked me to help them find out what happened to Martina. They don't trust the police and asked if I could look into the whole thing—kind of run my own investigation. So, I agreed. My mom's been watching Lucas."

"How's Lucas doing? I mean with the death. He's only four, and this is a lot different than losing a pet hamster. He knew your cousin, right?"

"To be honest, he's not very clear on what's been happening. He knows everyone is in a tizz, and that my mom has family visiting from Italy. He knows that I'm busy doing some work. But how much can a kid really understand?"

"Okay. Well, it's good that you can help your family. After that whole incident in Italy with the American student being wrongfully convicted of murdering her roommate—was her name Amanda? With that story and all the other negative news about innocent people being convicted, it's no surprise the parents don't trust the police. We all know that Eliza Fox loves a mystery. It's great that you're available to help."

Then Eliza had an idea of how David could help her. "Hey, do you know Detective Byron Comstock at SVPD? Or his partner, Detective Jessica Fonseca?"

"No, sorry," David replied. "Are they the detectives assigned to the case? It's been so long since I worked as an intern in the DA's office. I don't know any of the detectives or prosecutors anymore."

"Okay." Then Eliza had another idea. "What about Professor Timothy O'Keefe? Have you crossed paths with him?"

"The guy from Silicon Valley? Yeah. I've been to dinner with him a few times. One of the firm's partners invited me to tag along. I'm mostly working on intellectual property and patent cases now, and the firm has been helping O'Keefe with patents. Is he involved in the mess with your cousin? Why do you want to talk to him?"

"I'm not sure, and please don't say anything to anyone else about this. I want to talk to O'Keefe as a witness. He was Martina's faculty advisor. Do you think you could contact him this morning and let him know I'll be in touch? You can be upfront about why. Say I'm a private investigator who's helping the family. He doesn't need to know I'm related to Martina."

"Sure. Happy to help. I've been looking for an excuse to call him. It's always good to stay connected with clients. I'll text you when I reach him."

"Really? Thanks, David. The sooner the better. So, your turn. Why did you call?"

"Right. Okay. Yeah, it was to see about having Lucas stay with Stephanie and me sometime this weekend. I was going to text you, but it was still early, and I was afraid your phone would ping and wake you up. So then I sent an email and got your auto reply. Then I wasn't sure what was going on."

Eliza's radar strongly signaled that something was out of whack with David. She knew her ex well enough to know that he blathered when he was nervous. Further, he almost never spent time with Lucas without Eliza in the near vicinity. David always wanted easy access to a parachute in case their son transformed himself into a screaming mess.

"David, you know that I'm immune to your bullshit, right? What's up? Why are you making a last-minute request to have a messy four-year-old hang around your very clean house?"

"He's my son, Eliza," David replied, half defensively, half jovially. "Isn't that reason enough?"

"Alright, point taken. But really, why?"

"Okay, Stephanie is pregnant, four months along, and I want to do a better job of melding us into a family. I figure the best time to start is now."

"I see," said Eliza, the wind suddenly knocked out of her. "I didn't know you two were starting a family," quickly adding, "which is a good thing for sure. Yes, take Lucas for a night. It would be a big help to me. There is so much happening with the investigation."

David agreed to pick Lucas up on Saturday afternoon, and Eliza would collect him on Sunday evening after the vigil for Martina. Before hanging up, David reminded her to pack a button-down shirt with a collar and some slacks for Lucas because they would probably go to a nice restaurant for Sunday brunch.

"Yeah, I'll make sure he brings some nice clothes. Talk later." Setting down her phone, Eliza asked herself for the thousandth time how she could have married David. Was she so wowed by his good looks and charming personality that she ignored how fundamentally different they were from each other? "Yep, that explains it," she said aloud, answering her own question. Eliza also did a mental litmus test to see how she felt about David's news of his wife's pregnancy. The short answer was she felt numb—not jealous, not hurt, not disappointed. Only numb. On the plus side, Eliza was happy for Lucas because he would have a sibling, realizing a little too late that she neglected to ask David if they knew the baby's gender. She decided to end her thoughts there. She had a case to solve, which had priority over her personal drama.

Later that morning, Eliza sent a carefully worded text to Jason Chang, explaining who she was and that Kendra had given her his number. A few minutes later, Jason replied that he was free to talk that afternoon. He proposed they meet at a deli near campus so he could eat while they spoke.

With more than twenty minutes to spare, Eliza arrived at the place Jason suggested, a new business she hadn't tried yet. She wanted time to pick the best table, hopefully one that was outside and away from other patrons. A habitual eavesdropper herself, she wanted to be sure no other customers could overhear them. Thankfully, the deli had a lovely patio. After laying some books on the most private table, she went inside and returned shortly with a large cold drink. Eliza anxiously checked the time again—still twelve minutes before Jason was due. To tamp down her nerves, she pulled out her laptop and, for the third time, tweaked the questions she planned to ask him.

Thirty minutes later, Jason had still not shown up. Disappointed, she composed a text to him, but before sending it, she looked around one last time. A tall, lanky guy with long, dark hair and smooth, tanned skin was walking toward the deli. His straight posture and confident stride suggested that he was an athlete. If this was Jason, she could see why Martina had been drawn to him. They would have made a striking couple.

Waving her hand, Eliza caught the guy's attention. "Jason?" she said as he approached the outdoor tables. When he nodded and got closer, she said, "Thanks for meeting me on such short notice. Do you want to order some food before we get started?"

He disappeared inside and returned ten minutes later with a huge sandwich, chips, and a large bottle of water. Once he was comfortable, he reached out to shake Eliza's hand. "How can I help?" he asked.

"First, I'm curious if the police have contacted you? Let's start there."

"They have," Jason said. "Some detective left a voicemail this morning. Your text arrived about the same time. I didn't get in touch with the cops. Not yet."

"Why did you agree to meet with me? I really appreciate it, but you could have easily ignored me."

"I heard from Kendra that you wanted to talk, and that you were Martina's cousin. I'm struggling with what happened to her. It's hit me hard," he said, looking at the ground. "And you know the cops. They're an effing joke! Ah, sorry, maybe you're some sort of cop. I just mean the campus police or SVPD will probably mess things up. I'm sure I'll talk to them at some point, but I wanted to talk to you first."

"No worries. I don't have any law enforcement background, and I appreciate that you were close to Martina and want justice for her. Were you and Martina a couple for a while? Tell me about that."

Jason smiled and talked for several minutes about how he met Martina at a Wexford soccer game. They were playing a home game against a rival college. During the match, Jason, a midfielder, was fouled hard by a player on the other team, which led to that player being ejected from the game. Jason had heard someone yell from the stands, "*Ciao, bella!*" as a taunt to the player being sent off. After the match, Jason made a point to find out who had yelled in Italian. It sounded like a woman's voice, and Jason was intrigued.

It hadn't been hard to figure out who Martina was, owing to the sparse attendance at Wexford's soccer games. As people were leaving the stands, Jason asked his teammates who had shouted the "*Ciao, bella!*" and they pointed toward Martina. He caught up with her and found himself immediately smitten.

After that, he and Martina dated for a few months until she broke it off, saying she didn't want any serious entanglements. Jason was sorry she'd ended it with him, and he'd clung to a small hope she would change her mind.

"Not gonna happen now," he said wistfully.

Eliza was quiet for a few seconds before asking about Martina's friends and acquaintances. Could Jason think of anyone who would be so angry with her that they'd want to hurt her?

"Not really," he said. "She was kind of a loner on campus, aside from being friends with Kendra—who is chill and devoted to Martina. The other kids may have been jealous of Martina—she was talented and beautiful and so smart—but no one seemed obsessed with her. It was more like they wanted to *be* her, but not like literally so much they wanted to destroy her. Sorry, I'm not making much sense."

"I get what you're saying," Eliza said. "It's like she was a novelty. She didn't fit the mold."

"Yeah," Jason nodded. "She was a rare bird on campus. Maybe that's weird to say."

"What about her backpack?" Eliza asked, delving into the specifics. "What did it look like?

"Just a regular black backpack. The only unique thing about it was

Martina had attached a pink, puffy ball to make it more colorful."

"And her laptop? Anything you can tell me about that?"

"No, not really. I mean she was pretty freaked out when the other one got stolen while she was in yoga class. Did you hear about that?"

Jason explained that Martina had some important data modeling on it for a computer science project she was working on. She was worried someone would hack into it, so she had protected the laptop with a program to erase it remotely, and she always kept it backed up to the cloud.

"So luckily there were no serious repercussions when the first laptop got lifted from the gym. Except that she had to get a new one," Jason said.

"Did she report it missing?"

"Oh yeah, campus police were all over it. I think Martina talked a few times to the cop who was investigating it. A few other lockers were broken into at the same time. Wallets, phones, credit cards, and tablets all went missing. My guess was an inside job. Some of those guys they hire for the wellness center are pretty sketchy. Coach expects us to go there two or three times a week to lift weights. Some of those dudes are 'roided."

"Pardon me?" Eliza said.

"You know. On steroids," Jason pointed to his upper arms and made an exaggerated gesture as if he had huge biceps. "I heard from guys on the baseball team that you can buy steroids from a dude at the wellness center. I'm not interested in that, but they're available to anybody."

While Eliza found this interesting and noted it as a future problem to worry about in raising her own son, she felt he was veering off topic.

"Jason, tell me how this relates to what happened to Martina?" She was looking for a connection between steroid sales at the wellness center, Martina's stolen laptop, and her murder at Carter House.

"I don't know," he said with some consideration. "I don't know."

"It's interesting, and the campus police should be told about illegal drug sales," Eliza said. "But I need to think more about this.

Maybe it's important," she told Jason. "Do you know the name of the person from campus police who was looking into the locker thefts?"

"I think it was Thompson—or wait, Kennedy? Or maybe Thompson Kennedy. Something like that, I'm not sure."

"Okay." Eliza then circled back to something he had said earlier. "Do you know any more about the computer science project she was working on? You said she was worried about her computer being hacked."

"Not too much," Jason said. "I couldn't tell if she was being paranoid about computer security, or if the threat was real. I know she had some partner she was working with, a graduate student, I think. And it had something to do with helping the disabled. But she kept pretty hush about it. I wanted to write an article for the *Wexford Times* about Martina's project. I'm a journalism major, so I'm always looking for stories. But she was adamant that the project was off limits."

"Okay. Do you know the name of the graduate student?"

"I think it was Levi, but I'm not sure."

"Is Levi a first or last name?"

"Sorry, I don't know. Could be either."

Eliza thanked Jason as she packed up her things. "You know how to reach me," she said. "If you think of anything, truly anything, send me a text. I'll get right back to you."

Back in her car, Eliza looked over her notes. She realized that she hadn't asked Jason where he'd been on Tuesday morning, or the last time he'd seen Martina? What was Jason's alibi?

"Damn, damn, damn," she said, pounding the steering wheel. "Stupid rookie mistake."

She glanced back at the table where they'd been sitting, but he was gone. Feeling incompetent, she realized she'd been charmed by his agreeable demeanor and his forthright concerns about Martina. She had also given weight to Kendra's good opinion of Jason, which further clouded her ability to see him as a suspect. Despite her gut saying Jason was not Martina's killer, Eliza was still mad at herself. She needed to be more dispassionate and view everyone as a potential perpetrator. Adding to her distress, she had to admit she was biased in favor of good-looking guys—Jason and her ex-husband, to name a couple. They threw off her gyroscope and caused her to make careless mistakes with potentially big consequences. "You better watch this," she told herself, "before it trips you up in the investigation."

Her confidence waning, Eliza wondered if conducting a criminal investigation, especially without a more seasoned PI supervising her work, was beyond her ability. She considered calling her boss for a check in about the Noto case. Then, just as quickly, she backed off that idea. While Marty could be a good sounding board, it was likely he'd overstep. Eliza was certain he'd snatch control of the case, and somehow bring it under the purview of his firm, Fowler & Haverford, something she would surely regret. In lieu of contacting Marty, she took a breath and found some music on her phone that matched her mood.

After listening twice to Amy Winehouse's rendition of "Will You Still Love Me Tomorrow?" she had wallowed enough. It was time to refocus. Next up was the interview with Tim O'Keefe. Also on the list, find out whether there was a connection between what happened to Martina and the break-in at the wellness center. Was the theft of the first laptop significant? Eliza also wanted to see the autopsy report. She would ask Martina's parents to request a copy. Surely the family could get access to it.

Eliza started the Volvo and headed home. She needed to change into a more professional outfit before approaching Professor O'Keefe. As she drove, she found that the blues were still chasing her. Her mind was fixated on her dating life, or rather, the lack of dating in her life. *Maybe indulging in a soulful song about love and commitment was a bad idea,* she thought. "Time to change it up and get out of this crappy mood," she told the empty car.

When she found herself feeling glum, Eliza could sometimes reset her frame of mind by approaching the problem like an investigator—stepping back and looking unflinchingly at the facts. She took stock of her physical and emotional being: slender, but not skinny, medium height, with attractive blue-gray eyes, nice teeth, and good skin. She was smart, occasionally funny and knew how to flirt when it mattered. To be fair, she could do with some new clothes and fresh highlights to brighten her wavy brown hair. And maybe, if she wanted to face the truth, she could own up to being a little lonely. It was possible that she still hadn't recovered from her divorce and may have buried herself too deeply in the role of Lucas's mother. There, she'd admitted it. She had taken herself out of the dating pool, and she wasn't ready to go back in, at least not yet.

FILE 19-00537
VICTIM: Noto, Martina

21-year-old female, white non-Latino
Body found in basement practice room at Carter House by Kendra Reid, victim's roommate

Relevant Information from Medical Examiner:

Time of death: approximately 10 a.m.

Cause of death: Blunt force trauma. Head injury was likely caused by her skull colliding with hard object, possible stone foundation. No weapon found at the scene.

No food ingested for prior 12 hours

Toxicology: TBD. Preliminary evidence suggests victim was not under influence of alcohol or narcotics at time of her death. Parents reported victim used birth control pills and antihistamines, but no other known medications.

Forensic Analysis:

Crime scene was a public space used by multiple people. It was not possible to isolate DNA. The exterior area below the window of the practice room where victim was found did not yield viable footprints or other evidence, except for a cellophane wrapper from a hard candy or throat lozenge. This piece of evidence is still being analyzed.

Relevant data on victim's cellular for prior three months:
iPhone, model 8.

Call Log—Recent Calls (obvious spam calls not listed)

1. Roberto and Laura Noto (Parents)
2. Jason Chang
3. Francesca Noto-Fox
4. Kendra Reid
5. Levi Newcomb
6. Timothy O'Keefe
7. Wexford Campus Police—Internal line

Relevant text history:

Text messages only go back 60 days. Prior texts have been deleted from phone and victim's cloud acct.

1. Roberto Noto
2. Laura Noto
3. Ana Maggio (living in Europe, identified by Noto family as victim's childhood friend)
4. Timothy O'Keefe
5. Jason Chang
6. Kendra Reid
7. Francesca Noto-Fox
8. Levi Newcomb
9. Wexford campus library
10. Officer Kennedy Thompson, Wexford Campus Police
11. Texts regarding scheduled delivery of computer to victim's off-campus residence
12. Various messages from Europe, appear to be school friends of victim

CHAPTER TEN

Friday, May 10—Midday

Jessica was feeling wrung out and not yet ready to face the day as Detective Fonseca. She had been in the ER with her mom since 3 a.m. Thankfully, Dolores was fine and back at home although the fact that she had fallen during a 2 a.m. bathroom trip was worrisome. The emergency device her mother wore 24/7 was activated in the fall, which led to the paramedics and Jessica being notified.

This morning, she had planned to study the forensics from the Noto murder in a quiet space before Byron arrived at work, but that opportunity had evaporated. Given that it was nearly noon, her partner had ample time to digest the evidence, and he'd be expounding on his theories of the case before Jessica's purse hit her desk. Honestly, she was in no mood.

"Fonseca, you're late," Byron bellowed as she approached her desk.

"Yeah. Couldn't be helped. Family emergency. Mom took a fall in the middle of the night. I just left St. Joe's an hour ago. Didn't you get my message? I called the Watch Commander to say I'd be late."

Changing his tone, Byron asked, "Is Dolores okay? Are you okay?"

"She's fine, but I'm fried. Can you give me a minute with the file?"

"Yes, in fact, you can have a full ninety minutes with the file. Why don't you order in some lunch, read your emails, and then spend some time reviewing what's new with the Noto file."

"That seems like a very relaxed approach," Jessica replied, grateful that Byron wasn't being an asshole.

"Don't get too relaxed. I need you on your game this afternoon. We're going to drop in on Tim O'Keefe, our victim's faculty advisor."

"Timothy O'Keefe? Isn't he worth a gazillion dollars?"

"Oh, yeah. Guy's loaded. Anyway, while you were helping your mom, I was looking at what the tech team pulled off Martina's cellphone record. O'Keefe shows up on the call log, and he has a prominent role in her text messages."

Literally shaking off the tiredness, Jessica turned her complete attention to Byron. "What do you mean by prominent?"

"Read the file. You won't be disappointed."

"Roger that," she fired back.

Jessica did as Byron suggested and ordered a falafel wrap from her favorite Middle Eastern restaurant for delivery. While waiting for lunch to arrive, she called her sister to reassure her that Dolores was fine and to plant the idea that they needed to reconsider their mom's living arrangements. She knew her sister was in denial about their mother's decline, but Jessica was the daughter in charge. It wasn't possible for her sister, who lived in New York, to observe the subtle changes that Jessica noticed. Given that both sisters were busy with work, they made their call brief and agreed to talk in a few days.

With food in hand and her family crisis temporarily handled, Jessica found the printout of Martina's text messages and started reading. Oddly, the messages only went back about sixty days, which gave the impression that Martina deleted them regularly. While it was possible Martina only had limited storage on her phone, this seemed odd. Did Martina have another reason to clear out her texts periodically? If so, what was it?

Jessica thumbed through the printout of Martina's messages, finding exchanges with Kendra, with Martina's parents, and with friends in Italy and other parts of Europe. The texts had not been translated yet, and Jessica didn't understand Italian. She spot-checked a few with a translation app, and they seemed like harmless chatter among old friends. For now, she was going to assume they were from other young people in Martina's circle.

There were also other messages: some from Jason Chang, a former lover of Martina's, and some from people sharing information about a music recital. Eventually, she found the O'Keefe texts. They started off professionally enough with Martina asking for a meeting about one of her computer science classes and O'Keefe suggesting she stop by during his office hours. The texts continued in a friendly but appropriate professor-student vein for a couple weeks.

But on April 17, the messages took a more intimate turn.

> T. O'Keefe: What are you doing tonite would love to see u again! My place?
> M. Noto: Sorry gotta work. So much going on. I had fun did you find my earring?
> T. O'Keefe: Yes to the earring. I'll keep it for you—as a way to lure you back
> M. Noto: Hahaha don't lose it. It was a gift from my nonna. Mama will be very unhappy if I lose it. Cu soon.

April 24 (one week later):

> T. O'Keefe: Uncorking an excellent Tuscan chianti. How soon can you get here?
> M. Noto: Ooooh I like chianti but I need food. Do you have any?
> T. O'Keefe: Pizza ordered and on the way—the one u like with thin crust and mushrooms. CU at 8?
> M. Noto: Add a salad and ur on
> T. O'Keefe: [lettuce emoticon, heart emoticon, wine glass emoticon]

The texts start again on the following Wednesday, May 1:

> M. Noto: Sorry can't make it tonight. Gotta practice for my recital and study.

Another time?

T. O'Keefe: [Sad face emoticon] very
disappointed—u can practice here. Bring
your electronic keyboard.

M. Noto: No, I need an actual piano and
ur a distraction

T. O'Keefe: I'll leave you alone. Promise.
Just want to see you

M. Noto: Not tonight I'll c u in a few days

T. O'Keefe: Ok but not happy. Remind me
to buy a piano for you.

M. Noto: Hahaha

The last group of texts were from O'Keefe to Noto with no reply from her. They were sent on Monday, May 6, and after midnight on May 7.

T. O'Keefe: Miss u come over now [8:52
pm]

T. O'Keefe: Call me plz [10:12 pm]

T. O'Keefe: Worried and not laughing if
this ghosting me is a joke. Call me [11:45
p.m.]

T. O'Keefe: Martina, I'm truly worried
about you [1:15 a.m.]

Jessica checked the call log. O'Keefe had called Martina's phone several times on the evening of May 6 but never reached her, which was even more troubling given that Martina was found dead only hours later. If Kendra hadn't told them that she'd heard Martina in the condo that morning, Jessica would be questioning the whole premise of the case.

CHAPTER ELEVEN

Friday, May 10—Mid-afternoon

*E*liza wanted to present a professional yet alluring image when she walked into O'Keefe's office. After digging through her closet, she settled on a low-cut tank top and some skinny jeans, which she topped with a lightweight blazer. She then found a pair of sexy designer heels in a shoebox on her closet shelf. She remembered paying the equivalent of several weeks' groceries for those shoes— and hadn't worn them since before she was pregnant with Lucas. Looking at them now, Eliza felt equally silly having paid so much for a pair of shoes and pleased that she could have a frivolous side. The peek-a-boo toe was a statement. She gingerly maneuvered her right foot into the soft leather and immediately felt a crush of pain and pressure on her heel.

"Damn," she exclaimed. "No one tells you that having a baby makes your feet bigger! For the rest of your life!" She tossed the heels back into their box, making a mental note to donate them somewhere. Eliza slipped on a pair of sandals, put on some lipstick, and headed to campus.

Lucky to find parking near Janus Hall, which now served as the campus computer science building, she made her way upstairs to O'Keefe's office. She wanted to time her arrival so it would be close to the end of O'Keefe's office hours. While the lower floors of the old building had been remodeled with fancy computer labs and state-of-the-art classrooms, the upper floors of Janus Hall, where the faculty offices were located, still cried out for renovation. Faculty mostly worked out of oversized closets, and that was if they ranked highly enough to get a solo office. If not, they shared larger spaces with adjunct or visiting faculty, sometimes three or four professors to a room. But not O'Keefe; he had secured a spacious corner office, which would have normally gone to a dean or department chair. "Right. This guy has a personal fortune and the clout that comes with it," Eliza observed, a note to herself about the power Timothy O'Keefe could wield.

She tapped on his office door and, without waiting for a response, stuck her head in the office, smiling broadly.

"Professor O'Keefe? I'm Eliza Fox. I believe you know my ex-husband, David Rutledge. He contacted you this morning to say I would be in touch. I'm looking into Martina Noto's death, and I understand you knew her."

Eliza was caught off guard by O'Keefe's good looks, his appearance enhanced by his expensive haircut, designer glasses and nicely pressed shirt. His unlined face and athletic physique belied his true age. Having grown up around college professors, Eliza expected them to be sloppy and wrinkled, but not O'Keefe.

"Yes, come in," O'Keefe told her, half-standing and pointing to an empty chair. "I spoke with David this morning. He said you'd be reaching out, although I expected a phone call... but you're here... in person. I'm terribly sorry. I don't have a lot of time just now and can only talk for a minute. Please tell me how I can help. Martina was one of my students. A brilliant girl."

Eliza settled herself in the chair O'Keefe had pointed to while she took in the expensive oriental rugs, the trinkets from global travels placed tastefully among the books, and the peaceful view of the nearby foothills.

"Wow, what an office! Do you share it with anyone?" Eliza said, a bit more pointedly than she'd intended. She again made a mental note to play nice.

O'Keefe replied, with a half-smile, "No, the dean has been very gracious to let me use this space without an officemate." O'Keefe then checked his watch, reinforcing his point that he had limited time. Eliza could hear his computer pinging with alerts to announce incoming emails.

"I know you're very busy, so let me jump in," she said. "I'm a private investigator, and Martina's parents have asked me to look into her death. For whatever reason, they don't have much faith in our local law enforcement."

"Why would that be?" O'Keefe asked. "I mean, aside from the general news stories about problems with police agencies, is there something particular about the San Vicente police that worries them?"

"Maybe I overstated that," she replied. "Their mistrust of the local cops probably overlaps with a poor opinion of the Italian police. I'm sure you remember that botched investigation in Italy a few years ago involving a dead college student on a semester abroad from Britain. That investigation led to the wrongful conviction of the girl's American roommate and her Italian boyfriend. It was a big deal."

"Yes, the Knox case. I read about it at the time," O'Keefe said, nodding.

"Seemed like everyone followed that case," Eliza said. "Anyway, I'd like to figure out what was going on with Martina while she was here at Wexford. Did she say anything about problems with anyone? Anything that caught your attention? Either her death was random—wrong place, wrong time—or she was involved in something that went awry."

"I didn't talk with her about personal matters. We talked about her project. It had a tie-in with the business school. It's one of the reasons students come to Wexford, you know, the connections across departments. There is an excellent entrepreneurial program that intersects with our computer science courses."

"Did she have an advisor at the business school too?"

"Yes, she did," O'Keefe said, looking blankly at Eliza.

When Eliza simply returned his gaze, O'Keefe replied, "Oh, you want his name. I don't recall it off the top of my head, but I can email it to you. Send me a reminder later."

"Sure. I can do that. Since you were her advisor, I was hoping that you could explain Martina's project to me."

"Well, it was a great opportunity for her," O'Keefe said. "An excellent way to help people with dexterity impairments. A doctoral student with a background in biomedical engineering had the idea. This student came up with an improved prosthetic device to help people with disfigured hands, either due to injuries or birth defects. Martina was working with this student on the prototype. If they were successful and could work out the kinks, it would be a game changer for some people. One of the problems was the devices needed to be personally engineered for each patient, which added considerably to the costs. Martina was working on that angle, looking for ways to streamline the computer integration. She is—rather, was—excellent at problem-solving and often found elegant solutions. I hoped it would be a good match to have her work with Levi."

"Sorry," Eliza said. "I didn't catch this student's name."

"Levi. Levi Newcomb or Newbaum, something like that."

"Can I get Levi's contact information, please?"

"Sorry, I can't release that to you. Student information is private. We're not allowed to share it with anyone outside the Wexford community."

"Right, of course," Eliza nodded.

"Is that all? I have another appointment in a few minutes."

Seeing that she was being dismissed, Eliza thanked him and put her notepad into her purse. Before stepping into the hallway, however, she turned back to look at O'Keefe directly. "Professor O'Keefe, I meant to ask. Where were you on Tuesday morning? It was such an awful time for the entire campus."

O'Keefe paused noticeably, as if to keep his emotions in check. "Yes, awful," he said. "I can't imagine what it must be like for her parents. I'm curious why you'd ask me such an obvious alibi question? Do you suspect me of something?"

"No, of course not," Eliza quickly back-pedaled. "I was only asking to see if you were with any students at the time the news broke. I was wondering how people reacted—if you observed any odd responses."

"I was home on Tuesday morning, preparing for my class that afternoon. My cleaning lady can confirm this."

"Right. Many thanks," she said, closing the office door behind her. Slowly, Eliza walked along the corridor toward the staircase, mulling over what O'Keefe had told her and what he seemed reluctant to reveal. Eliza would have liked to talk to O'Keefe much longer than the fifteen minutes he gave her, but he was clearly impatient for her to leave.

As she reached the stairs and was about to descend, the elevator doors opened, and a man and a woman stepped out. The man, beardless and quite tall with short-cropped hair, wore a shirt and tie with an ill-fitting jacket. The woman was dressed in a gray pantsuit, her dark hair rolled up neatly and clipped at the back of her head. They looked out of place in the computer science building, which was confirmed when they consulted the wall directory for information. Eliza had a hunch they were Detectives Comstock and Fonseca on their way to talk to O'Keefe.

As soon as the two had moved down the corridor, she turned and retraced her steps, walking slowly behind them toward O'Keefe's office. She was ready to act like a lost student if they noticed her. Except for a few professors quietly working in their offices, the floor was largely empty.

As Eliza spied from a few yards back, Comstock and Fonseca knocked on O'Keefe's door, walked in, and closed it behind them. Eliza moved quickly toward the small single-occupancy restroom right next to O'Keefe's office. She stepped inside, flipped the lock on the bathroom door, and stood quietly, hoping she'd be able to eavesdrop on their conversation.

At first, she only heard muffled voices. As a child, Eliza had visited similar offices with her parents and was amazed that the deans had their own bathrooms and sometimes even private showers. Eliza was certain the restroom she now occupied was replicated in O'Keefe's office on the opposite side of the wall she was staring at. Eliza looked for an air vent, hoping she might be able to pick up a few words if she put her head close to a duct. "Lucky, ducky," Eliza murmured, quoting her son. In the corner, behind a tall metallic trashcan filled with used paper towels was a big, grated air vent near the floor.

She quickly moved the waste can and tugged on the grate. Its screws held fast. However, with her ear close to the duct, the voices in the next room seemed a little clearer. Eliza eyed the gross bathroom floor, scrunched up her face, and knelt next to the vent. Almost immediately, the mingled odors of mold and old urine triggered a few waves of nausea, which Eliza struggled to suppress.

"Look, Professor, we don't want to play hardball here," Eliza heard a woman say, assuming this was Fonseca. "But we know you were sleeping with Martina. We have the texts from her phone and the call log. We know you tried calling her several times the night before she died. This makes you a person of interest."

"We can do this at the station if you'd prefer," a man said, presumably Comstock.

Eliza couldn't make out O'Keefe's response, but it was hard to imagine that he'd replied anything other than that he wanted to contact his attorney. As Eliza pressed her left ear closer, straining to hear more, her peripheral vision picked up an odd brown thing on the floor, only inches from her face. She bolted to her feet, letting out an audible scream. In the process, the metal trashcan was upended, creating a bang and spewing paper towels and tissues. A giant cockroach scuttled peacefully among the wads of paper littering the floor.

In a momentary panic, Eliza righted the trash can and began cleaning up the mountain of dirty towels. She heard a pounding on the bathroom door and saw the door handle jiggle.

"Everything okay in there?" a woman asked, and Eliza realized it was Fonseca. The crash must have reverberated in O'Keefe's office.

"I'm fine! Sorry. There's a gross cockroach in here. It startled me," Eliza yelled through the door.

"Ohhh, okay," Jessica said. "As long as you're not injured or need help."

"No, I'm fine. Bit of a fright, but all's good. Thanks."

She flushed the toilet and turned on the tap, hoping Jessica would accept that she was fine and lose interest in her. Jittery, Eliza took a few deep breaths to collect herself. Then she gave her hair a quick brushing and touched up her makeup. After a few minutes, she heard footsteps in the hallway and assumed the detectives had left O'Keefe's office. She figured they had cut some deal with him to reconvene when his attorney could be present. After another half-minute passed, she slowly opened the bathroom door and looked around. Seeing the empty corridor, Eliza stepped out, walked full speed to the stairs, and left the building. As soon as she was clear of Janus Hall, Eliza found a secluded bench and took out her notepad. She wrote down what she thought she'd overheard in O'Keefe's office:

Janus Hall, Office of Professor O'Keefe
Detective Fonseca said Martina's phone had texts and calls from O'Keefe that showed he was sleeping with her. O'Keefe is a person of interest, called Martina several times the night before she died.

Eliza took a minute to consider what this meant. It explained why O'Keefe had been quick to get rid of her. He didn't want to let slip that he was hooking up with a student half his age. Even if he was innocent of anything criminal, it was a bad look to sleep with a student. Now Eliza wanted to know more about the connection between Martina and Tim O'Keefe. While it was doubtful the detectives would share anything with her, they might share information with Martina's parents. It was also interesting that Kendra hadn't said anything about Martina having a fling with O'Keefe. It was possible she hadn't known about it, which made her wonder just how secretive Martina was.

Eliza regretted not putting her phone on record while in the bathroom. That simple step would have created an exact record, so she wouldn't have to rely solely on her memory. In a calmer frame of mind now, there were many things Eliza regretted about her time in the bathroom: crawling on the disgusting floor, getting uncomfortably close to a cockroach, knocking over the trashcan, emitting an audible yelp, and the final regret, being fundamentally a good girl and picking up the soiled paper towels with her bare hands. Yuck!

On the plus side, she was happy with herself for following the detectives and placing herself in the bathroom. That maneuver had yielded some very useful information.

Eliza found her car and turned toward her mom's house. As she left the Wexford grounds, she saw a couple of campus police vehicles headed toward Janus Hall. A few seconds later, two San Vicente police cars passed her, also rolling toward Computer Sciences. Shortly, Professor O'Keefe would likely be escorted to the station for questioning where he would be met by his extremely well-paid legal counsel. Eliza wondered if David's firm would have a role in O'Keefe's defense. The practice included a criminal defense group, although it mostly focused on white-collar crimes, not murder.

Eliza's heart was no longer racing, but she was still amped up from her afternoon. As she sat in traffic, she thought about whether O'Keefe was guilty. Had he entered Carter House and killed Martina while she practiced the piano? It seemed unlikely. He would have known the police would eventually find his texts and calls to Martina. Even if he deleted every interaction with Martina on his phone, her phone would still have a record of them. O'Keefe's deep financial resources were also a factor. Assuming he had fatally struck Martina in a fit of rage, why was O'Keefe still quietly sitting in his office a few days later? Wouldn't he have immediately fled to Morocco or the Maldives, somewhere without extradition? On the other hand, maybe he had orchestrated a murder for hire scheme, and he figured he had enough money and power to get away with it. That could explain his reaction to her question about his whereabouts and his handy alibi.

Eliza realized, of course, that she didn't know what evidence the police had against O'Keefe, beyond what she'd overheard. All in all, he was a good-looking White guy with money. Eliza was curious to see how the professor, who was used to having things go his way, would navigate the ensuing days and how the campus community would respond to whatever transpired.

Her immediate plan was to collect Lucas from her mom, take a long shower, put on her sweats, and cuddle with her son on the couch while they ate take-out fried chicken and watched a movie. She needed a night off from Martina's complicated life.

CHAPTER TWELVE

Saturday, May 11—Morning

*E*liza nodded off in Lucas's bed after they finished his favorite book. Her nightstand clock read 2:13 a.m. when she crawled into her own bed. Waking up a little stiff, she told herself it was nothing a few yoga stretches and some physical activity couldn't put right. First, she reached for her laptop to check for news coverage linking Timothy O'Keefe to Martina's case.

Bingo. Two local television stations were running footage of O'Keefe entering San Vicente police station, but none of the TV news outlets had much more than that. Eliza also checked the online edition of the *Wexford Watch,* the campus paper. Sometime after midnight, the *Watch's* reporting team had filed a story about Professor O'Keefe—his business history, his path to joining the Wexford faculty, and his role as a student advisor. The article quoted a couple of female students who found the handsome professor "flirty," but there was no mention of any specific incidences of sexual harassment. Within a day or two, Eliza knew that coverage of O'Keefe's connection to Martina would mushroom in the national press.

She next phoned Francesca. Even though it was Saturday, her mother would be awake and already on her second espresso. Eliza called to propose a family dinner for later that night. Eliza needed to talk with Martina's parents about O'Keefe and what had been happening in the investigation. She also wanted to see how they were holding up and talk about what to expect at the campus vigil. It was scheduled for sunset the next evening. With Lucas heading off to his dad's house, tonight would be a good time to do that.

As expected, Francesca quickly agreed and proffered a plan. She would send Roberto to the market for groceries and then enlist Laura's help to make chicken cacciatore with linguini and a green salad. Eliza was directed to pick up a baguette and a fruit tart for dessert. As Eliza well knew, Francesca believed in the curative powers of staying busy, which she saw as a salve for life's difficulties—loneliness, anxiety, addictions of all sorts, even unspeakable grief. Being active and connected to community were Francesca's guardrails, and she told her daughter that the familiar tasks of preparing a Saturday night meal would be good for all of them.

With the evening plans resolved, Eliza set about fixing Lucas's breakfast and then turned to vacuuming, changing sheets, doing laundry, and all the other chores that normally consumed her Saturday mornings. Lucas was excited about his rare sleepover at his dad's. She had instructed her son to pick out some toys and a few books to bring along. He was a decisive child and quickly filled a backpack with some treasured items. He also checked over the clothes Eliza had packed for him. After verifying that his favorite dinosaur pajamas were included, he went happily to the yard to dig for bugs.

With her personal life temporarily organized, Eliza opened the spreadsheet she was using to make sense of her investigation. The document laid out what she had done so far and what she planned to do. She added Levi Newbaum to her witness list (contact information unknown) and the professor (name unknown) who was Martina's advisor at the business school. Martina's project with Levi was intriguing, and Eliza wanted to find out more about it.

Eliza googled "Levi Newcomb" and "Wexford" to see what came up. She found several hits for Professor Elijah Newcomb, now retired, who used to teach linguistics at Wexford, but nothing about a student named Levi Newcomb. She then added "engineering" to the search. These results brought up a donor to the School of Engineering named Livie Newbaumer, but still no mention of Levi. Eliza tried some social media searches for Levi Newbaum and Levi Newcomb, but still no useful hits. "What the heck? Who is this Levi?" she said aloud. "And where does he live?"

It was time for the next level of research. Eliza navigated to the proprietary database that she used at her job to find personal data about people to use in lawsuits. The database compiled and categorized information from public records such as home addresses; dates of birth; ownership of large assets, like real estate, boats, or airplanes; bankruptcies and other court filings, and more. She typed in LEVI NEWCOMB and zip codes for San Vicente to see what the database would cough out. The results showed no listing for anyone named Levi Newcomb in San Vicente. She expanded the search to all of Los Angeles County and checked the search box for "similar sounding names."

There were three possible matches:

> Leviticus Newcomb, age 48, living alone in Santa Monica
> Levi R. Newcomb, age 79, living in Pasadena with Sara
> Newcomb, age 75
> Elvis M. Newbaum, age 60, living in the mid-Wilshire
> area of LA with Deborah Newbaum, age 86. Her hus-
> band, Levente Newbaum, died in 2009

"Damn!" Eliza yelled. All of them were too old to be the Levi she was looking for. While the results from the database were annoying, they weren't surprising. Levi was young, so he might not have enough employment history or other on-the-grid activities to be included in the databases.

Eliza thought it might be possible that one of these people had a son or a grandson named Levi. She printed out the search results and decided to stop by the home of Levi R. Newcomb, the older man living in Pasadena. Conveniently, David didn't live too far from Levi and Sara's address, so she could drive there after dropping Lucas at his dad's. Eliza figured she would learn something from this exercise, even if it was that she had the wrong address.

Thinking about other loose ends, she also considered Martina's old laptop, the one that was stolen from the campus wellness center. Hopefully, Levi—once she found him—would be able to shed some light on that, since he was working with Martina when it was stolen.

She also added the names of the students who told the *Wexford Watch* that Professor O'Keefe was flirty with them into a "maybe interview" category. With the police focused on O'Keefe, Eliza's instinct was to let the two detectives pursue that angle, especially since her own gut said that O'Keefe was not the killer. Eliza thought more deeply about motive—or lack of it—in O'Keefe's case. She reasoned that Martina would have needed to do something very serious to have thrown O'Keefe so far off balance that he would want to kill her. While it was possible O'Keefe had hurt Martina in a crazed state, it was hard to picture. He had a cushy life that would be devastated if he got embroiled in a crime of passion. It was possible he'd tried to rattle her with the idea of exacting some kind of revenge, and maybe something had backfired. But again, why would O'Keefe risk it?

Eliza was very clear with herself that she was not in competition with SVPD; her goal was to give her family peace of mind that Martina's murderer would be apprehended, and justice would do her thing. If the detectives, who had lots of resources, solved the crime first—and proved that O'Keefe had caused Martina's death—that would be an acceptable outcome to the situation.

Finally, Eliza entered Ana Maggio, Martina's childhood friend, to her short list of people to talk with. Martina's parents had given her Ana's name as someone their daughter was in regular contact with. It made sense to connect with her, although Eliza was worried that her mastery of Italian was too limited to conduct an interview, assuming Ana was not conversant in English.

"Problems. Problems. Problems," she said aloud, closing the laptop and heading to the yard to check on Lucas.

∼

A few hours later, Eliza made her way to David's to drop off her son for the night. After giving the boy a hug and a kiss, she was back in her car and making a quick retreat from David's large contemporary home overlooking the Rose Bowl. She surprised herself by being on the edge of tears. While Eliza didn't want to be married to David, she envied his financial resources, his new spouse, and his baby on the way. She literally shook herself to dispel a growing bad mood and refocused on the night ahead of her. Her phone was set to navigate to the Newcomb house, located in an area of Pasadena known for its older craftsman bungalows. Eight minutes later, with her navigation app chiming that the destination was on her right, she parked in front of an aging house with overgrown shrubs and paint peeling from its eaves. Eliza disliked knocking on anyone's door without an appointment, but cold calls were a necessary part of the job. She got out of the car and climbed the porch steps. Summoning cheerful memories of selling Girl Scout cookies door-to-door, she pressed the doorbell and waited.

Less than a minute later, a short, round woman whose apron said, "Kiss the Cook," opened the front door a few inches. Peering through silver-framed glasses that coordinated with her curly, gray hair, she looked firmly at Eliza and said, "I'm not signing any petitions, nor am I giving you any money."

"Then I'm in luck," Eliza said, laughing lightly. "I'm not here for your signature, and I don't want any of your money. I'm so sorry to bother you, but I'm looking for someone named Levi Newcomb. Do you know him? I'm looking for a man who attends Wexford College, where he knew my cousin Martina."

The woman looked up and down, assessing the stranger on her porch. She then opened the door wide enough to squeeze herself through it. Standing on the porch, she took another long look at Eliza.

"Dear, you must have the wrong Levi. Levi is my husband's name, but he was never a student at Wexford. Decades ago, he was a Caltech man, but he's nearly eighty now."

"I see," said Eliza. "Do you have a grandson named Levi, or a nephew? A young cousin?"

"No, we don't have any grandchildren. Sorry, I wish I could help."

"Okay, I won't take any more of your time then," Eliza said, acknowledging she was at a dead end. "Thank you for talking to me."

"No problem, dear. I hope you find your cousin's friend. It must be important for you to knock on a stranger's door late on a Saturday afternoon. Good luck with your search."

Eliza got back in her car, drove a few blocks, and parked. She wanted to think for a minute, without Mrs. Newcomb peering out her window at her. Clearly, Levi wasn't living at the Pasadena address she'd located for the elderly Levi Newcomb, the Caltech man.

Eliza texted Kendra and Jason Chang to see if they knew Levi Newcomb or Levi Newbaum. She had wasted enough time chasing Levi on her own. On a positive note, Eliza still had enough time to stop at her favorite bakery before it closed to pick up the tart and baguette her mom had requested.

∿

Twenty minutes later, as she stepped out of the bakery, Eliza's phone pinged with a reply from Kendra.

> Kendra: Yes to Levi NEWCOMB. Martina
> was working with him.
> Eliza: Excellent! Do you have his contact
> info?
> Kendra: Yeah, I'll text it.
> Eliza: Thanks. Appreciated.

Eliza made a mental note to send Kendra some flowers. Martina's roommate was proving to be helpful.

∿

A short time later, Pavo greeted Eliza with enthusiastic tail wags and joyous barks as she walked through her mother's front door. The house smelled of tomatoes and garlic. Caught by the familiar aromas, she stood in the entryway and attempted to time travel back to her life as a child in her parents' house. She envisioned her dad reading in his brown leather chair, sun streaming over his shoulder to illuminate the page. After a moment of memories, Francesca's voice cascaded from the kitchen, breaking the spell. *"Figlia, vieni qui!"* her mother shouted. Eliza found Francesca and Martina's parents sitting around the kitchen table, with glasses of red wine and plates of olives and cheese in front of them. A short time later, the four were resettled in the dining room around the large, comfortable table.

Over the chicken cacciatore and linguini, Eliza brought Roberto and Laura up to speed on her investigation, including the news that their daughter had likely been involved with an older, wealthy professor. Eliza didn't want to upset them needlessly, but the truth was what it was. As they absorbed this information, she asked what the police had shared with them so far. Laura said that Detective Fonseca had called earlier to say Professor O'Keefe was now considered "a person of interest."

"Did Fonseca say why O'Keefe was of interest?" Eliza asked.

"No, the detective was vague," Roberto told her. "Something about finding text messages between him and Martina."

Roberto, now zeroing in on the O'Keefe angle, reasoned, "Maybe Martina told this man no when he tried something sexual with her. That could make some men very angry, even violent. You say that this professor is a rich man, much older than Martina. Then maybe he would react strongly if he was rejected by a young girl."

"Yes, we should ask the police more about it. I'm curious if you've received the results of the autopsy yet?" Eliza asked, trying to pivot away from the O'Keefe angle, but Roberto wasn't ready to let it go.

"Laura," he said, in a measured voice. "Did you know about this relationship our daughter was having with this man? Did she talk to you about it?" Roberto pounded a fist lightly on the table as he said this, looking as if he were ready to punch anyone who crossed him.

"No, *amore mio,* she didn't talk to me much about her personal life," Laura replied quietly. "She was in a rebellious phase and thought I was overprotective. I think it's why she wanted to study so far from home. I was hoping that when she was a little older," her voice breaking, "we would become close again."

Roberto reached over and hugged his wife for a long minute while they both regained their composure.

"We haven't seen a written report, but we asked about the cause of death," Laura said. "The detective confirmed it was a homicide. They believe it was blunt force trauma, that she'd hit her head, but this was still preliminary. They don't think Martina was raped."

"Did the police say anything about defensive wounds? Was there a struggle?" Eliza asked. "Really, anything they said would be helpful."

Laura continued, "There was a visible bruise on her forehead. On the left side of her skull. Roberto noticed it when we went to the morgue. The police are assuming it happened when she fell, rather than her being struck with something. Apparently, the room where she practiced had a stone foundation." Roberto and Laura both agreed this was everything they knew from the police.

Eliza considered whether Martina had known her killer. Was the perpetrator someone she greeted and invited into the practice room, or a stranger who snuck up on her? And how did the killer exit Carter House after the murder?

There was so much that was unanswered. If the police were focused on O'Keefe, Eliza had to wonder if they saw the professor as an easy solution—or if they had solid information linking him to the scene of the crime. Eliza needed to talk to Detectives Comstock and Fonseca.

"I have an idea," she said. "Let's call Detective Fonseca tomorrow and set up a meeting with her and Detective Comstock for Monday morning. I can take you to their offices. I'd like to be there when you talk with them."

"I'd like to be there too," Francesca joined in. "I can offer support at a minimum. Or translate into Italian if the police say something you don't understand. And the more brain power we have, the better. Let's see if they can meet while Lucas is at school."

With all in agreement, Eliza turned to the idea of talking with Ana Maggio. She wanted to contact Ana the following morning, which would be Sunday afternoon in Italy. But she was worried that her Italian wasn't good enough to do the interview. Eliza needed a translator on the call.

Roberto immediately offered his help, but Eliza gently quashed this approach. She didn't want either of Martina's parents on the call. The presence of Roberto or Laura—and the reality that they were Martina's parents—might cause Ana to withhold information in order to protect them. Eliza turned to Francesca, who readily agreed to translate. They would get together the following morning at Eliza's house to try to reach Ana. Laura had Ana's contact information in her phone and sent it to Eliza.

These details resolved, Francesca said, "*Cara*, cut into that tart that you brought us. I'll get the dessert plates. Does anyone want coffee or tea?" Francesca was doing her best to create a normal environment, and they all tried to play along. But they all knew normal was transitory, and it would elude them long into the future.

CHAPTER THIRTEEN

Sunday, May 12—Morning

Francesca arrived at Eliza's before 9 a.m., eager to place the call to Italy. But first, she wanted to know if Eliza had spoken to Lucas.

"How is our boy?" Francesca asked. "I worry about him when he's with his father and his new wife."

Eliza had already Facetimed with both David and Lucas. Other than being unhappy that his dad wanted him to dress up for brunch, their boy was in good spirits.

"He's fine, Mama," she assured Francesca. "I'm the one who's a little unnerved. David is suddenly showing an interest in Lucas, who will have a new brother or sister next year. They're building a family with my son, and I'll be sidelined, relegated to onlooker."

"Oh, my," Francesca responded. "You didn't tell me that David and his *moglie* were expecting a baby. When did you find out?"

"David told me a couple days ago. So much has been going on with the investigation. I didn't get a chance to tell you until now."

Francesca could see that Eliza, who was usually so calm about everything, was struggling. She opened her arms to embrace her, and Eliza stepped into the semi-circle.

"*Cara,* maybe it's time you found yourself a partner," her mother said quietly. "We all crave intimacy and companionship, and you don't want to turn into one of those women who hates men and is angry all the time."

Francesca felt Eliza's body tense up, and she regretted her words, even though she was pretty sure Eliza knew they were true.

"We have work to do," Eliza said coldly, an unambiguous signal to Francesca that there would be no discussion of Eliza's non-existent love life. "Let me find my phone. I probably left it in the kitchen. Do you want coffee?"

"Okay," Francesca replied. "A coffee would be nice. We'll talk more about finding a husband for you later."

Eliza reasoned it was unlikely Ana would answer a call from the United States if she didn't know the caller. Many people also didn't listen to their voicemails, especially from unknown numbers. They decided the best approach was to text Ana first to make an introduction.

Eliza dictated a message for Francesca to translate into Italian. Francesca then typed it into Eliza's phone. They sent it and waited. Fortunately, they didn't have to wait long. Ana quickly texted that she would be free to talk in about twenty minutes, when she got back to her apartment. They agreed to connect by Facetime.

Eliza and Francesca used the extra time to think more about what they wanted to ask Ana, and how they would handle Francesca's role as an interpreter. Eliza had worked with bilingual interpreters in the past and found the experience frustrating. She was never sure they were repeating her questions exactly or if they accurately conveyed what witnesses had said. Eliza made sure her mother had a notepad and pen. If Ana's English was good enough that an interpreter wasn't necessary, Francesca could help by writing down what Eliza asked and what Ana said in response.

Twenty minutes later, they were connected with Martina's closest friend. "*Ciao, Ana,*" Eliza greeted the young woman whose face filled the screen. Ana wore glasses with a thick red frame, her long dark bangs spilling over the edge of the eyewear. "Good afternoon," Ana replied with a noticeable British accent. Within minutes, Eliza determined that Ana had just returned to Rome from a semester in London and was conversant in English. Comfortable that she would be understood, Eliza moved forward with her questions.

However, only a few minutes later, Ana's composure melted away, and she was emotional and tearful. She had lost her dear friend, and her feelings were still raw. Given Ana's unsettled state, Eliza was grateful to have Francesca on the call. Her mother, poised to take notes, was always steady in a crisis. While Eliza worked to calm Ana down, Francesca focused on capturing exactly what the young woman said. Their witness sometimes went seamlessly from English into Italian as her demeanor teetered between forthright and tearful.

They learned that Ana had talked to Martina the previous weekend, and Ana told them what she could remember from the conversation. Later, Eliza scanned her mother's notes from the call into her laptop:

Sunday, May 12, 9:30 a.m. PDT—Call with Ana Maggio by Facetime re: Martina Noto

(EF=Eliza Fox/Ana=Ana Maggio)

EF: When did you last talk to Martina?

Ana: Saturday, May 4 (three days before Martina died). Martina was in a good mood. The semester would be over in a couple weeks, and Martina was busy with final exams and practicing for a piano recital. *Note: Ana broke down in tears at this point and had to collect herself before she could continue talking.*

Ana: Martina had been seeing an older man, someone well-known, but wouldn't tell Ana his name. Ana thinks the guy was in the film industry or the music industry, but Martina wouldn't say for sure. Ana's impression was that Martina liked that he was an older man, more mature.

EF: Did Martina say if she was still seeing this man, or if the romance was over?

Ana: They were still seeing each other.

EF: Was Martina troubled by anything or anyone?

Ana: Ana was at school in London when she talked to Martina. They talked about missing Rome and how different Americans and Brits were from Italians. No kisses on the cheek, no hugs, no yelling or waving their hands about. Ana thought that while Martina liked being in California, she was ready to go home. Martina didn't mention any specific problems and seemed happy. Martina liked living with Kendra and had enjoyed Wexford.

EF: What can you tell me about Martina's computer project?

Ana: Martina was planning to work on it over the summer from Rome. She mentioned something about needing money for the work to continue. Martina planned to talk to her previous computer science professors in Italy about the project to see if they could help find investors.

EF: What did Martina's project entail? Do you know specifically what she was working on?

Ana: It was a prosthetic device for someone's hand. It was somehow better than the devices people currently used, but Ana didn't understand what made it better. A student named Levi was leading the project. Ana believes Levi had submitted a patent application to the US government and maybe Martina's name was on it.

EF: Again, was anything troubling Martina?

Ana: No, nothing. They had planned to see each other in June, when both were back in Rome.

Call ended at 9:52 a.m.

~

Once her mother left, Eliza sat at her desk to think more about the call with Ana. A minute of quiet in her house, so hard to carve out in her typical day, allowed her the mental space she needed to decompress. Ana had been understandably emotional, and Eliza felt bad about drawing her into such a difficult conversation, one that was probably made worse by the confines of video chat. If they had all been in the same room, Eliza could have offered Ana a tissue, patted her hand, or given the young woman a hug if she were open to it. Eliza, close to tears herself as she reflected on Ana's frame of mind, had not fully appreciated how taxing this case would be. She headed to the kitchen for a cup of tea.

An hour later, after some Earl Grey and a restorative walk to the park, Eliza was able to focus on what she had learned that morning.

One, Ana confirmed that Martina was sleeping with an older man, which made Eliza revisit whether Tim O'Keefe could be the killer, either with malice and forethought, or spontaneously. Another possibility was that he hired someone to kill her. O'Keefe, or someone working for him, could have followed Martina from the condo to Carter House that morning. Although Eliza's gut told her a murder-for-hire scheme was too reminiscent of a Hollywood script to play out in sleepy San Vicente, she also accepted that it was possible.

Two, Eliza placed the likeable Jason Chang low on the list of suspects, based on instinct rather than actual evidence. She still had to find out exactly where Jason was on Tuesday morning. Maybe Kendra or Francesca could cover this angle and look into whether Jason had an alibi. Eliza realized she could use help with the legwork.

Three, Levi Newcomb remained an open question. Checking her phone, Eliza realized that Kendra had not sent Levi's contact information yet. Levi was turning out to be elusive. Why was that?

Four, a random whacko from the neighborhood could have slipped into Carter House, which made Eliza consider whether

Martina's attacker was a stranger. She needed to find out how many registered sex offenders lived near campus, and then she wondered if registered sex offenders were even allowed to live near colleges.

Eliza caught herself. "Avoid rabbit holes!" she chided aloud. The perpetrator could be someone with a history of sex crimes, but whether this person lived near Wexford was immaterial. Southern California was a big place where millions of people lived, and some of them were very capable of violence, especially against young, attractive women like Martina. That was an unfortunate fact. Martina also could have crossed paths with a depraved stranger who had no prior history with the police. All criminals had to start somewhere. "Jeeez!" Eliza literally threw her hands up. "How am I going to figure this out?"

Lastly, Eliza thought more about Martina's laptop being stolen from the wellness center and wondered if it was a relevant fact. And if so, how was it relevant?

She pinged Kendra to remind her to send Levi's contact info. She also sent a text to Roberto, nudging him to call Detective Fonseca to schedule a face-to-face meeting for Monday morning. Both responded right away.

Kendra provided Levi's cellphone number and email address. *Finally.* And Roberto confirmed they had a 9 a.m. meeting the next morning with the detectives at police headquarters. According to Roberto's text, Detective Fonseca wanted to invite a victim liaison officer to the meeting, which Roberto declined. Instead, he had advised Detective Fonseca they might need a small conference room because he and Laura were bringing their own people—family members—for support.

∿

The vigil for Martina was scheduled to begin at 7 p.m., but students and members of the community had been arriving at the campus since about 5 p.m. People were scattered on blankets on the lawn or resting on benches in the quad. The overall tone was respectful, sans loud music, shouting, or the horseplay that typically emanated from students before an event. Many people had brought their dinners, eating pizzas or deli sandwiches while they made a half-hearted effort to hide bottles of wine or beer. Eliza could smell marijuana scenting the early evening breeze. She reasoned that campus police were instructed to look the other way and not pursue minor alcohol or drug violations during the vigil. Cigarettes, pot, and alcohol were all restricted on campus, except for the faculty club, where a dry martini was still available to professors and donors.

A small stage had been erected in front of the quad with a sound system and a piano. There were plans for a performance of *Clair de Lune,* the third movement of Claude Debussy's "Suite Bergamasque," which Martina had been practicing at Carter House that fateful morning. It seemed to Eliza like a fitting tribute, and she knew she'd be in tears when it was performed. Just then, Eliza's attention was dialed into finding Levi Newcomb. Slowly she scanned the crowd. Shortly after receiving Levi's phone number, she had sent him a text. He agreed to meet her at the campus fountain about an hour before the vigil started. Eliza wasn't sure what he looked like, only that he'd be wearing a white cap and that she'd recognize him. Eliza positioned herself about thirty feet away from the fountain at the crest of a small, grassy hill. At that point, people were mingling near the fountain, but they weren't packed in. From her vantage point, Eliza could distinguish the individuals standing around it. Her plan was to surveil Levi for a few minutes before she approached him, although she had no clear idea why she was doing this. By watching him from afar, it was possible she'd learn something that might give her an advantage over the elusive Levi. Eliza stood near some tall boxwood and pretended to scroll through her phone, one eye lasered in on the comings and goings around the fountain.

Levi was late. Eliza had expected him close to 6 p.m., and it was now 6:10 p.m. Maybe she'd missed him among the crowd. She checked her phone again for a message from him, but there was nothing. Eliza decided to initiate contact and sent a text:

> Eliza: Where r u? Been waiting
> Levi: Approaching. C U in 2 mins
> Eliza: K

With that, she gave up her idea of spying on Levi, walked down the small hill, and found a seat on the fountain's wide, circular edge. Within seconds, a tall, thin student wearing black jeans and a tattered Sonic Youth T-shirt plopped down to her left. His hair was mostly hidden under an orange knit hat, but a few dark wisps had broken free and skated along the top of his eyebrows. Eliza saw that his arms were darkened with tattoo ink as he propped his skateboard against the fountain's edge. While he wasn't wearing a white-billed hat as promised, he had one in his hand.

"Are you Levi?" she asked, and he nodded in response.

"How'd you recognize me?" her curiosity in the forefront.

Levi suppressed a smile. "I googled you," he said, incredulous that she would ask this. "You look a lot like your headshot. The one that's on your company's website. What's the name of that law firm you work for? Fowler something?"

"Right," she replied, feeling disadvantaged. She shifted her bodyweight and tilted a bit toward Levi, working to make the most of her five-foot-five frame. This was her meeting, and she'd better grab control of it.

"Thanks for coming, Levi," Eliza said, using a professional tone. "I know you were working with Martina, and I've been looking into her death for the family. Have the police contacted you yet?"

"Yeah, they left me a few messages," he replied. "But I haven't talked to them. I mean, I will. I've been laying low and couch surfing a bit. This thing with Martina has been pretty nuts, you know."

"I do. It's a lot," Eliza said, feeling that the tone between them had shifted again, this time in a positive way. "What can you tell me about working with Martina? Was she troubled about anything? Or anyone?"

"Not that she told me about. She seemed ready to go back to Italy. It had been a long two semesters for her at Wexford."

"Why do you say that?" Eliza queried.

Levi paused before answering, taking time to assess Eliza more fully. His dark eyes scanned her floral print dress, her cotton blazer, her pink Chuck Taylor high-tops, and the large Coach handbag resting to her right. Eliza suddenly grew very conscious of how she presented. Was Levi making assumptions based on her job? Her outfit? The absence of visible tattoos? Probably so. But Eliza had no way to shape-shift into a younger, less established version of herself. She was a divorced mom in her thirties who lived in a rented house and drove an aging station wagon. Continuing to hold Levi's gaze, she waited for his answer. Why did he think Martina wanted to go back to Italy and leave Wexford?

"I don't know if you went to Wexford, but sometimes the kids here can be judgy," he said. "Maybe they didn't make it easy for Martina. She was an outsider who didn't have a lot of friends. I think she missed her peeps back home."

His answer caught Eliza off-guard. Kendra had mentioned something about Martina not having many friends at Wexford, and Jason had described her cousin as a loner. But Eliza hadn't given much attention to this thread. Now the idea was resurfacing, and it needed her focus.

"Was someone threatening her? Did Martina have an enemy? Or enemies?" she pressed.

"No. Wait, that's not accurate. I don't know. You asked if she was troubled, and I gave you my best answer. I think she was ready to put Wexford behind her. That's all. A lot of kids like the idea of going to school far away from their parents, but then they get homesick and miss what's familiar."

"Sure. I can understand that. Tell me about the project Martina was working on with you. I know it was to help the disabled, but I'd like to understand it better."

"No comment," Levi said, his expression blank.

"Excuse me?" Eliza responded. "I don't understand."

Levi looked at her again in disbelief. "You do understand what 'no comment' means? I'm not discussing the project. Hard stop. I don't mean to be rude, but I have to maintain secrecy around my concept. Anything else you'd like to ask?"

She paused for a beat, deciding whether to press him further. Levi was showing little patience for social norms, and she felt he might walk off in a huff if she pushed about the project. "Okay, Levi. What about Martina's other laptop, the one that was stolen from the wellness center? What can you tell me about that?"

"That was effed up. Luckily, she had everything backed up, so no data was lost. You should talk to campus police. They took down all the information and were in contact with Martina about who could have taken her stuff."

"Okay. Do you know who she was talking to at Campus PD?"

"Yeah, a tubby dude. Officer Thompson, I think he was called. Talk to him."

"Got it. So going back to Martina not fitting in on campus, you brought it up for a reason. I really want to know if anyone was threatening her?"

"Okay," Levi sighed, giving up his earlier resistance. "You didn't hear this from me, but she was having problems with a few sorority girls—Chelsea Miller and her pal, Dahlia something. I don't know if they were just talking shit about Martina, or if it was more serious. Maybe they were into some cyber-harassment trying to make Martina look bad. I'm not really sure."

Eliza took this in. "What do you mean? Can you tell me more about that?"

"No, not really. Martina was obviously savvy with computers, so I doubt they did much damage, but you should check it out. Maybe they tried to make Martina look like a slut with a fake Tinder profile."

"What sorority do they belong to?" Eliza asked.

"I don't know. Gamma Hamma Bamma," he said, showing his

annoyance. "Look, that's all I got. I want to get out of here before this place fills up more. Not a fan of crowds."

It was clear she'd reached the end of Levi's cooperation. Eliza considered whether to ask another question and then decided there was no real risk to it: "Levi, I'm curious. Did you apply for a patent on the project?"

Levi's eyes widened. "Whoa, you've gotta be kidding me. I already told you no comment about the project. There is a real need for secrecy around it. That's non-negotiable. Sorry, I'm out."

Levi threw his skateboard to the ground and maneuvered down the concrete walkway leading away from the fountain. Those standing in his path quickly jumped clear, as it seemed unlikely he'd stop for anyone.

"Yeah, that went well," Eliza said under her breath. She pulled her cellphone out of her pocket and turned off the record button. Even though she knew it was illegal in California to record someone without their permission, no one needed to know about her small recording. When she got home, she'd jot down some notes from her talk with Levi and then double delete all versions of the audio clip, including the cloud backup. Eliza promised herself not to make a practice of relying on this small illegality, but Levi had been so hard to connect with, she wanted to capture every word he said.

At this point, Eliza was feeling both pumped up after her meeting with Levi and drained from the weekend. It was time to shift mentally into family mode. The vigil would start soon, and she needed to find her mother and Martina's parents and Kendra, too. The next couple of hours would be emotional for all of them, and Eliza wanted to stand together with this chosen group who had all been close to Martina. She wanted to experience the vigil as someone related to the victim, not an investigator looking for a killer.

CHAPTER FOURTEEN

Monday, May 13—Morning

Detective Jessica Fonseca scanned the department's open-plan workspace looking for her partner. She wanted to find time to connect with Byron before the Notos were due to arrive for the briefing. Over the weekend, the two detectives questioned Tim O'Keefe, and on Sunday morning, O'Keefe voluntarily surrendered his passport and was released with a caution not to leave Los Angeles County. While the professor's behavior with Martina was sordid and would probably get him fired from his cushy job at Wexford, it wasn't illegal. Martina was not underage, and there was no evidence that she had been an unwilling sexual partner.

Moreover, Jessica had spoken to Kendra, who confirmed that, while Kendra had not actually seen Martina before she left for Carter House, there was evidence that her roommate was present in the condo Tuesday morning. Kendra recalled hearing the shower and seeing the silver espresso pot on top of the stove. Martina typically stored the little Italian coffeemaker in the cupboard, so it was clear Martina made a coffee before leaving the condo that morning. Martina's bed also looked slept in, but since it was rarely made, it was hard for Kendra to know for sure if Martina had actually slept in it Monday night. Kendra herself had fallen asleep early. She had gotten up very early to surf that morning and had crashed around 10 p.m. Monday night. She didn't know what time Martina arrived home.

While there was no explanation yet for why Martina had not answered the calls from O'Keefe the night before she died, Kendra's statements about hearing the shower and seeing the espresso pot supported that their victim had been in the condo that Tuesday morning. She had walked to Carter House from there and not from some other location. Comstock and Fonseca were now focused on retracing Martina's steps the prior week, hoping this approach would generate some new leads.

And what had happened to Martina's laptop and backpack? Kendra told Jessica that she still hadn't found them anywhere.

With almost a full week having passed since the murder, Jessica felt mounting pressure for her and Byron to produce a suspect. Understandably, the Noto family wanted answers. Now the community was getting antsy. The *Los Angeles Daily Post* had published a front-page piece in its Sunday edition, written by reporter Vanessa Delaware, that laid out O'Keefe's connection to Martina. While local TV news stations had also run clips of the vigil and of O'Keefe entering the police station, Delaware's involvement with the story worried Jessica. Delaware had a reputation for fomenting anxiety in the community and pitting residents against the police. She openly suggested in her reporting that a killer was preying on young females at Wexford and warned students to go out in groups and "be hyper-prepared, as if you were armed for bear." Jessica wondered if Delaware owned stock in a company that manufactured pepper spray.

Delaware's piece also scratched a constant itch in San Vicente about how much of the city budget should be allotted to police and crime prevention versus community services like parks, street repair, and new bike lanes. Jessica found that residents didn't make police a priority until something scary happened. Then police were top of mind. Citizens wanted police to be fully staffed, fully armed, and fully trained with access to all the latest law enforcement tools and technology. It was just like the people who hated lawyers because attorneys were too aggressive and combative—until they had a legal problem. Then they wanted to be represented by the meanest mad-dog attorney they could find.

Jessica mentally checked off the tasks they had accomplished. Byron's hunches about Abel Trenton, the registered sex offender, had not panned out. Evidence on Abel's video game system gave him a solid alibi for Tuesday morning. During some of this period, he was chatting online with a fellow gamer, all of it timestamped. Mrs. Trenton had also provided the police with a formal statement that Abel had not left the house during this period. While she might have been lying to protect her son, it was more likely that Abel was ensconced in his mother's garage waging war against his video opponent while Martina practiced at Carter House.

As Jessica again considered whether the killer was someone known to Martina, she eyed Byron across the room and shot him a text. She then watched as he pulled out his phone and looked in her direction. Jessica waved him over. She wanted a few minutes with her partner to make sure they agreed on their talking points with the Notos and on what to say about how the investigation would move forward.

"Hey, partner," Byron said, his cheerful morning demeanor fully visible.

"Good morning," Jessica said. "Let's talk about this family meeting. The Notos will be here in about twenty minutes."

They moved into an empty conference room. Byron, who liked to be in control, jumped in: They would bring the family up to date on O'Keefe. This story was being covered in the press anyway, so there was no downside to sharing details with the family. He suggested they also talk about their work surveying local sex offenders and acknowledge that this hadn't produced any real leads. They should also bring up the department's use of social media, putting notices about Martina on several community sites and digital billboards. And, of course, they could refer to their talk with Kendra Reid, letting the family know the police had spoken to her.

Jessica and Byron were aligned on not bringing up the interviews with Dahlia Moreno and Li-Ann Wong, especially since both students had solid alibis, nor would they talk about Jason Chang and Levi Newcomb, who had yet to be interviewed.

"We still need to interview Chelsea Miller. Let's get that done," Byron said.

Byron noticed his partner's strained expression and conceded, "I know, Jess. We need a lot more staff working this case. I'm meeting with the deputy chief at noon about resources. I'll make him understand that we're on our back heel here, and it's a bad look. SVPD and campus police need to work together. We gotta throw everything we can at this one. We should call in other agencies too."

Jessica reminded him that their task list was actually longer. They agreed to make Chelsea, Jason, and Levi their priority for that afternoon. This meant that another set of detectives would talk to the other Wexford kids that Li-Ann and Dahlia had suggested. She checked her notes for their names—Aidan, Zoey, and Olivia—and then corrected herself that they were not kids; they were fully responsible adults. If any of the Wexford students had a role in Martina's fate, they would face serious consequences.

Jessica next checked to see if Byron wanted to tell the family their working theory that the murderer was known to the victim, rather than a stranger.

"No," he answered flatly. "I don't want to share that, Jess. I hate family meetings. I do them because they're required, but during a pending investigation, information should be a one-way street. Witnesses, the family, the community tip-line—they all provide pieces of the puzzle, and we take this information in. We don't have to reciprocate and share facts with them. It's our puzzle to solve."

"Okay. I agree," she said. "Go. You have fifteen minutes. Get something to drink and answer some emails before the family gets here. I've reserved this conference room for us. Also, I decided not to have the victim liaison officer present. Mr. Noto reacted negatively when I suggested it to him on the phone."

A half hour later, they were all situated around the large conference table: the victim's parents and close family, Professor

Noto-Fox from Wexford and her daughter Eliza Fox. Jessica had stopped at a bakery earlier that morning for pastries and orange juice. She wanted the family to feel cared for, even if she had to pay for the refreshments herself.

Byron nodded at her to take the lead just as she had during Kendra's interview. In this meeting, with these particular people, it made sense to rely on his partner's likeability and empathy, a point that he could literally taste as he bit into one of the buttery croissants she provided.

∾

Jessica thought the meeting with the Notos had gone well for the first twenty minutes, until Eliza assumed the role of family spokesperson. She wanted a list of who the detectives had interviewed, who they planned to speak with, a copy of the coroner's report, and an update on the search for the victim's backpack and laptop. Additionally, she wanted video surveillance from the basement level of Carter House. Roberto and Laura Noto remained mostly silent during the meeting, allowing Eliza free rein.

Jessica had done her best to not react to Eliza's tone, which was business-like and insistent. It was evident the family had put Eliza in charge of a parallel investigation. Adhering to the script she and Byron had worked out, Jessica batted away Eliza's requests. She was practiced at offering non-committal responses: "Yes, I understand." "Let me look into that." Byron stayed largely quiet, which Jessica found irksome. As this meeting unfolded, it became clear that the detectives would have benefited from looking like a united team doing their best to help the Notos. Instead, Jessica was the only one speaking, offering them unsatisfactory answers.

However, reflecting now on the things Eliza had asked for, Jessica saw no compelling reason to release any of it. After a quick minute on Google, she learned that Eliza Fox was a private investigator who worked for Fowler & Haverford, a firm that occasionally defended celebrities and white-collar criminals. Jessica was quickly reminded of one of her cases that involved the Fowler firm. They had represented the defendant, a rapper who had beaten up his fiancé. Jessica was still mad about it because the defendant had gotten off with no more than anger management counseling. Jessica questioned why Fowler & Haverford would take that kind of a case, which sent a message that the firm condoned domestic violence. Jessica recognized that she was on a rant, and if she continued, it would throw her into a lousy mood. She shook it off and turned to the immediate problems.

Over the course of the prior week, Jessica had learned that the video cameras on the lower level of Carter House were non-operational. While badly functioning CCTV was a dirty secret in law enforcement, the public didn't need to know the truth. It would upset the Noto family—and do nothing to help find the perpetrator—if word got out that the cameras at Carter House were merely props installed to deter vandalism. The calculus had been reasonable at the time: pianos were big, heavy items that were impossible to steal, and functioning CCTV at that location would not have been cost-effective. In retrospect, that analysis looked short-sighted and miserly. Until last week, San Vicente's murder rate hadn't been a concern. Jessica sighed. "It's all a big balancing act, isn't it?" she asked no one in particular.

∽

Eliza had begged off having an early lunch with her family after the meeting. She told them she needed to run a few errands before picking up Lucas from school, but she really wanted time alone to think. She was mad. She was mad on behalf of her family, she was mad as a taxpayer, she was mad as a long-term resident of San Vicente. The meeting with the detectives had been useless. They'd offered nothing of substance and asked the family to wait patiently while SVPD, campus police, and everyone else did their jobs. While Eliza didn't expect full disclosure about every nuance of the investigation, she thought the detectives would have shared *something* meaningful. But Roberto and Laura were told *niente.*

For better or worse, forbearance and restraint were not in Eliza's constitution. Francesca famously told stories about her daughter scouring the house each year for hidden gifts weeks before her birthday. This included episodes of Eliza taking her mother's art history books off a shelf, stacking them three-feet high, and climbing precariously atop the pile to get a better view of a closet shelf. One time, the stack of books toppled with a huge bang, causing Eliza's parents to run from opposite ends of the house. They found her amid the books, unharmed but surprised. Given that Eliza was so incorrigible, Francesca began hiding her gifts at her campus office in a locked file cabinet.

"No, being patient is not my thing," Eliza said, deciding it was time to turn up the pressure on SVPD with a multi-pronged plan. First, she'd send her mother for a friendly *tête-à-tête* with Carole Gardener, Wexford's president; Francesca might be able to wring some details about the investigation out of her long-time colleague. Second, she would put Kendra and Jason to work on a social media effort, dubbed #neverforgetmartina. Finally, she'd reach out to Vanessa Delaware at the *LA Daily Post.*

CHAPTER FIFTEEN

Monday, May 13—Afternoon

Byron's noon meeting with the deputy chief went well enough. The department authorized more overtime and committed more staff to the case. They would also rely more heavily on Wexford's campus security and work in sync with Chief Mendoza. With the extra resources, the department wanted Byron to produce a result within the next week. The deputy chief promised that the chief of police would hold off the mayor, the city council, Carole Gardener, and the other birds of prey circling over Detectives Comstock and Fonseca.

Byron would be happy when the Noto investigation was stamped "Case Closed." He was propelling forward on very little rest and craved a day off. He wanted to jump in the pool with his daughter and play some tennis with his neighbor. He wanted to barbecue a tri-tip, drink a few beers, and have sex with his wife. Then he wanted to sleep deeply without dreaming. But wishing these things wouldn't make them so. Byron softly sang Eric Bogle's "If Wishes Were Fishes" to himself—a tune he had sung to his baby daughter as she rocked in her cradle. The melody made him think of his own mother, Annie Comstock, born in the north of England in the Lake District, a petite woman with a sharp wit and a quick smile. Byron missed her and still thought of her every day since her death two years ago. He was getting a bit maudlin, but he knew Annie would not have tolerated any whining about the long hours he was putting in, or the idiots who controlled the budget, or the lack of trained personnel. She would have told Byron to do his job and get the bastard. She had no tolerance for anyone who took a human life. "No one can play God," Annie had said. "Let the murderers rot in prison and then in hell."

He and Jessica were now en route to the campus, fully apprised of Chelsea Miller's class schedule. She was supposed to be in an anthropology class that ended at 2:30 p.m. Byron had asked the professor to send a text verifying that Chelsea had shown up, so the detectives were certain she was there. He and Jessica would position themselves in the hallway and corral her as she left class, while other students gawked and snickered. Byron didn't like to embarrass people, but Chelsea had brought this drama on herself. She could have talked to them in the relative privacy of the provost's office, but she didn't, and Byron wasn't sure why. Was it a false sense of entitlement because her dad was a lawyer? If that was the reason, she'd run the clock out on that tactic. Or was it because Chelsea was guilty about something related to Martina, so she was hoping to avoid answering questions?

He had looked over Kendra's statement again from their interview with her shortly after Martina was found.

> *Martina was not well liked by some of the kids here, mostly a clique of popular girls. They fixated on her in a hateful way. I assumed they were jealous of her, with her beautiful face and Italian upbringing, but I didn't think they'd ever hurt her.*

Kendra's words resonated now in light of Chelsea's effort to avoid questioning. They had motivated Byron to scour the internet looking for ways that Martina's so-called friends could have targeted her online. It was also significant that Li-Ann and Dahlia had solid alibis for that Tuesday morning, while Chelsea had yet to provide one.

At 2:30 p.m. exactly, both doors for Hickman 204 swung wide and students poured out, faces in their phones, Chelsea included. "Hello," Byron said, as he stepped to her left side and Jessica fell in step on her right. He saw a fearful look cross Chelsea's face. She seemed exposed, like a quarterback about to be sacked with the game on the line. Minus her bravado, Chelsea appeared as she was—a twenty-year-old—someone teetering on adulthood but who harbored all the misconceptions and false expectations that young people have about life after college. He almost felt sorry for her.

"What are you doing?" Chelsea asked, alarmed.

"Maybe keep your voice down to not draw attention to yourself," Jessica told her. "We'd like to go somewhere for a chat."

Byron had arranged with the campus to have a golf cart waiting outside of Hickman Hall. The three of them jumped in, and the driver took them to campus police headquarters at the eastern edge of Wexford, where the campus abutted a residential neighborhood. Chief Gil Mendoza stood in front of the building as the golf cart arrived. He greeted Chelsea warmly and handed her a bottle of water.

Within minutes, Byron, Jessica, and their witness were seated in a small room around a stained particleboard table. Byron informed Chelsea of her right to keep silent and her right to an attorney. He told her that whatever she said could and would be used against her in court.

"Lawyer," Chelsea responded. "I want to call my dad."

"Sure," Jessica said. "You can call him. But isn't he in trial this afternoon? I looked at the court docket. He has that big construction defect lawsuit against those investors from Singapore. The ones who built that high rise downtown with all the problems. Weren't there headlines about the floor tiles cracking and the roof leaking? And the air conditioning fails any time it gets above eighty-five degrees? I love that Wesley Miller is representing the people who bought condos and leased offices in that building. Your dad is doing important work. I gotta hand it to him."

Chelsea looked wordlessly at the detectives. Her expression conveyed both confusion over their praise for her father and her own fear that she was about to be held accountable for whatever crimes the detectives thought she'd committed.

"Do you want to call him?" Jessica continued. "You can sit here for three hours, or however long he takes. I know Chief Mendoza would be happy to have you hang out. Or, my partner and I ask you a few questions, and we see where it goes. You can stop the process and call your dad any time. Okay?"

Chelsea considered her situation. She knew she'd have to talk to these detectives eventually. A student was dead, and that problem was not going to disappear without someone being blamed. Daddy would be in a rage about her talking to the cops without him in the room, but Chelsea felt the walls closing in. She bobbed her head slightly in agreement.

Jessica began by asking Chelsea some questions about student life at Wexford, the names of people in her friend group, and how she and Martina had gotten along. Then Jessica quickly shifted gears and asked about Chelsea's whereabouts on the morning of Tuesday, May 7. The young woman paused for more than fifteen seconds before she answered, as if she were carefully considering her words. Chelsea described getting up early that Tuesday, leaving her dorm, and wandering the campus looking for a quiet place to read. She was behind in a literature class. Her chore for that Tuesday morning was to plow through the assigned Octavia Butler novel and then, relying heavily on study guides, write a paper on the novel's dystopian motifs and their relevance today. Once the cops and media had arrived on campus and all the excitement erupted around Carter House, Chelsea had gone back to her dorm to continue reading and working on the paper. Chelsea offered to show the detectives the essay; she was pleased with her effort and expected an A.

"Exactly where on campus were you sitting with your book, Chelsea? Did any of your friends interact with you? Did you buy a drink or some breakfast anywhere that morning? *Think!*" Jessica prodded.

"I took a blanket and spread it on the grass outside of Hickman. It was a nice morning, and I wanted to get some sun. I had a travel mug full of hot tea. No one knew where I was. I even turned off my phone.

I remember thinking how nice it was to be offline for a while." Aware of how lame this sounded, Chelsea mumbled, "Sorry, that's all I can tell you. It's the truth."

Jessica threw her partner a skeptical glance, and she and Byron stepped into the hallway to confer. "This girl has no alibi," Jessica announced, stating the obvious. "Her answer felt rehearsed to me. What'd you think?"

"Agreed," said Byron. "It's too convenient. This is a student who thrives on social connections. She never turns her phone off, and now she wants us to believe she was out of contact at the exact time her classmate was being murdered."

"Right," said Jessica, annoyed. "But her story about sitting on the grass catching up on her homework could also be true."

They took a second to mull this over before Jessica went to her next topic. "How do you want to handle all the crap she did to Martina with the cyberbullying?"

"We ask her about it, of course," Byron said. "She can ask for an attorney if she doesn't want to answer. She watches TV. She's a very bright girl. She can say, 'No comment.'"

"Okay," Jessica said. "It's your turn. Bad cop time."

Going back into the office where Chelsea waited, Byron noticed tiny bits of torn paper on the table, a mound that hadn't been there five minutes earlier. Chelsea had pulled the label off the water bottle and ripped it into a hundred little pieces, evidence of the stress she was feeling.

Byron pulled out an iPad from his briefcase and motioned for Chelsea to look at the screen. Byron slowly scrolled through five or six doctored images of Martina that had been posted on an internet dating site. The profile described this woman as in her early thirties, looking for hook-ups, and up for anything. The mock-up of Martina had been named Tina Naughty.

"Chelsea, who is Tina Naughty?" Byron quietly asked. "These posts have our victim's face, but the body is different. Tina is described as a decade older than Martina, and she has much bigger breasts, lots of cleavage. Did you come up with the porn-star name, or did you get help from your friends? The photoshopping isn't bad. Are you studying graphic design, Chelsea?"

Tears streamed down Chelsea's cheeks. "I want my dad," she whispered.

"Okay," Byron told her. "Take out your phone and call him. But just so you know, cyberbullying, online harassment—whatever name you want to give it—is a crime. And even if the DA doesn't want to prosecute, it's certainly a code of conduct violation at Wexford, one that can get you suspended or expelled. And let's remember that the target of these fake posts is now deceased."

As her new reality permeated, Chelsea crumpled and slid down toward the floor; Jessica jumped to cushion her fall. Folded into the fetal position on the dirty carpet, Chelsea's sobs were audible now. Jessica's calm voice guided her to breathe. "In through your nose and out through your mouth. Slow and even, Chelsea. Slow and even."

As she cradled Chelsea, Jessica made a mental note to ask her neighbor to feed and walk her dog that evening. She still hoped to talk to Jason Chang and Levi Newcomb before it got too late, except that Chelsea was eating up precious minutes. Jessica still wondered about the young woman. If Chelsea was guilty of something, was it murder? Jessica didn't know, but there was something about Chelsea that made her uneasy.

As Jessica and Byron talked with Chief Mendoza about how to deal with Chelsea, the chief's phone pinged. Martina's backpack had been found in a campus dumpster behind the main dining hall. One of Mendoza's officers was bringing it to him now.

Jessica called for a squad car to transport Chelsea downtown to SVPD headquarters, where she'd be questioned further. Even though the young woman would certainly be released into her father's custody in a few hours, Jessica wanted Chelsea to experience the humiliation of riding in the back of a police cruiser. She'd catch up with Chelsea and Wesley Miller later that evening.

Just as Chelsea was driven away, Officer Kennedy Thompson arrived at the campus police station in a golf cart with a dark gray trash bag resting on the back seat. He carried it into the station and laid the bundle on a vacant desk. With Chief Mendoza, Byron, and Jessica looking on, he cut away the plastic to reveal a dirty black backpack with a soiled pink fuzzball hanging from a zipper. All four of them stood and stared at it.

"Where was it? How'd you find it?" the chief asked.

"It was luck, really," Thompson explained. "I was driving around doing routine patrols when it was time for my break, so I got a soda in the dining hall. I sat there a minute, caught up on the baseball news on my phone, and then I got back to work. I was going to south campus next, to check the athletic fields, so I circled the cart around the back side of the dining hall—you know, so I'd be pointed in the right direction. When I passed the dumpsters back there, I stopped to throw away my empty soda cup. If it wasn't for that pink thing hanging on the backpack, I wouldn't have seen it in the garbage. It blended in with the other trash bags."

"Did you touch it?" Byron queried.

"No. Of course not. I mean, I don't think I did. I might have poked at it. I went and got a trash bag from the dining hall. Then I used the trash bag as a protective layer to grab it out of the garbage and flip it inside the bag. I didn't have any gloves with me and nobody else was around. I left it in the dumpster for only a minute while I went to get the trash bag."

The others exchanged looks. "Kennedy, the next time you find evidence, *do not* touch it without gloves or leave it unattended. That's why you have a radio and a phone," Chief Mendoza gently admonished. "Call for help so we can always maintain the evidence properly." The chief then changed his tone. "We can talk more about procedures later. This is a great development. Really important," he said, clearly proud of Thompson.

Byron was not as sanguine about Thompson's approach to handling evidence and was surprised at the chief's overall calm.

Making a show of putting on gloves, Byron pulled gingerly at the zipper and opened the backpack enough for them to see a silver laptop gleaming inside.

"Let's take this downtown and get forensics working on it," Jessica said. "I can take custody of it now. I need to go back to the office to deal with Chelsea anyway."

Byron agreed. He called ahead to let forensics know about the backpack and computer and to plan for a long night.

∼

Monday, May 13—Early Evening

Carole Gardener, having just returned home from a day of campus meetings, was caught off guard when she saw Francesca Noto-Fox maneuvering into a parking spot in front of her house. She had to admit the professor's visit was not a surprise, not really. Carole had, of course, sent a hand-written note and flowers to Francesca when she learned the victim was a member of the professor's family. She also reached out to Martina's parents, but they had refused any contact with the campus administration. Now Francesca was approaching her front porch without an appointment, and Carole felt she might be opening the door to a verbal pummeling. She had only seconds to choose a strategy: hide in the bathroom until Francesca retreated, or graciously invite her inside.

As college president, Carole enjoyed the perks of living in the sprawling single-level home that Wexford had owned for decades. A few blocks from the campus, the modern house was built on an expansive lot at the end of a cul-de-sac. Located just far enough from campus to discourage students from staging spontaneous protests, the residence was close enough that Carole could attend countless evening meetings, have a social glass of wine with donors, and make it home without a designated driver. Its contemporary lines mirrored the work of Eichler. Carole loved its light-filled, mid-century feel, and she would be sorry when it was time for her to move out. The question was whether recent events putting a spotlight on campus safety heralded her departure sooner than she'd planned. If a suspect was not apprehended soon, campus stakeholders would look for a scapegoat, someone to bear responsibility for the death at Carter House. Why not blame Carole Gardener? During her tenure, she had grappled with declining funding, low enrollment, faculty scandals, #metoo, Title IX nightmares, and sports teams that rarely got a win. Admittedly, she'd made some unpopular decisions over the years, which had cost her the support of powerful alumni and donors. They'd be sharpening their talons for her now. These thoughts were running through Carole's mind as she weighed whether to open the door when Francesca knocked.

On the verge of hiding in the bathroom, Carole had vacillated too long. She had been seen. It was clear from Francesca's friendly wave that Carole was visible through the expansive front window. She would now have to slip into several roles: empathetic colleague, good listener, and the one she portrayed most often, community leader facing a terrible set of circumstances. She fixed her expression to convey caring and concern and opened the wide, wooden door.

A few minutes later, the two women were situated in the terraced patio with a northward view of the nearby national forest, birdsong carried on the breeze. Each had a glass of wine, and they were picking at a plate of hors d'oeuvres, leftovers from a donor meeting earlier that afternoon. With the niceties taken care of, Carole didn't waste any time. "Francesca, tell me why you stopped by. How can I help?"

Francesca focused on her colleague's frameless glasses and faded blue eyes. "We've known each other for many years, Carole, and my husband and I always supported you, even when many of the faculty wanted you removed. I need your help now. Bring me up to speed on what's going on with the investigation into my young cousin's death. What are SVPD doing? What are campus police doing? I know you have information that law enforcement isn't sharing with the family. I need a full briefing," Francesca declared, showing she wasn't in the mood for bullshit answers.

"I can understand why you're asking," Carole acquiesced. "I'll tell you what I know. You're her family, and you have a right to basic information. There's no good reason to keep you in the dark."

∿

An hour later, Francesca pulled into Eliza's driveway, eager to share what she'd learned. After kissing Lucas and admiring the new toys he had brought home from his visit to his dad's, she sat down with her daughter for an update. Her visit with Carole had been fruitful.

"*Cara*, did you know the police questioned some of our students? At least two of them so far." Francesca said. "I have their names written down."

Eliza opened her laptop to her witness list, ready to type in the names Francesca dictated. According to what Carole told Francesca, the same detectives the family met with that morning had interviewed students Dahlia Moreno and Li-Ann Wong.

Eliza made a mental note that the detectives had not shared this information during the family briefing. However, Levi had mentioned some tension between Martina and her classmates, and so had Kendra and Jason. Eliza needed to know more.

Francesca recounted that, based on intel from Carole Gardener, a third student had elected not to participate in the police interview. This was Chelsea Miller.

"Carole thinks the police still haven't spoken to Chelsea," Francesca explained. "Her dad, Wesley Miller, is a real estate lawyer active in the San Vicente Civic Association, and Carole would have expected to hear from him if police had questioned his daughter about something related to Wexford without notifying him first. Since all's quiet with the Millers, Carole thinks the detectives haven't been able to corral Chelsea, at least not yet."

"Interesting. What else did President Gardener tell you?"

"This next part was no surprise. They are moving to end Wexford's relationship with Tim O'Keefe. He doesn't have tenure, which makes it an easy process. Carole hinted that other complaints about O'Keefe had surfaced, but nothing with real teeth."

"Didn't Martina have a faculty advisor from the business school too?" Eliza asked. "O'Keefe was the computer science advisor. Who heads up the entrepreneur program? Do you know anyone on the business faculty you can ask?"

Francesca pondered for a moment and nodded decisively. She'd make some inquiries at the business school in the morning.

Eliza was gathering steam now; she could almost feel the electrical charges firing in her brain. "Mama, did President Gardener tell you anything about what they're finding on the CCTV? Aren't there lots of cameras around Carter House? And what about keycard access? Isn't the front door to Carter only accessible to students and faculty with keycards? It's not like the campus libraries, which are open to the community. Don't you need a valid swipe card to get into Carter? Staff could get in, of course, but not the public, which limits who would have access to the basement practice rooms. And why is all of this just occurring to me now?" Eliza said, questioning her own process.

Francesca was aware of how her daughter approached problems and could tell from the expression on Eliza's face that she was in "combustion mode," as she and her husband had referred to Eliza's creative bursts when she was a girl. Her daughter was not an organized, logical thinker, but an intuitive one who had the ability to pierce the core of a problem and find a novel solution without necessarily following a linear path. Francesca stayed quiet, giving Eliza space to think. The human brain, its hemispheres and processes, fascinated Francesca, who had learned so much from the thousands of college students she had taught over the decades.

"Sorry," Eliza said. "My brain's in overdrive. I asked you too many questions at once. The video cameras. What did campus police or the SVPD learn from the cameras?"

"I don't know," Francesca said. "Carole didn't talk about the video cameras, and I didn't think to ask her. We might get this info from Chief Mendoza. Should I try asking him?"

"Yes," Eliza said. "Try to work your magic with the campus police. You're the best person for that job. What about access to Carter House? Who can come and go from that facility?"

"I don't think the public can just wander into that facility. It's designated for use by art and music students. Unless an event is underway, like a live performance or an opening in the art gallery, you need to swipe a keycard to get in. This would limit foot traffic to students, faculty, and staff. Maybe a few very high-level donors who sit on the leadership board have keycards, but I'm only guessing about that."

"Right. That makes sense. Did President Gardener say anything to you about card swipes? They would know who swiped into Carter House on the morning Martina was killed."

"I was getting to that. She said they were consulting with campus IT about 'various angles.' When I asked what kinds of angles she meant, Carole was vague. She said something about checking Martina's college email account for leads, but that seemed like a dumb answer, one that she pulled up to placate me. Wouldn't the campus police have already examined Martina's Wexford email account for leads?"

Eliza nodded and said, "Yes. Probably. Can you ask Chief Mendoza about that too, when you talk to him about the video cameras?"

"Anyway, there was something in Carole's body language that made me think she wasn't being fully forthcoming, that there was another source of information that campus IT was checking. I don't know what it was," Francesca trailed off.

"Great work, Mom. *Molto utile*. You should get home. Laura and Roberto are probably holding off on dinner until you get there. Can you follow up with Chief Mendoza tomorrow? And can you ask if Martina's laptop has been found? And please reach out to your contact at the business school."

Francesca was soon headed toward the door, but then doubled back. "Eliza, there's something I forgot to tell you this morning. So much has been going on. I met a man at the vigil last night. He approached us as we were leaving the campus. You had already gone to get Lucas."

"Yeah? Who was he?"

"William Ducane was his name. He goes by Willie. He wanted to tell Roberto and Laura how impressed he was with Martina and the work she had been doing for disabled people like himself. It looked like he had some disfigurement with his hand. Anyway, he was offering his condolences."

"Ahh, her Helping Hands project. I asked Levi about the project at the vigil, but he wouldn't say anything. He was kinda weird about it. Did this guy say anything else? Do you know how he was involved in the project?"

"I could see that he was missing fingers, so I assumed he was serving as a test subject for them. I'm sure he'd talk to you. He's an Iraq war veteran. He said to contact him if he could help in any way with finding who hurt Martina."

Francesca reached in her purse and found a card with Willie's name and phone number.

"Thank you, Mama. I'll call him. Now go home."

Once Francesca was driving away, Eliza grabbed a bottle of mineral water and some peanuts and then sat down with her laptop. She composed a list of next steps in her investigative plan:

- ☐ Meet With Vanessa Delaware
- ☐ Review Recording Of Interview With Levi Newcomb
- ☐ Consider If There's A Link To The Theft Of Martina's Old Laptop And Her New Laptop Disappearing From The Crime Scene
- ☐ Call The Campus Cop Who Martina Was Dealing With About The First Laptop. What Was His Name?
- ☐ Check With Kendra About Student Access To Carter House
- ☐ Talk To Chelsea Miller

One thing seemed clear to Eliza; with the advantage of 20/20 hindsight, Martina was most likely killed by someone she knew. And the updates from Detective Fonseca that morning about known sex offenders were nonsense.

It was also clear that this investigation was too big for Eliza to handle alone. She needed help from Francesca and Kendra, who could cover different areas. Francesca had untapped connections to faculty and in the community, and Kendra had contacts to other students. Eliza needed to build a team. Before closing her laptop, she made one more entry:

☐ Call Willie Ducane

MARTINA'S JOURNAL

February 14—Three months earlier

Salve Journal,

I have a minute and thought of you. It's the feast of San Valentino today. They celebrate here as they do in Italy—with lover's cards and chocolates. Jason made a reservation for us for dinner. I'm sure it will be at a nice place. He's easy to be with, and I'm looking forward to the evening. I'm even going to dress up for it.

I haven't told Jason this yet, but soon, I'll have to stop spending so much time with him. He wants too much. I can't commit to being his exclusive partner. Definitely, I will go back to Italy this summer. It's been great to study in California—a dream from my childhood. But my home is in Italy, and that's where I'll live. Not America. I know that now. Once I'm back in Italy, it won't be realistic to have an American boyfriend. Why have all the drama of a long-distance relationship, even if Jason is a very nice guy.

Something I'm excited about: The piano teacher I study with here asked if I would perform in a piano recital three months from now. It will be toward the end of May. Only a couple of pieces, including Debussy's moody "Clair de Lune," which I love. It's a difficult piece to play well. And as my friends all know, I don't do things halfway. The recital gives me another reason to cool things with Jason. I'll need time to practice.

Basta, enough about breaking up with Jason. Negative thoughts will derail (is that the word?) our dinner tonight. For fun, I googled San Valentino, who lived in my home city of Roma. Aside from lovers, Valentino is also the patron saint of beekeepers. Who knew? I'll buy Jason a jar of honey as a small gift.

CHAPTER SIXTEEN

Tuesday, May 14—Morning

As soon as she dropped Lucas at school, Eliza parked on a side street and called Vanessa Delaware. The reporter was obviously still asleep at 8:30 a.m., but they arranged to meet in an hour. Moving through her to-do list, Eliza decided next to listen to the recording of her conversation with Levi from Sunday night. She focused on his comments about Martina being harassed by other students. This had an unexpected and immediate impact, causing Eliza to feel melancholy and regretful that she hadn't been a better cousin to Martina.

She tried to put herself in Martina's situation and considered how she would have felt. More importantly, how had Martina reacted when she found out she was being harassed online?

"Maybe they tried to make Martina look like a slut with a fake Tinder profile," Levi had said.

Eliza had had her own run-ins with bullies, and these encounters still caused an ache in her gut decades later. There was Candace, the menace in third grade who demanded every day for a week that Eliza turn over the small dessert her mother routinely packed in her lunchbox. Acting like a mafia don, Candace had demanded her payment. When Eliza either refused or tried to broker a deal and offer the girl half a cookie, Candace threatened to confiscate the entire lunch, including her My Little Pony lunchbox. These encounters left Eliza feeling powerless, neither physically strong enough nor ballsy enough to fend off the determined Candace. Twenty-five years later, she still regretted not showing more pluck in those playground moments. Eliza had wordlessly turned over the cookie on four consecutive days until she tearfully confided in Francesca. Her mother, always the peacemaker, resolved the matter by packing a few extra cookies, so Eliza could share the bounty. Only years later did Eliza learn that Francesca had also talked to her teacher, who arranged a special assignment for Eliza to work in the school office during lunch, out of Candace's reach.

Now she wondered how Martina would have reacted when targeted. Had she confronted the sorority cyberbullies directly? Or worse, had she set up some sort of revenge plot that backfired and led to her own demise? Eliza needed more. She needed more details about her cousin's whereabouts in the days before her piano session at Carter House. Aside from spending time with Tim O'Keefe, who else had Martina seen or talked to? Or conversely, who else had laid eyes on Martina? Had Martina caught the attention of someone, a stalker, maybe?

"I need to talk to Kendra," Eliza said aloud to no one. They had loosely arranged to get together on Monday following the vigil, except it was now Tuesday morning and they had yet to meet up. She shot off a quick text to Kendra. Hopefully, she'd be free, and they could talk face to face that afternoon.

Eliza was also struck by Levi's reference to Officer Thompson. Martina's missing backpack and the two missing laptops—one stolen during a yoga class and one missing from Carter House—was another angle that needed attention. As far as Eliza knew, these items hadn't been found yet, although only the detectives knew for sure. She was still peeved over Detective Fonseca dodging every question she posed, including the status of the missing computer. Could the disappearance of the first laptop have a nexus to Martina's death? *So many paths*, Eliza thought, feeling like an octopus with many arms and no clear idea of which one was pointing forward.

~

Vanessa was definitely awake now. She regretted sounding groggy when Eliza phoned fifteen minutes earlier, but she made no apologies for being nocturnal. Some of her best writing and most creative ideas blossomed after midnight.

For the past few days, Vanessa had been trying to think of other angles for reporting on the Noto case. There was the mushrooming fear on the Wexford campus angle and the bumbling detectives from SVPD angle, but she had already filed some version of those stories. She had also covered the breaking news about Tim O'Keefe. Hopefully Eliza would have something Vanessa could pursue. Otherwise, she was left with reporting on the police department's progress. Even though the *LA Daily Post* had run her story about O'Keefe in the Sunday edition, it was now Tuesday, and two days was a lifetime in the news cycle.

Sadly, the *Post's* coverage on Monday of the campus vigil had been little more than an oversized photo of Wexford students standing with lighted candles. Vanessa was still in a froth over it. TV news and bloggers were fully sensationalizing the story, and she realized it was hard for old-school print publications like the *Post* to compete. But the *Post* could do more. Even the students who ran the campus-based *Wexford Watch* seemed to be throwing all they had at the story. Vanessa's competitive nature wanted the *Post*, as the hometown paper, to shine and maybe win a Pulitzer or two during award season next year. Vanessa knew in her soul that she was the best person to write about Martina and cover many of the spin-off articles as well. She needed to focus.

For certain, there would be no Pulitzer if Raffa, her editor, didn't step up. Citing staff shortages, he had pulled Vanessa off covering the vigil on Sunday and sent her in the literal opposite direction to report on the opening of new hiking trails in the Santa Monica mountains. "Unfricking believable," was Vanessa's response to the assignment, considering the last time she'd been on a hike was when her parents sent her to Camp Bearhaven. But like a good soldier, instead of complaining to Raffa, she pulled up her socks, literally, and covered the hiking story. A staff photographer had attended the vigil alone, which was a definite missed opportunity in Vanessa's view.

Now, it was Tuesday morning, and she needed to make sure Raffa was putting her back on the Noto story. Certainly, the murder at Carter House had the sizzle to engage readers and drive-up hits to the *Post's* website. Sometime around 1 a.m. she had jotted down storylines she could use to persuade Raffa in case he gave her some other crazy assignment:

1. A young life cut short in San Vicente—stoke community outrage and increase readership.
2. The death dovetailed with growing anger nationally around the treatment of women on campuses and in the workplace, fomenting more anger and engagement on the *Post's* social media pages.
3. Write about tension between spending tax dollars on crime prevention versus other community needs (homelessness, climate change, and public transportation). Put a spotlight on local elected officials who can't get anything done.
4. Headline that a killer is still at large, someone who could target other women, generating fear. It's worth repeating this story since it brings in lots of hits to the website.
5. Repeat the angle that the police aren't doing enough. This approach generates outrage and anger over local government gridlock.

Vanessa knew she was right about all of it. Once she presented her list, it would be obvious to Raffa that he should reassign her to the Noto story full-time. To make everything work, Vanessa still needed a closer connection to Martina's family. Hopefully her meeting with Eliza Fox would fill that void.

Nearly ready, Vanessa searched for the right jewelry to complete her look, something to convey to Eliza that she was put together and prepared, but not formal or stiff. Details mattered, and she hoped to impress Eliza and win her confidence. Her silver hoop earrings and a matching chain necklace met the mark—businesslike, but not overly so.

~

Driving slowly and then parking some distance away, Eliza arrived late to the meeting with Vanessa Delaware. It was a small power move, but she wanted to get the upper hand. The reporter could worry for a short while whether Eliza would be a no show. Bottom line, Eliza didn't trust journalists. Anytime she had to interact with the press in her job at Fowler & Haverford, she was on full alert, careful not to say anything that could be misconstrued or misquoted. She approached Vanessa's table with her guard up.

"Vanessa," Eliza said, plopping down into the chair opposite the reporter. "Sorry to keep you waiting. My son had a meltdown. It couldn't be helped."

Vanessa reached out and greeted Eliza with a handshake. "No problem. I was catching up on a few things. Would you like a coffee? Cup of tea? I'm buying."

"A large latte would be great," Eliza said, grabbing the opportunity to let Vanessa wait on her. Then once they were both settled, Eliza took control. "I understand you tried to contact my cousin's roommate, Kendra Reid. I'm curious. Why'd you want to talk to Kendra?"

"My hope was to talk to a few people who were close to Ms. Noto. I'd like to give our readers a real sense of who she was. Sorry, I know I'm speaking of your cousin in the past tense. Do you know Kendra? She didn't return my texts. I also tried to reach another student, Jason Chang. But neither got back to me."

"You don't need to talk to Kendra," Eliza said in a quiet, steady voice. "She's devastated by what happened to Martina, and I'd like you to respect her privacy, please."

"I hear you," Vanessa said. "Now it's my turn to be curious. Why did you want to meet in person? If you wanted me to back off from contacting sources on this story, you could have said that on the phone."

"Fair enough," Eliza replied. "I don't want to waste your time. I'm pretty single-minded right now. I want Martina's killer to be apprehended and prosecuted. That's it. That's the only thing that will give her parents—our family—some peace. Figuring out what took place that morning at Carter House can't happen fast enough."

"That makes sense," Vanessa said. "But how do I factor in? I'm not a cop."

"Right. My guess is that we share some mutual interests. For example, I'd like to see a fire lit under San Vicente PD, campus police, and any other agency they call in. I think you have a knack for getting under the skin of SVPD and the politicos on city council. I'm betting that your reporting could nudge them to throw more resources at the police investigation. That would benefit you, wouldn't it? If you have a prominent role in a big story? Can we help each other here?"

Vanessa tried to hold back her smile. "You and I are definitely on the same page," she said. "But do you have an angle that I can take to my editor? I get that you want me to steer clear of Kendra and your family, but the personal approach is what grabs readers' attention. It's the thing that makes them care."

"Right. Kendra and my family are off limits. I need your word on that," Eliza said, not that she had much trust in Vanessa's promise.

"Of course," said Vanessa. "Scout's honor."

"What if I text you contact information for Martina's best friend in Italy, Ana Maggio? Ana has already agreed to talk to you. She can speak to what Martina was like as a girl, her aspirations and quirks. Ana is also prepared to give you the names of other childhood friends. She'll probably have some photos, too. Talking to Martina's friends in Italy should give you enough to write a compelling profile of her and generate more sympathy here in San Vicente—all of which will push the police and local officials to make the investigation their top priority."

Eliza waited to gauge Vanessa's reaction. "Do we have a plan?" she asked.

"We do," Vanessa replied. "We definitely do."

∾

Eliza still had doubts that Vanessa could be trusted, but she'd done her best to steer the reporter away from Martina's inner circle. The news media was always going to be in the mix. She went back to her car and called Willie Ducane, leaving a voicemail when he didn't answer. She also tried following up on Levi's tip and reached out to Chelsea Miller, now that Kendra had provided the sorority girl's number. Chelsea also didn't answer, and her voicemail was full. Eliza texted them both; maybe one of these people would text her back.

Martina's room was next. Eliza knew she had put it off too long. To understand Martina's fate, she needed to organize the disparate pieces of information she'd learned in the past week. Maybe being in Martina's space and retracing her cousin's steps up the hill to Carter House would help Eliza comprehend the bigger picture. The police had already been to the condo. Eliza didn't know what they found, but she needed to see the place for herself.

Forty-five minutes later, she had collected the key from Kendra, who was on her way to class. The two had arranged to meet later that afternoon at Francesca's house, where Kendra could also talk more with Roberto and Laura.

Eliza now stood in the kitchen that Kendra and Martina had shared. First, she used the little pot on the kitchen counter to make herself an espresso, and she sipped it while she eyed the adjoining living room and dining area. The décor had elements of both a student's budget and high-end castoffs. The walls were adorned haphazardly with vintage travel posters from Fiji and Hawaii and museum posters of works by Leonardo da Vinci and Fra Angelico. The black leather couch looked expensive but worn, probably a piece

Kendra's mother had handed down. A wooden floor lamp, which Eliza recognized from Ikea, arched over it, and an oval glass table, strewn with books and dirty glasses, stood guard in front of it. From her perch on a kitchen barstool, Eliza observed the objects around the room: a stack of unopened mail, a vegetarian cookbook, and a couple of books of sheet music. She circled the room, grabbed the mail, and returned to her seat on the barstool.

Among the utility bills, catalogues, real estate ads, and restaurant flyers, Eliza found an unopened envelope addressed to Martina Noto from the US Patent-Trademark Office. She hesitated a tick, feeling weird about opening someone else's government mail, and then felt silly about being reticent. The letter was from a patent examiner, who was writing to both Levi and Martina in their roles as inventors. It identified several deficiencies in their patent application, including problems with the drawings they'd submitted and questions about the medical evidence supporting the device. They had eight weeks to submit an amended application. The letter, which was sent from Alexandria, Virginia, was dated May 6, meaning it had likely arrived after the police had searched the condo. Eliza tucked the letter back in its envelope and stuffed it into her purse.

She then moved onto Martina's bedroom and ensuite bathroom, looking for anything that might provide a clue—a pregnancy test, morning-after pills, prescription meds, bank statements, electronic devices, handwritten journals—but nothing seemed relevant. The room was tidy, and it was likely Kendra had put things in order after the police left. In a way, she was glad she found nothing. It meant that Martina's parents could go to the condo and organize their daughter's things without finding anything disturbing. At least, Eliza hoped that was the case.

She glanced at the clock by the bed and decided she had enough time to walk from the condo to Carter House. Eliza still wanted to retrace Martina's likely route to the practice rooms. If she didn't linger, she'd be able to get Lucas from school on time. Then they'd head to Francesca's. Leaving the key to the condo with Kendra's neighbor, Eliza set out on the path that Martina probably followed that Tuesday morning.

The street was lined with massive camphor trees that shaded the road. Three-story apartment buildings were interspersed with single-level homes and duplexes, making the parking competitive. Eliza figured that Wexford students rented places on this side of campus, evidenced by the aging cars, the selection of bumper stickers, and the young people coming and going from the apartment buildings. There was also a dearth of baby strollers, swing sets, and the sounds of young children.

Eliza walked along Whitmore Road, looking for CCTV cameras as the street rose upward. She considered finding a photo of Martina on her phone and showing it to random people to see if they knew her. Maybe she'd get lucky and someone would recognize her, but that also felt like a fishing expedition. Eliza kept walking, simply observing, until she reached a corner market situated a block from Carter House. Appropriately called Snack & Go, it was the kind of place you'd stop at for a bottle of water, chips, a packet of gum, or cigarettes. Eliza also noticed that the store's surveillance cameras were mounted above its front entrance, where they would capture a wide swath of the intersection. She pushed open the door, triggering the annoying buzz that signaled a customer.

The shop was dark with high windows and poor lighting, but it also had a neighborhood feel, less cookie-cutter than the usual chain stores that offered similar quick-sale items. Circling around the shelves, she noticed some unusual items: boxes of European chocolates, imported British teas, and a selection of Indian spices. She grabbed a cold apple juice for Lucas and some potato chips and approached the counter. A tall, reedy man with a dark beard and a brown turban stood at the cash register. Eliza set her items on the counter and pulled out her phone, preparing to show him Martina's photo.

"Hello. I wonder if you could help me," she said. "You must have heard the news about the Wexford student who was killed last week.

I'm trying to figure out what happened to her. Were you working that morning?"

His dark eyes assessed Eliza, scanning for why she was asking such a question. "No," the man said. "I don't work in the mornings. I don't know anything. Are you the police?"

"Can I show you a photo of her, the girl who died? She was my cousin. Maybe you'll recognize her from the neighborhood. She lived close to here. And, no, I'm not the police. Just her family. My name is Eliza."

After looking at the photo, the man shook his head. "No, I don't remember her. I'm sorry for your loss. Come back in the morning when my cousin Jay is here. Maybe he can help you."

"Thanks. I'll do that. I'll be back tomorrow. One more thing, are you able to access the video feed for your surveillance system? Your cameras look like they cover much of the intersection. It could help. I'm guessing that my cousin walked by this corner the morning she died."

"Ahh. I see. I'll look for you. I'll try to retrieve the feed."

"I'd appreciate that. Would it be possible to go back the week before it happened. That would be the first full week of May. I know it's a lot of data. Whatever you could provide would be a big help."

"I'll try. If I can get the video, I'll leave it with Jay on a flash drive, so you can pick it up when you come back."

"Thanks. That would be great. Sorry, I didn't catch your name."

"Call me Samay."

Eliza paid for her items and took a few steps toward the door before she thought of one last question. "Samay, do you know if the police were here? In the past week, I mean, asking about this?"

"Not that I know of," he replied. "But I'm aware of this incident. Of course, it was in the news. But my family, we own this business. We talk to the other merchants—the dry cleaners, the bakery, the pet store—and we keep watch. There was a post on the police's social media about your cousin. They were looking for leads. It seems like the police are trying."

"I hope so," Eliza said. "Thanks for your help."

She continued up the hill to Carter House, thinking more about where Martina might have gone that last morning, and where she'd been the night before. Who were the last people to interact with Martina? Maybe the detectives had this information, but they hadn't shared it with the family.

Reaching the top of the hill, Eliza could feel her heartbeat as she neared the graceful Carter House, with its cedar shingles and forest green window trim. Her body was either reacting to the stress of being so close to the crime scene, or she had exerted herself walking up the hill. Probably both, she figured. Eliza stopped to observe the path that snaked through the sloping front lawn and led to Carter's wrap-around stone porch. From where she stood, it looked as if the venue was closed, even though it was early afternoon. She watched as a small group of students approached the front door and unsuccessfully tried their keycards. Eventually, the door opened a few inches, and the students appeared to talk to someone before they retreated. Eliza caught up with them as they walked away from the property.

"Hey, can people get into Carter?" Eliza asked.

"Not yet," one young woman snapped. "Which sucks because my art project is locked in there."

"Did they say when it would open again?"

"Nope. The person inside said I should talk to the art department to get an extension on my senior project. I *need* to graduate at the end of May. That's like in two weeks. I don't need this shit!" the student yelled as her friends tried to calm her and guide her back toward the main campus.

"Bummer," Eliza said, sardonically. "You know somebody died there," she called after them. "There's a good reason it's closed!"

With her raised voice drawing looks from pedestrians, Eliza took a breath and checked the time. Her conversation with Samay at the Snack & Go had taken longer than she thought. If she hurried, she had just enough time to circumnavigate the exterior of Carter House and still make it to Lucas's school for pickup, assuming traffic was light. With more urgency now, she veered left and headed up the grassy hill toward the western edge of the property. At the corner of the house, Eliza turned right and quickly walked past the planting beds bordering the west side of Carter. At the rear corner of the grand house, she stopped short, reaching the point where police caution tape flapped in the breeze. The yellow stripe was a clear message the area was closed. Eliza inched closer to the flimsy barrier to snap some exterior photos of the area with her phone.

Most of the space was planted as a native California garden, probably to promote water conservation. Unobtrusive green benches and small wooden chairs were tucked in among the low shrubs. With the area cordoned off and no people trekking through, small birds were comfortably pecking at the ground and a couple of squirrels cavorted on the property's rear fence. Eliza thought more about the slope of the property as the hillside continued its angle upward from the rear of the house. The windows on the lowest level, where the practice rooms were located, were set about a foot above the ground. It would have been easy for someone to escape out one of them. She imagined that on a typical Tuesday morning the area behind Carter House would have been devoid of people, although it was possible a groundskeeper was working behind the house. Eliza made a mental note to ask the garden crew if anyone was working behind Carter then.

She looked more closely at the caution tape. "Damn!" she said. There was no place behind the house where she could step without crossing under it. She didn't want to contaminate the turf behind the property, but she also wanted a closer look at the property's rear side. When the killer approached, Martina had been inside a practice room on the basement level, probably immersed in her music. The perpetrator had gotten in and out of the building somehow. But how?

Eliza hovered at the edge of the yellow tape, still toying with the idea of slipping under it, when she realized that a drone could get the perspective she wanted. A novice at spy craft, Eliza didn't have a drone sitting on a closet shelf but figured one could be rented. She'd consult with her neighbor, a drone fanatic, about the best way to shoot some footage of the area. Yes, this was a better plan than slipping under the ominous yellow tape. Almost ready to leave, she snapped a couple more photos with her phone, then a deep male voice shouted, "Hey, you! Stop right there." Eliza's reconnaissance mission was officially over.

She turned to see a uniformed campus police officer taking big strides toward her. Under the brim of his police hat, his round face looked reddish, and his eyes were scrunched into small orbs. His expression made him appear hard, but also clownish, as if he were pretending to be tough. He stopped only inches from where she stood, and she smelled garlic emanating from him.

"What are you doing! This is a crime scene. You can't be here," he barked, mimicking an army drill sergeant.

"Really sorry," Eliza said. "I was out for a walk on the campus. Just looking at the pretty gardens. I was about to turn around and go back the way I came."

She stepped to her left to navigate around him when she noticed the nametag on his chest and stopped. It read "Officer K. Thompson." Eliza made the connection. This was the campus cop Levi had told her to talk to, the guy who had taken the report about Martina's laptop after the theft at the wellness center.

"Why were you taking photos here behind the police tape, if you're just out for a walk? Answer that one," he demanded.

"Okay, sure. I saw some unusual birds. They're so pretty. I'm a birder and you gotta document. I was just about to leave though."

"I see," he said, still scrutinizing Eliza. "Birds. Right. Let me see your phone."

"No, I don't think so, Officer Thompson. Look, I need to go. It's time to pick up my son from school, so I can't chat anymore. Sorry."

"Do you have a Wexford ID? Are you a reporter? Give me your name!"

"No, I don't have a campus ID. Not a reporter. And you don't need to know my name," Eliza said sharply. "I was out for a walk, and I snapped some photos of birds. I said I need to go now," her voice growing more defiant.

As Eliza stepped forward to pass him, Officer Thompson surprised her by reaching out for her right arm, grabbing ahold just above her elbow. His fingers dug into her flesh. "Don't let me see you here again," he said. "Today I'm gonna look the other way and let this incident go."

Eliza, locking on his brown eyes, annunciated, "Let. Go. Of. My. Arm." He waited a beat to comply, then made an exaggerated gesture of suspending his open palm a few inches from her shoulder, as if he'd touched something hot and dropped it. His lips transformed into an odd grin. Eliza walked forward without saying anything more, without looking back.

"You know you're in the wrong, lady," Officer Thompson called after her. Eliza heard the radio on his belt crackle. "Area secure. I sent her off. Probably a reporter. Clear," he said officiously.

"Asshole," Eliza mouthed, as she walked down the hill at a rapid clip, adrenaline pumping. She was unnerved over her encounter with Officer Thompson for so many reasons. She was furious about being manhandled, and he clearly had a power thing. Their unexpected meeting also complicated the fact that she had planned to talk to him about the theft of Martina's first laptop. Approaching Kennedy Thompson for any reason now would be more complicated.

She eventually reached her car parked at Kendra's condo. Settled in the driver's seat, Eliza dug into her purse and found the bag from the corner market. Even though the apple juice was intended for Lucas, she took a big swig of it. She then confronted the chips, also meant as a treat for the boy. "What the hell," she said, ripping the bag open and stuffing a handful of salty crunch into her mouth.

Lastly, she found some music on her phone, something that she could sing along to, and headed for Lucas's school. It was time to transform herself into a mom again, without distractions or stress, for at least the first thirty minutes after collecting her kid. He would need to download his day and she wanted to be—needed to be—fully engaged in that conversation. Later they would go to Francesca's, where Kendra was meeting her, and she could return to being a working mom. But for the next little while, it would be Lucas's time, and Eliza needed it as much as he did.

~

Francesca was feeling pulled in too many directions. Although she was semi-retired, she was still advising graduate students and had navigated three such meetings today. Knackered was how she felt, stealing a term from her husband and his British roots. Aside from the stress in her own family, one of the student meetings had turned unpleasant when Francesca told a student that she needed to redraft large portions of her thesis. There were tears over this, and Francesca was sure the student was venting now to her friends about how unreasonable Professor Noto-Fox was. "Too bad," she thought. "Whatever happened to high standards and a desire for excellence?"

On the bright side, she had found time to track down Fernando Guzman in the business school, who had been Martina's advisor for entrepreneurial programs. Professor Guzman was very helpful with background information about the project Martina was working on with Levi Newcomb, a doctoral student in biomedical engineering. According to Guzman, Martina and Levi began work in October and had made excellent progress over the ensuing eight months. Martina was working on the algorithms, and Guzman thought her experience as a pianist gave her a unique insight into the project. He knew that she and Levi had been close to producing a rough prototype of their prosthesis and were applying for patents.

Francesca asked specifically about Levi, and Guzman's carefully chosen adjective for him was "difficult." He saw Levi as one of those students who worked better individually, rather than in groups. Initially, Guzman had doubts about pairing Martina with Levi, but the two seemed to resolve conflicts easily and had made amazing progress together. Guzman speculated that because they were both strong personalities, maybe they had respected that trait in the other.

It turned out that Tim O'Keefe was the snake, Guzman observed, given that he had crossed ethical boundaries by sleeping with a student. Guzman asked Francesca her thoughts on whether O'Keefe was linked to Martina's death, but she dodged the question, mostly because she had no idea who was to blame. At least not yet.

The whole day had made Francesca reflective. Her thoughts kept returning to the work Martina and Levi had been doing with their aptly named Helping Hands project. As an art historian, she found representations of hands both beautiful and evocative of our shared humanity, whether the hands were at work or at rest, whether they conveyed affection or anger.

Francesca mentally flipped through the catalogue of images she had shared with her students over the years. There were the flat depictions of human hands that dated back more than ten thousand years to cave drawings. During the Renaissance, da Vinci made hands true to life with his anatomical studies and sketches. Around the same time, Michelangelo used the expansive canvas of the Sistine Chapel to demonstrate the power of touch. Francesca thought, too, of Albrecht Dürer's *Praying Hands,* which instilled a sense of stillness and peace in her. In a more modern depiction, M. C. Escher drew two hands drawing each other in a circular image that turned in on itself. All of these depictions—even the cave drawings—told a story, and she loved trying to decode the illustrator's message.

Francesca was proud of her young cousin. After talking to Willie Ducane at the vigil, she was starting to grasp how he would benefit from Martina and Levi's work. The device could interface with a person's nervous system, facilitating a more precise communication between the brain and prosthetic fingers and thumbs. Francesca wanted to talk to Eliza about meeting with Levi again. He was turning out to be a central player in Martina's life, yet none of the people who were close to Martina seemed to know very much about him.

"*Nonna!*" Lucas shouted, running through the house to find Francesca in her study. She was happy to see him. The boy's rambunctious spirit contrasted with her pensive mood, and she welcomed the atmospheric shift.

"*Ragazzo mio, com'è andata la tua giornata?*" she greeted him warmly.

"Fine, *Nonna*," he replied. "I was the fastest runner today at school. I flew like a jet airplane."

"Lucas, can you tell me that in Italian?"

"I don't want to speak Italian, *Nonna*. My dad and Stephanie talk in English, and the baby won't understand Italian."

"I see," Francesca said. She knew he would balk at being bilingual eventually. It was common for children to push back when their parents wanted them to converse in a mother tongue.

"Can we do this, Lucas? I'd like to speak to you in Italian sometimes, even most of the time, but you can respond in either English or Italian. It will be your choice. Can we do that?"

"*Si, Nonna.* We can do that."

"*Perfetto, un bacio, per favore.*" He placed a big kiss on Francesca's forehead and bound from the room to find Pavo. It was time for the dog's afternoon stroll, and she could hear Roberto gathering the leash, preparing to take the dog around the neighborhood. Lucas would join them. It was nice to see new routines being established, small steps forward for all of them. Lucas was a gift, a touchstone toward recovery and resilience. Francesca was curious now to find out if Lucas spoke with Roberto in English or Italian or a mash-up of both.

~

Francesca found her daughter in the kitchen talking quietly with Laura. Kendra was expected soon, and Eliza was explaining that the Notos should talk to Kendra about finding a time for them to visit the condo.

The three women sat down, each with a cup of tea and biscotti within reach. Eliza asked Francesca about her progress, and she recounted her meeting with Professor Guzman and her idea that they should talk with Levi further. Eliza agreed that Levi was a mystery, and they needed to know more about him. She brought out the letter from the patent office and showed it to Francesca and Laura. It was proof that the two inventors had applied for a patent or patents, as Ana Maggio had told them, but the application was deficient and needed amending.

"Laura," Eliza said. "Finding the letter confirming that they'd filed for a patent made me think of something else. Obviously, the patent application was submitted before Martina died. But I'm wondering if Martina's interests as an inventor are transferable to you and Roberto as next of kin?"

Both Laura and Francesca quietly considered the ramifications of this.

"*Cara*, was it possible Levi wanted to remove Martina from the patent so he wouldn't have to share profits with her?" Francesca asked. "Wouldn't that provide a motive for him to want her gone?"

"Sure. It definitely would, except I have no information about the law in this area. I'm not sure if a patent application is an inheritable asset. If Martina's interests in the patent would revert to her next of kin, then the profit motive would evaporate. Do you see what I mean?"

"I get it," Francesca said. "If Laura and Roberto could legally collect their daughter's share of the proceeds, Levi wouldn't have gained financially from Martina's death."

"That's right. But again, I'm in the dark here. I'd like to talk with David about it. But I'm stretched too thin already. Laura, would you and Roberto mind talking to my ex-husband about this? It's a practice area he's working in, so I don't think he'd need to do a ton of research. As Martina's parents, you need to know the answer to this."

"*Certo,*" Laura replied. "We have lots of free time here, maybe too much, and we want to help."

"One thought though. Even if the law says that you, as her parents, will inherit Martina's interest, it's possible that Levi didn't know this.

We need to find out two things: what Levi understood the law to be and what the law actually says. Mama and I can take care of the first part if you and Roberto talk to David about the second part."

"Agreed," they said, each raising their teacup in a toast.

Francesca then blurted, "Wait, I have more." She had almost forgotten her conversation with Chief Mendoza earlier that day. She had talked to Gil in the faculty lounge that morning, which now seemed like the distant past.

"I learned something about the video cameras in the basement of Carter House. The police don't have any video feed from them."

"Wait. Why not?" Eliza asked. "Was it erased?"

"It seems the system didn't function. Gil was a little coy and avoided answering me directly. I'm not sure if the feed was erased or if the system was offline for some reason. But there was no recording from the basement of Carter House that morning."

Eliza considered this. "I don't know that building. Is there a surveillance system in place where the practice rooms are?"

"I haven't been down to that level. Whenever I've been to events at Carter House, they're on the main floor in the performance space. I can't picture what the basement or the practice rooms are like."

"Okay," Eliza said. "I went to Carter House today, and it's still closed. I watched as some students tried to use their keycards to access the main door, but the cards didn't seem to work. Eventually someone opened the door and turned them away. Did the chief mention accessing keycard swipes from Tuesday morning? If the police don't have video, they would at a minimum have a list of who swiped into the building that morning."

"You're right about Carter House not being open to the public," Francesca said. "Chief Mendoza confirmed that unless there's a performance or a gallery opening, one needs a Wexford ID to enter the space. This means the person who went into Martina's practice room that day carried a Wexford ID of some kind," Francesca reasoned.

"Or Martina brought someone along with her, maybe her piano teacher. I guess that's possible," Eliza said, "but not likely. In that case, she would have gone to the teacher's studio rather than Carter House."

"What if someone slipped in behind a person who used their keycard?" Francesca asked. "You know, before the door closed. Most people, especially students, are not very careful about security."

"That's also a possibility," Eliza agreed. "But let's not overcomplicate things. I think the police are working on the theory that Martina knew her attacker, that it was someone from the Wexford community. It's why the detectives told us yesterday they had ruled out sex offenders in the neighborhood, people who presumably don't have Wexford keycards."

"It also explains why no one in the other practice rooms heard Martina scream," Laura said. "Remember, we asked the detectives that question yesterday—if anyone heard loud noises or cries for help. My daughter probably knew the person who hurt her. I've read a lot about women being attacked. Statistics show that women are more often hurt by their boyfriends, their husbands, or someone in their trusted circle. Attacks from strangers are much less common, although we shouldn't rule it out entirely."

Eliza and Francesca both looked intently at Laura. She had spoken very little since arriving in San Vicente, mostly allowing Roberto to provide information and talk to Eliza about the investigation. Laura was visibly stronger than when she'd first arrived in Los Angeles. While she still wasn't the vibrant woman Eliza remembered from her trips to Italy, Laura's posture was straighter and her voice was stronger than a few days earlier.

"You're right, Laura. I've read those statistics too," Eliza said. "It is more likely that we're looking for someone Martina knew rather than a total stranger. And presumably the police have narrowed that circle to the people who swiped into Carter House that morning."

Responding to sounds in the house, they all looked toward the kitchen door. Roberto, Lucas, and Pavo had returned from their walk, bringing Kendra inside with them. It felt good to have a house full of people, Francesca thought. She opened the freezer and found a large tub of lentil soup and a frozen baguette. There were enough tomatoes and lettuce on hand to make a salad. She naturally fell into preparing dinner without asking whether anyone was hungry. Of course, they needed food, and of course, they would eat.

∿

Leaving Roberto and Laura to do the dishes, Eliza took a few minutes to talk to Kendra before heading home. Although she had already asked Kendra about Martina's work with Levi, he continued to be enigmatic. She wanted to dig a little deeper to see if Kendra knew more than she realized.

"Did you ever meet Levi?" Eliza asked.

"No, never."

"How would Martina seem after working with him?"

"Fine, I guess. She didn't talk much about Levi. I figured he was paranoid about privacy and very worried that someone would steal his concept, or rather the concept that he and Martina were developing."

Eliza kept going. "What about a man named Willie Ducane? Did Martina talk about him?"

"Yeah, she did a little," Kendra answered. "He was the guy who had the hand injury, right? Martina and Willie were fine-tuning the prosthetic device. I think she liked working with him as a test subject. He came by the condo once. Seemed like a nice guy."

"Okay," Eliza said, writing a note to herself to keep trying to reach Willie. "Do you have any idea where Martina might have been on Monday night? When was the last time you saw her or connected with her? Can you check your phone?"

Kendra did as Eliza asked and pulled her phone from her back pocket. She opened her text messages, then scrolled and read for several seconds without speaking.

"That Monday, I was either in class or in the library," Kendra said. "I was behind on my work and spent the day trying to catch up. I have some texts from Martina. I remember being in the library when I read them. You can see they were sent a little after 4 p.m. Take a look. Martina was worried about the piano thing."

Eliza scanned the texts between the two roommates:

Martina: Nervous about recital not sure why I'm doing it. Over committed and overwhelmed. Is it 2 late 2 back out?
Kendra: Hahaha u rock whatever u do will be fine.
Martina: Not so sure. Classical music ppl are judgy and harsh.
Kendra: [heart emoticon]
Martina: Gonna be out tonight. Can we do bfast tomorrow around 11. gonna hit piano at Carter House early tomorrow, so after that?
Kendra: Sure. see u then if I miss u tonite

Eliza considered the messages. "Can you think where she might have gone on a Monday night? Her text says 'gonna be out,'" Eliza pressed.

"I'm only guessing. She could have been with Levi. She was secretive about him, so the fact that her text is vague about where she was going might mean she was with him," Kendra said.

"That's my thought too," Eliza agreed. "But what are other possibilities? Let's not get tunnel vision."

"Okay. Maybe Jason? They were still friends and maybe regretting their break-up. Maybe Tim O'Keefe? For lots of reasons, she and the professor were keeping their hook-ups quiet. I doubt it was other girlfriends. Other than me, she didn't have female friends at Wexford."

Eliza thought for a moment. "Kendra, did she say anything to you about some guy who works for Wexford campus police? Kennedy Thompson?"

"Yeah, I know who you mean. He called her a few times about the stolen laptop. She was submitting some sort of insurance claim about it. She needed the police report as proof she'd reported it stolen. He stopped by the condo at least once, so Martina could sign some paperwork. They talked on the porch. He didn't come inside the condo. I remember that."

"When was this? When did he go to your place?"

"Maybe two weeks ago. It was a Sunday morning. I went out early to surf at Zuma. When I got back, he was on the front steps talking to Martina. I just walked past them and went to shower."

"Was there anything that stood out to you about him or the way they were interacting?"

"No, not really. He was just some campus cop. Martina thought he was nice to help with the police report. Her computer was expensive, and she wanted the campus—well, its insurance company—to reimburse her. That was it."

"Okay, thanks. That's very helpful. I need to ask you for something else. This investigation has so many loose ends. Would you be able to talk to Jason for me?"

"Sure. About what?"

"Can you ask him when he last saw Martina and where he was that Tuesday morning? I should have asked him this stuff when I met with him, but I messed up. He's your friend. You'll have a sense if he's lying or not."

"Wait, do you seriously think Jason would lie to me? Or that he would hurt Martina?"

"No, I don't," Eliza replied. "If I thought Jason was dangerous, I wouldn't send you to do this. I just want to cover all the details, and I don't have time to get to everything. The questions I want you to ask are better asked face to face. It would be a big help if you could talk to Jason. Then afterward, let me know exactly how he answered, as close to verbatim as possible."

"Okay," Kendra agreed. "But I'm not gonna lie. This makes me a little nervous. I'll text him. Maybe he can meet up later tonight."

"Perfect. You'll be fine. You'll find a way to ask that seems natural."

"I hope so," Kendra said, unconvinced.

"*Grazie mille*," Eliza said. "I need to go. I have a kid who should be getting ready for bed, and I need some downtime. I've had a very long day."

Eliza encircled Kendra in an appreciative hug before calling out to Lucas that it was time to leave. She was exhausted and hoped to fast-forward their family ritual of the extended *arrivederci*. She made her way to the den where the three adults and Lucas were gathered around the TV, watching an animated movie about a family of superheroes.

Eliza smiled at the scene, but she didn't feel like a superhero. Although with every detail they nailed down, she did feel closer to the truth. They were ruling out possible explanations for what happened to Martina. What were the detectives focusing on, Eliza wondered. Should she try to talk to them again? *Seems pointless* she thought. *Unless*—she had an idea—*I take a different approach.*

CHAPTER SEVENTEEN

Wednesday, May 15—Morning

After negotiating with Wesley and Chelsea Miller until midnight, Detective Fonseca slept badly and was spent when she woke up. Jessica needed a day off, but even such a brief respite wouldn't be possible until…. *Until when?* she asked herself. "Until the Wexford community felt safe again," she answered aloud. "That's the job." If students were fearful as they navigated the campus, that anxiety would permeate everything they did. Jessica was duty bound to fix that problem. Her personal needs and desires, like getting a pedicure or going ballroom dancing, could wait until the case was resolved. She wasn't ready to accept, at least not yet, that the SVPD team would be dismantled without someone in custody. They were still a long way from that, thankfully.

She had come into work early. With the department still quiet, she sat at her cubicle and thought back over the past week, focusing on the things in the investigation she and Byron had zeroed in on and the things they'd let slide. She scanned her notes, looking for scribbles to herself, reminders to do something later. The words "lovers or ex-lovers" caught her attention. She remembered telling Byron that they needed to look into the victim's boyfriends or sexual partners for motive and opportunity. It was a classic scenario for good reason; jealousy, rage, and revenge were powerful emotions that could trigger deadly consequences. They had looked closely at Professor Timothy O'Keefe for that very reason. While the woman who cleaned the professor's house provided an alibi for him, the notion that the killer was someone desirous of Martina, someone she may have rebuffed, still rang true. She would have attracted men like bees to a sunflower. Martina's recent whereabouts, especially the night before she died, were still in question. Who had their victim been dealing with, and who had she run afoul of?

Jessica had hoped the forensics on Martina's laptop would be ready by the time she arrived at the station, at least a preliminary readout. Thankfully, the department, now putting more people power on the case, had okayed overtime for the tech team to work all night. While she waited for the forensic report to come through on the computer, Jessica stood by the large bank of east-facing windows. The sun was on the rise, and the calm that permeated the large open workspace wouldn't last much longer. Stifling a gaping yawn, she grabbed her phone and dialed her sister, Sylvie. With the time difference on the East Coast, Sylvie would be at her desk and hopefully able to talk.

"*Mi hermana*," Sylvie said cheerfully. "It's still early in California. *Cómo te va?*"

"Fine. The same. I had a minute and wanted to catch up with you."

"I talked to Mom this weekend. She sounded good. We talked about the usual stuff: her roses, the cat, the latest *chisme* from the neighborhood."

"You must have caught her on a good day," Jessica said.

"What? What does that mean?" Sylvie asked.

"She's getting frail, Sylvie, and I worry about her living alone. I don't have time to get into it right now, but I have an idea, and I hope you'll agree. Can you take a week off and come out for a visit? Spend a week with her. Once you've seen things for yourself, we'll talk."

Jessica heard her sister's deep sigh. She envisioned Sylvie twisting a thin strand of long, dark hair with her index finger. It was a habit from their childhood, something Sylvie did when she was nervous or unsure. Jessica had an urge to speak, to fill the silence with a sales pitch about her plan, but she held back and waited. It was better to let her sister reach her own decision.

"Okay," Sylvie finally agreed. "I'll send you some dates. Mid-June looks good. I can take Mom to a Dodger game. She'll love that."

"Ahh, thank you. It'll be great to see you. We'll eat at all your favorite restaurants, I promise. I have to go. My day is about to get crazy," Jessica said, ending the call and the momentary connection to her past. It was almost 7 a.m. and the office atmosphere was already getting chaotic as street cops, command staff, and civilian employees filtered in and took their posts.

As Jessica settled back at her desk, her computer sounded a familiar chime, the arrival of another email. It was from the forensic tech team, and she didn't waste any time opening it. Unfortunately, the news wasn't good. They had not cracked the password on Martina's laptop yet. Frustrated, Jessica called Kendra, who was still sleeping by the sound of her voice. Kendra had provided the password for Martina's phone, and Jessica wanted to be sure she'd been asked about the laptop password. Kendra confirmed that someone from the forensic team had called her the previous night. Kendra had scoured Martina's room looking for a list of passwords, but no luck. She promised to call Jessica if she found anything that might help.

Jessica was beyond disappointed at this setback. She needed to walk off her sudden bad mood, which led her to the building cafeteria, where she gobbled up a stack of pancakes in a puddle of syrup. "I need the sugar to think," she fibbed to herself, licking drops of sweet goo from her fork. A short time later, she was back at her desk and revisiting the data on Martina's phone. *Maybe we missed something,* Jessica thought, recalling the first time she'd looked at the phone data. It was the morning her mom had been in the hospital and she'd arrived late to work. Byron told her to look at the phone's text messages, which led to them learning about their victim's illicit relationship with Tim O'Keefe. Maybe, in their haste to go after O'Keefe, she and Byron had missed something important. Jessica looked more closely at the photos and videos in the phone's storage.

Many of them she had already seen—photos from a beach day with Kendra, shots of various restaurant meals, and videos of Jason

Chang clowning around with a soccer ball. Jessica considered again whether Jason was their killer. Like O'Keefe, he fit the category of lover or ex-lover. She wrote a note to check the status of Jason's alibi for the time of the murder.

There were also selfies of Martina with other young people in San Francisco and at the Grand Canyon. Jessica looked closely at the clothing, sunglasses, and haircuts of the others in these photos and decided they were probably friends of Martina's visiting from Europe.

She then turned to a trove of pictures in a different folder labeled *Mani,* a set of photos she didn't remember seeing before. Jessica figured "*mani*" meant hand in Italian, and she clicked to open it. The first images were of a grizzled-looking man, maybe in his late forties, with short, graying hair and deep lines around his eyes. Despite the effects of the sun, he was still appeared youthful, but it was clear he either had an injury or he was born with a disability. He was missing several fingers on his right hand.

Jessica wasn't sure exactly where these photos were taken, although the location data pinpointed a spot on the western edge of San Vicente. Numerous close-ups depicted the man's bare hand and fingers, or lack of fingers. In various photos, his hand was encased in different prosthetic devices, and he was filmed picking up a pencil, trying to button a jacket, and holding a toothbrush. The most recent video opened with a tight shot of him wearing a more advanced prosthetic device, one that looked like a tight glove. As the camera moved around his arm capturing the scene from different angles, one could see that his hand was hovering over a piano keyboard. A woman's voice, presumably Martina's, could be heard offering encouraging words—"You can do this, Willie. Slow and steady, just relax." He first pecked hesitantly at the piano keys before gaining momentum, eventually playing a simple piece of music to the end. Judging by the ecstatic reactions from the two of them, the brief performance was a huge accomplishment.

As Jessica watched the video clip over and over, she began to grasp more deeply the significance of the work Martina and her collaborator, Levi Newcomb, were engaged in and its potential for big monetary rewards. Several inventors of medical devices had become very wealthy people. Years ago, doctors didn't use sonograms, MRIs, or CAT scans, but now they were common diagnostic tools. Perhaps the prosthetic device Levi and Martina had developed was a breakthrough of similar significance, one that would generate huge financial gains. Jessica's sugar rush now fully firing, she saw a piece she'd missed before: a disagreement between Levi and Martina—about ownership rights, about the plan to market the device, about financial backing, about anything, really—could have led to a heated argument, which may have turned deadly.

"Maybe it wasn't about romance and possessiveness," Jessica said. "Maybe it was about greed and fairness and proper compensation." Could this be as simple as a woman standing up for herself and being knocked down for demanding her due?

∿

Since finding the backpack the previous night, Kennedy Thompson had been receiving all kinds of accolades, and the praise felt good. Damn good! Even though he knew he was a good cop, one who deserved to be rewarded, his coworkers usually treated him like an outsider, someone not to be taken seriously. But today had been different. This morning, he was receiving congratulatory emails and texts from President Gardener, from command staff at SVPD, and even from the mayor. He liked being top dog, and it hadn't taken much effort on his part to become the subject of positive attention. If finding one missing backpack was generating this much goodwill, imagine being the cop credited with solving the Wexford College killing. That would be sweet.

He thought more about the night before. When Kennedy arrived with the backpack at campus police headquarters, Chelsea Miller was being questioned by the SVPD detectives. Then they took her downtown to the police station. He remembered seeing Chelsea in the oak grove with her friends the previous week and how strangely they had acted toward each other. Kennedy hadn't done much since then to track down Chelsea's friends. Chief Mendoza was keeping him busy with extra patrol shifts. Kennedy didn't blame the chief, given how unnerved the campus community was. Working the swing shift over the past week, Kennedy had been called several times to escort female students or faculty to the dorms or to the parking lot. It was a service he was happy to provide. But he needed to stop getting distracted. If he was going to be recognized as a hero, one thing was clear: he needed to track down Dahlia and Li-Ann and maybe some of the others who had known Martina. It was very likely they had useful information about Chelsea and Martina, and they needed to share it with him.

~

Eliza fought the urge to call Willie Ducane as soon as she woke up because phoning him before sunrise would have been rude—definitely rude. During her restless sleep, she obsessed about things Francesca said about Willie's connection to Martina and her project with Levi. Eliza added this topic to her own list of questions about Levi and the patent application. But obsessing was incompatible with her real life. The second Lucas woke up, he required her full attention, which forced all other thoughts to the sidelines until her son was ready for the day. Thankfully, she didn't need to drive him to school. Carpools were a blessing when it wasn't your turn to drive.

The first second she was alone, she dialed Willie's number, only half expecting him to answer. "Hello?" a deep voice crackled from her phone.

"Hello. I'm trying to reach Willie Ducane. My name's Eliza Fox. I left you a few messages. I believe you knew my cousin, Martina Noto."

"Wait," the man said. "Who are you?"

"Eliza Fox. I think you talked to my mother, Francesca, at the vigil. She said that you had nice things to say about Martina and that

I should contact you. I've been trying to investigate what happened to her."

"Right, you're the cousin. I meant to call you back. Sorry. I just forgot. What did you want to ask?"

"Full disclosure, it's more than one question. Would you have time to meet me in person? I know it's last minute, but I'm free this morning. I'd like to talk about the project that Martina was working on with her collaborator, a doctoral student named Levi."

"Yeah, sure. I can meet you, except I know those two were obsessed with keeping their project hush hush. Maybe I'm not the best person to discuss it. Maybe you should talk to Levi directly."

"Okay, do you know where he's staying?" Eliza said, remembering that Levi could be difficult to find.

"He's here now," Wille offered. "Levi's been crashing on my couch since the thing with Martina happened. Want me to wake him up?"

"No," Eliza said quickly. "Don't do that. Look, would you mind if I come over to your place now? I'd like to talk with you both. I know it's still a bit early. I can bring bagels," Eliza offered as an enticement.

"Yeah, sure. Bagels would be nice. And cream cheese? I can make you a cup of coffee. But you better bring milk if you want it. I'm out."

"Of course," Eliza laughed. "Bagels. Cream cheese. Milk."

"Should I text you the address?" Willie said.

"That'd be great. Hey, Willie, one thing," Eliza said. "If Levi wakes up before I get there, can you not let on that I'm headed to your place? I don't want him to freak out and take off. I'm worried he might try to avoid me."

"Oh, okay. He can be skittish. You got that right." Willie said. "I won't tell him."

~

Forty minutes later, Eliza was driving down a road in San Vicente she'd never been on before. The area was a mix of industrial and residential buildings situated near the railroad tracks that skirted the city's western edge. She was able to park directly in front of the address Willie had sent, a two-story apartment house dating from the 1970s. Its yellow stucco walls were marred by brownish patches, and the dirty white railings sadly needed paint. The lawn was weedy and brown. Despite the apartments' worn appearance, Eliza had to smile at the massive hibiscus bush growing near the staircase, its enthusiastic orange flowers bringing a touch of tropical décor to the street. She climbed to the second level and knocked on unit 204. As she stood, she could feel the warmth of the bagels through the large paper sack tucked under her arm.

Willie was quick to unlatch the door and grab the bag from Eliza. "Come on in," he said, his mouth in a wide grin. "It didn't take you long. I'll get some of these toasted."

"Can I help with that?" she asked, seeing no sign of Levi.

"Actually, yeah, things will go faster if you do the slicing."

"Sure," she said, following him into the kitchen area. In no time at all she was cutting bagels in half and making small talk with Willie. She asked him about Martina, how often they met, and whether Martina had talked about having problems with anyone.

"I'm so sorry about your cousin," Willie said, directly meeting Eliza's gaze. "I liked her very much. She and Levi were doing such important work. They were going to help so many people. I hope they still do—that is, that Levi can keep the work going. You know what I mean."

"Thanks," Eliza said. "I know you talked to her parents and my mom at the vigil. We appreciate you taking the time to find us. It's been rough."

Taking an empty mug from Willie, Eliza poured herself some coffee and then pulled out her laptop. "Let's wake Levi up," she said. "Where's the best place for me to sit?"

Willie cleared a few things off a small dining table and motioned for her to sit down. "I'll go wake up my houseguest," he said.

A short time later, Levi emerged from a hallway in the small apartment. Wearing sweats and an old T-shirt, he looked disheveled from sleep but otherwise congenial. "Hey, you found me," he said. "Maybe I underestimated you before. Maybe you are a detective."

"Ohhhh, not a cop," she reminded him. "But it's definitely a bad idea to underestimate me. Can we talk for a bit?"

He sat down opposite her and nodded his okay. Eliza didn't waste time on small talk, handing him the letter from the patent office. His surprised reaction said enough. It made sense that he hadn't seen the letter if he'd been sleeping at Willie's. His unopened mail was probably stacking up somewhere.

"When we spoke at the vigil, you put up a roadblock to any questions about your project with Martina. Why?"

He paused, considering his next answer. "What she and I were working on was groundbreaking—at least we believed it was. I insisted on absolute secrecy. Our computers were encrypted, and we rarely texted about it. I was worried that the professors at Wexford might betray us, but I can only control so much. I had agreements with the campus about intellectual property rights. Hell, Willie signed a confidentiality agreement. So, when you asked questions about it, I defaulted to 'no comment.' It's what I would have expected Martina or Willie to do."

"Understood. But now I need more. Did Martina agree with the level of privacy you required? It looks like she was part of the patent application."

"I think she mostly kept our work secret. I was not happy that she was sleeping with Tim O'Keefe. I didn't think he could be trusted, and I was worried she might let something slip. It was a plus that she didn't have many friends at Wexford. I liked her outsider status."

"When was the last time you saw Martina?"

"Okay, I guess we're doing this," he sighed, deciding to give Eliza the information she sought. Levi sipped from his large mug of coffee and took a bite of bagel, as if to prepare himself before answering. "I was with her that Monday night. Before everything went to shit the next day. We were here at Willie's place. We sometimes came here to talk or to work. Willie is solid, trustworthy. He'd let us meet here even when he wasn't home. On that Monday, Martina and I mostly argued. I regret that now. She was so smart and strong willed, and I loved those qualities, even if she could be annoying."

"You argued about what?" Eliza coaxed.

"About a lot of stuff—about sources of funding for the project, about her ownership rights, about her stupid relationship with O'Keefe. The guy seemed possessive and was texting and calling her repeatedly that night. I don't think she responded. At some point, she turned her phone off."

"What time did she leave here?" Eliza asked.

"Around midnight. Willie came back to the apartment about 11:30 p.m. At that point we decided to call a truce, and we talked with Willie for a while. Then I drove her home and went back to my place to crash. I drank some beers to unwind and slept late the next morning. The next thing I knew, I was getting texts from the campus about a safety alert."

"Did you tell the police any of this? You may be the last one in her circle to see her alive."

"I haven't talked to the police, although I don't think I can avoid them much longer. I can't hide here forever."

"Can anyone vouch for you? That you were in bed asleep last Tuesday morning?"

"For the past couple of months, I've been staying in a converted garage to save money. I don't have any roommates. The landlady, Mrs. Fuentes, knocked on the door when all the commotion started up around the campus, and I talked to her. But that was close to mid-day. I don't think anyone can verify that I was home alone before that."

"Okay. One more thing about the patent. I've been talking to Martina's parents. Do you have any idea whether Martina's interests in the patent would be transferable to them as next of kin?"

"I'm not a lawyer, but I remember hearing something about that. I believe her rights will transfer to her next of kin. I guess that's her parents. Before Martina and I started working together, I consulted a business attorney about lots of legal stuff. I think I was told at the time that patents were transferrable or became part of one's estate, but it seemed like an unimportant bit of legal detail, some contingency I'd never need to know. Shows how wrong a person can be."

Feeling that she had what she needed, Eliza closed her laptop and got ready to leave. "You might want to have that lawyer on speed dial, Levi. If I was able to find you, the detectives from SVPD will track you down soon. And your alibi for Tuesday morning is thin to non-existent."

She called out to Willie to say goodbye, and he emerged from the bedroom.

"Thanks for letting me stop by on short notice. This was very helpful. I'm guessing that you'll verify that Levi was here with Martina a week ago Monday night?"

"Yeah, they were here. Things seemed a little tense when I walked in, but they were all calm and friendly when they left," Willie said. "They were both joking and laughing."

"Okay, I'm off," Eliza said. As she opened the front door, she saw an electronic piano keyboard propped on its end in the corner. "Willie, is that your keyboard?" she asked.

He looked to Levi before answering, and Levi nodded his okay. "That belongs to your cousin. She brought it here and was teaching me to play a simple melody—something piano kids learn—using the fake hand those two developed. It was amazing," Willie said. "I've had a mangled hand for a long time. Since Iraq. I played piano as a kid and then messed around in a band as a teenager. But I never thought I'd put both hands on a keyboard again and make music. And then I did."

Willie was choking up by the end of this explanation. Eliza took a deep breath, wiping her own eyes as she processed what Willie had said. "Levi, has anyone else reached that level of dexterity with a prosthesis? Were you two in new territory with this?"

"I think we were ahead of everyone else, at least as far as I know. Now you have the full story. Please, please keep it to yourself. It'll become public eventually, but there's still a lot to sort out. I hope this helps you solve the case."

"*Mio Dio*," Eliza said. "I appreciate that you told me. I won't say anything about the piano part."

She walked slowly down the stairs and toward her car, thinking about what she'd just learned. Levi and Martina must have argued in their partnership. The whole family knew that her cousin could be feisty, and she and Levi were enmeshed in a complex project. Conflicts would naturally occur. While Levi had a financial motive to get rid of Martina, it was more likely that he benefited from having her as a business partner. He needed her help to get their invention produced and sold.

She thought about whether it was possible Levi had struck Martina accidentally and then reacted by hiding what happened. Now that she'd spoken to Levi a second time, it seemed unlikely that he was the killer, even an accidental one. Levi was a highly private person but also a straight shooter. He didn't appear to dissemble. It was hard to believe that he had caused a death and then had the hutzpah to lie to everyone about it. He would have to be an amazing actor to pull that off.

"Levi isn't the guy," Eliza told herself, pulling the Volvo away from Willie's apartment. *But who is?* she wondered, more determined than ever to get justice for Martina.

∼

Eliza drove to the neighborhood next to the campus and parked in front of Snack & Go. Out of habit, she checked her phone before leaving the car and saw missed calls from Kendra and Francesca. She tried Kendra first, curious about how things had gone with Jason.

"Does he have an alibi?" she asked as soon as Kendra answered.

"Hi, Eliza. Yeah, he does. He was out for a run that morning with guys from the soccer team. They left campus around nine o'clock and did a six-mile run."

"Six miles. Okay, let's do the math. How fast does a college athlete run? Eight minutes a mile? Faster? That would put their run time at about forty-five minutes."

"Sure, that's probably close," Kendra agreed. "Jason said he had a class starting at 10:15 that morning, and he went back to his dorm to shower first. The timing fits pretty well. I was supposed to meet Martina around 11 a.m. that morning. I got to Carter House about 11:30."

"Did you get the names of the guys he ran with?"

"I did. I'll text them to you."

"How'd Jason seem when you asked him?"

"I met him outside the library, and we talked for a bit. He seemed okay with me asking where he was that morning. I just said that Eliza needed to know, so we could rule him out as a suspect. He answered right away that he was out for a run."

"Did he explain how he was so sure he took a run that particular morning? Most people can't remember the day they went to the gym if you ask them a week later."

"Yeah, I asked about that. He said everything about that day is frozen in his brain. He cared about Martina, so it makes sense. He also said that he runs most Tuesday mornings with guys from the team, particularly in the off season. They gotta stay fit."

"Okay, that makes sense," Eliza said. "Anything else I should know about your talk with Jason?"

"Well... it turned into more than a talk," Kendra said, sheepishly.

"Kendra? What does that mean?"

"It was cold standing outside the library, so he came back to the condo with me. And... you know... stuff happened."

"Wait, did you have sex with Jason last night?"

"I know. It sounds bad, but yeah, we hooked up. I thought you should know. Did I mess up?"

Eliza stumbled for an answer. Although she wasn't that much older than Kendra, the decade between twenty and thirty was a significant one. She felt surprisingly off kilter grappling with a question about college sexual liaisons.

"Do you feel like you messed up?" Eliza responded, putting the question back to Kendra.

"I don't know. Not sure."

Eliza didn't answer right away. Then, finding her bearings, she said to Kendra, "I have to ask. Did Jason answer your questions about his alibi before or after the sex? Oh God, tell me you didn't ask for his alibi during the sex. It wasn't like foreplay or pillow talk, was it?"

"Nooo! I definitely asked before," Kendra snapped back. "I'm not some CIA chick with super sexy spy skills. We were at the library when we talked about him going on a run with the team."

"Okay, good. Somehow that makes me feel better. Look, I gotta go," Eliza said. "Thanks for talking to Jason. We'll talk more later."

Eliza shuddered as she ended the call. Sleeping with a witness was on a whole different level, but she didn't want to overreact. Kendra was a student, an unpaid volunteer, who had helped the investigation by asking another student, Jason, some questions. Eliza had lots to worry about beyond college libidos. She hoped Jason's alibi held up because things could get ugly if he lied or he misremembered about going for a run that morning.

Next she returned her mother's call. "*Cara*," Francesca said, almost breathless into the phone. "Did you see my text? The police found Martina's backpack last night."

"What? That's great. How'd you find out?"

"From Chief Mendoza. He called Roberto and Laura early this morning with an update. I was with them when he called."

"Did the chief say anything else? Who found it? Where?"

"On campus. In a dumpster. I don't know where exactly. One of Gil Mendoza's officers found it."

"Who specifically found it? Did he say?" Eliza asked.

"He did. Gil said it was Kennedy Thompson."

Eliza felt a weird twinge in her chest. She exhaled slowly. "Mom, do you know Kennedy? Have you met him before?"

"I don't know him well. He waited with me one night when my car wouldn't start. I was teaching an evening class, and it ended late. He stayed with me until the tow truck came. I knew his mother. She worked at Wexford for years. Why do you ask?"

"Well, I had a bit of a run-in with Kennedy yesterday. I don't have time to explain it all now, but I need you to do something. Can you call Kennedy and ask him to meet you later this afternoon at your faculty office? Say that you want to thank him in person for his excellent police work, which I'm sure you do. Maybe bring a bottle of wine for him as a gift. I'll be there, too, but I'm going to be incognito. I know it sounds weird, but I have an idea."

"Eliza, what kind of run-in? What do you mean you'll be incognito? I don't understand."

"I don't have time to explain right now. I promise I'll fill you in before you see Kennedy today. See if he can meet you around 4 p.m. Does that work for your schedule? Oh, and see if Laura or Roberto can watch Lucas then. I'll bring him to your house after school, and we can drive to campus together. We'll talk in the car."

"Okay," Francesca agreed warily. "I'll reach out to Kennedy. But you'll need to explain everything before I walk into this meeting. Okay?"

"I promise. I have a plan. Thank you, Mama. Text me when you've set it up, so I know it's a go."

Eliza threw her phone into her purse and took a deep breath. It was only 10:45 a.m., and her shoulders were noticeably tight, as if she'd worked a ten-hour day. She felt a little uneasy about dragging Francesca into her scheme to get information from Kennedy, especially since she was putting her plan together on the fly. On the other hand, it was likely Kennedy knew something about Martina. He'd been in contact with her recently. Kendra confirmed that he'd been at the condo, presumably about the burglaries at the wellness center, which struck Eliza as odd. Even by private college standards, where students were catered to, a campus cop going to a student's off-campus residence about a property crime seemed excessive. Why not email her the victim statement or make her go to the campus police station to review it? Something was off about Officer Thompson; Eliza felt it deep in her bones.

She had planned to ask Officer Thompson some questions, but that was before he'd caught her lurking around the backside of Carter House. Their encounter would make it awkward for her to approach him now. He'd be on guard. Alternatively, Francesca was the perfect person to vet Officer Thompson. Her mother was charming, and people warmed to her. Moreover, she was a high-ranking faculty member and related to the victim, both of which would elevate Professor Noto-Fox's status with Wexford police. Campus culture would dictate that Kennedy treat her respectfully. Even though Eliza still had to fine tune her plan and figure out how to eavesdrop on her mother and Kennedy, she felt optimistic for a change. The investigation was taking shape. Fingers crossed, Kennedy would offer something useful.

With one last thing to do before going home for a lunch break, Eliza got out of the car and walked into Snack & Go to look for Jay. The store appeared to be empty of both customers and its proprietor. She circled around the small space, calling hello a few times, but the only sound was jazz emanating from speakers resting on a shelf. Eliza eyed the imported chocolates while she waited. Eventually, a man emerged from the back of the store balancing a tower of boxed grocery items.

"Can I help you, miss?" he said, setting the stack on the floor. His voice sounded surprisingly like Samay's, the man she'd spoken to yesterday, and Eliza was briefly distracted by the way relatives could have such similar voices. He also had a similar appearance—tall and thin, with a toffee-colored complexion and a dark beard. The main difference was the absence of a turban. His wavy, black hair curled around his ears.

"Are you Jay? I'm Eliza. I talked to Samay yesterday. Did he say I'd stop by?"

"Ah, yes. Were you waiting long? I've been restocking. Samay told me about your cousin."

Eliza handed Jay her phone, a photo of Martina visible. Jay studied it briefly.

"Yes, I recognize that girl. She had a nice smile. Her English was different— with a foreign accent. She came in here once or twice a week. She'd buy Pellegrino or iced tea. Maybe a bag of peanuts or chips."

"Do you remember the last time you saw her?" Eliza asked.

"Must have been more than a month ago. I was on vacation at the end of April, so it was before that."

"I see. Did she usually come into the store alone?"

"Sometimes she'd be with a guy, maybe her boyfriend. I think he played soccer for Wexford. I noticed his soccer gear. But she was often alone. I would see her in the mornings. She seemed to be on her way to class."

"Thanks for looking at the photo," Eliza said. "Let me leave you my number. If you think of anything that would help us find her killer, please text or call. Also, did Samay leave anything for me?"

"Yeah," Jay said, producing an envelope from under the counter. "I'm sorry for your loss. There is a way we might be able to help you. Samay and I belong to the Merchants' Association. We work with many businesses in the neighborhood to stop the shoplifters, the taggers, the troublemakers. We help each other. All the store owners are very alarmed about what happened to your cousin. I can ask them to look at their surveillance video. Maybe they'll see her on the video. You never know what we might learn. What are the dates to focus on?"

"That would be wonderful," Eliza exclaimed. "It happened the morning of May 7. So maybe ask them to look at May 5 through the morning of May 7. I know I asked Samay for the footage from the full first week of May, but that would be a lot of data for them to sort through. I'd be grateful for whatever they can do."

"Don't worry. I'm sure they'll want to help," Jay said. "We're on the corner, so I'll also make a point to check with the businesses on the cross street. We might find something."

"Thank you," Eliza said, a little overwhelmed by the kindness of strangers.

MARTINA'S JOURNAL

April 30

Salve Journal,

I've been "crazy busy" as the Americans say.

Our *auitare le mani* project is moving forward now. I'm excited about it. Willie has been a gift. With his help, I can see how our prosthesis, if we can work out the bugs, could make dramatic changes in a person's life. Willie's excitement over playing the piano was its own reward. Meanwhile, Levi was grouchy about the patent application, but we finally submitted it. I'm still worried that somehow I'll lose out, and my work on the project won't be acknowledged. Or that Levi will get rich, and I'll never see one dollar from it. So many things could go wrong.

I'm stressing about my recital, too. I don't know why I agreed to perform. I said I'd do it months ago when I had fewer commitments. Now I feel overwhelmed. For certain, I need to practice on an actual piano at Carter House.

I broke up with Jason to simplify things. But then not seeing him made me feel even more alone. I miss my Italian friends so much. When Professor Tim started flirting, I flirted back. I guess I wanted to distract myself from missing Jason. I know Tim is older, and my mother would not approve. But can't I enjoy his attention for a while? He's a good-looking man who is very wealthy. He knows it's not serious, and he'll be fine when I break things off.

A small worry, though, is the policeman, Officer Thompson. He's sweet, and I appreciate that he wants to help with my insurance claim—except that he looks at me with puppy dog eyes. I know that expression. I've seen it too many times before. Boys get an idea that I'll go out with them, and then they're disappointed when I tell them *no grazie*. I've been praying that Kennedy doesn't ask me out. It was weird that he stopped by the condo on Sunday. I never asked him to come by. Maybe I'll talk to Francesca about him. She might have some good advice about turning him down without crushing his ego. *Dio Mio!*

Ciao for now.

CHAPTER EIGHTEEN

Wednesday, May 15—Afternoon

Jessica tracked her partner down as he was leaving a special closed session of the city council, and they arranged to meet at a small Mexican restaurant for lunch. Now she was pushing around the food on her plate as she half-listened to Byron rant about what had transpired at City Hall. A week after the murder at Wexford, Byron recounted how the city's leaders were in a froth. Reporter Vanessa Delaware was leaving voicemails for San Vicente's elected officials, wanting them to comment on the police department's handling of the investigation thus far.

Byron had heard from councilmembers that the *Post* was finishing up a major story about the victim, with statements from her friends and former teachers in Italy. The story would be published overnight in the paper's internet edition and above the fold in tomorrow's print edition. Jessica knew that Ms. Delaware, who was always an annoyance, would have done her best to make SVPD look hapless and portray Jessica and Byron as buffoonish at best. Jessica warned Byron that they would soon be confronting the backlash the *Post's* story would inevitably trigger. Her anger ready to erupt, Jessica questioned how someone as shallow as Vanessa Delaware could have such a big voice in the community and the power to undermine SVPD's reputation. Every good cop knew that detective work took time, and sloppy investigations produced sloppy results. What good would come from rushing the Wexford investigation if they got the wrong result? Apprehending the wrong person, and unwittingly allowing Martina's real killer to roam free, was like letting a rabid coyote wander around the playground with toddlers in reach.

As Byron ranted on about the city council meeting, Jessica paid little attention to him, thinking instead about finding Levi Newcomb, who kept falling off their radar. During the past week, she and Byron were twice sidetracked by evidence that now appeared to have no value. Tim O'Keefe was guilty of horrendously bad judgment, but the detectives hadn't settled on any real motive to explain why O'Keefe would go after Martina. Jessica again considered whether the professor had risked everything because he was ghosted by a woman half his age. It seemed doubtful.

Then there was Chelsea Miller, who had consumed a lot of Jessica's time during the previous week. While Chelsea's antics deserved to be punished, it didn't make sense that she would press things with Martina to the point of physical harm—unless there was something the detectives didn't know. Aside from the lack of alibi, where was the evidence that pointed to Chelsea?

"Hey, Jess! Are you with me?" Byron asked, tapping her hand. "I was saying that everyone's waiting for the *Post* to release the story."

"Sorry. I was thinking," she responded, now hyper-aware. "We need to talk to Levi Newcomb. *Today*, Byron. We need him today. I looked back over the evidence on the victim's phone, and I found some video we'd missed. Their project—the prosthetic hand thing—it was a big deal and has the potential to make mega bucks."

"Wait. Are you thinking that we have a dead student because of some invention she was working on? That this is a business deal gone bad?" Byron asked.

"Yeah, maybe. I'm thinking that if Martina pressed Levi about her financial interests in the project, he had a dollars-and-cents motive to want her out of the way. We both agree that our victim was not a passive woman who meekly did what others told her to do. If she didn't like the monetary arrangements with Levi, my guess is that she pushed back."

"Makes sense. Let's go find Levi," Byron said, waving to the waiter for the check.

~

Francesca let Eliza know that Officer Thompson planned to stop by her faculty office around 4:30 p.m. Eliza arranged to pick her mother up an hour before that. Tearing through her closet, she searched for the right outfit, something that would mask her appearance enough to prevent Kennedy from recognizing her. After a quarter of an hour excavating drawers and boxes, Eliza had amassed an oddball collection of possible disguises: a black beret, a blue Dodger cap, a gray hoodie from her college days, a large straw hat she wore to the beach, and a pair of oversized sunglasses.

The hoodie and the beret were quickly rejected as too cliché. With the Dodgers on a winning streak and playing at home a few hours later, the baseball cap was promising, but it needed something more. Kennedy had gotten a good look at her face, and if he recognized her in Francesca's office, it would ruin her plan.

With the sports cap in hand, Eliza moved to the hall closet and browsed through her collection of raincoats and parkas. Wedged between a heavy wool overcoat and a corduroy blazer, she found a silky jacket in Dodger blue, something she'd purchased years earlier during a baseball phase. "Progress," she said. Next, she opened a promising box labeled "Halloween" and laughed at its contents—a panda bear costume for Lucas that she'd sewn when he was a baby, a scary monster mask that David wore when he gave out Halloween candy, and a sexy black cat costume she'd worn a few times to parties. She briefly held each item, revisiting scenes from the past, letting the nostalgia seep in. Her nose to the panda costume, she sniffed to see if any of Lucas's baby scent remained. Then, feeling ridiculous, she scolded herself. "Get moving."

As Eliza lowered the lid on the box, her finger became entangled in a few strands of blonde hair that poked out of the monster mask.

Tugging the strands, she saw they were part of a long, blonde wig she'd worn for a project in college when she was cast in a tiny role for a student film.

Laughing now, she took her finds back to the bedroom for a trial run. With the blonde wig obscuring her brown, wavy hair, she affixed the baseball cap over it, and added the Dodger jacket and some red lipstick. The effect was surprising. Her look was so different from her quotidian self, she doubted her close friends would notice her if she passed them on the sidewalk. Confident in her plan, Eliza took off the costume and packed it up. It was time to pick up Lucas from school, and she didn't want to explain why she was wearing a wig on a Wednesday afternoon.

Thirty minutes later, the Volvo pulled up to Francesca's house. Lucas leapt from the car, calling for Roberto. In the short time her Italian relatives had been in San Vicente, Roberto had stepped into the role of *nonno*. With her own father gone and her ex-husband only recently showing an interest in Lucas, the boy could only benefit from a positive connection with a kind male relative. It was true that Roberto and Laura had come to town for the saddest of reasons, but hopefully the company of Lucas and Francesca was rejuvenating them. Eliza knew she'd miss them when they returned home to Italy.

Francesca must have been watching for Eliza's car because she opened the door before Lucas was halfway up the path and emerged from the house with her arms extended. Lucas gave his *nonna* a quick hug and a kiss. Once Francesca confirmed that the boy was safely passed off to Roberto, she took fast steps toward the Volvo and secured her seat belt in seconds.

"Drive," Francesca said. "You can explain on the way."

∼

Eliza was grateful that Wexford had never forced her mother to move to a smaller office after her father passed away. Because they were both tenured faculty and had some campus clout, her parents had secured a single large office for themselves. At their own expense, they'd furnished it with two desks, a nice rug, and attractive lamps.

Eliza was now situated at her father's old desk, a laptop opened in front of her. Her reflection visible in the window, it startled her each time she looked outside. The woman with long, blonde hair and a Dodger cap had little resemblance to the Eliza that everyone knew, and the transformation pleased her. Her mother was prepped for Officer Thompson. Eliza had given her talking points, and Francesca was ready to be the concerned cousin, a role she was already playing.

∼

Leaving their lunches half-finished, Jessica and Byron drove directly to the Wexford campus and parked outside of Janus Hall. Within minutes, they'd tracked down the faculty secretary who worked with Tim O'Keefe. The two detectives, with police badges visible, asked her to look up contact information for doctoral student Levi Newcomb. Amid grumbling and visible unhappiness, she complied. "The campus is very strict about this. We have rules against releasing private student information," she informed them while handing over a printout with Levi's name and mailing address. Jessica studied the street address the woman gave her. Unfortunately, it was the same one the police already had.

"What now?" Jessica said as she and Byron stood outside of Janus to confer.

"Let's call the post office and see what they're doing with his mail. I asked one of the patrol guys to check on this, but he got pulled off on something else. Did Levi submit a forwarding address? Get a PO Box? He must have mail."

"You want to call the post office? It might be faster to drive there," Jessica quipped. She climbed into the passenger seat while Byron verified which postal branch serviced Levi's former address. As she looked aimlessly in the car's side-view mirror, Jessica noticed a young woman standing on the curb about fifteen feet behind their vehicle.

The woman, who was dressed like a student, was looking toward the car with an odd expression. "Give me a minute," Jessica told Byron.

She got out of the car and motioned for the student to come closer. "What is it?" Jessica asked. "You look like you need some help."

"No, the opposite," the student replied. "You need help."

"What?" Jessica said. "I don't understand."

"I heard you upstairs talking to Sandra, the admin assistant. You're looking for Levi, right?"

"We are. Do you know where he is?"

"I can give you the address where he was staying a couple weeks ago. That was before all the craziness happened. I'm not sure he's still at that place, but you can check it out."

"That would be a big help," Jessica said. "Thanks."

The student pulled out her phone, scrolled a bit through her text messages, and then showed Jessica an address—different than the one the school provided.

"Do you know when he moved here?" Jessica asked.

"I don't know, maybe early in the semester. He was almost out of money, and this place was cheap. It's a converted garage with no kitchen, a space heater, and a crappy shower."

"Got it," Jessica said.

"Okay then," the student said, turning away.

"Wait. What's your name? Are you Levi's friend? What's your deal?"

"Can we skip the part where I say my name?" she asked Jessica. "Martina was my classmate, and so is Levi. I don't want to be pulled into this. But I do want you guys to catch the creep who was in Carter House. If Levi can help you do that, you should talk to him. That's all."

Jessica pulled a business card from her pocket and handed it to the woman. "This has my cellphone on it. Text or call if you think of anything else. I mean *anything*," she said.

Jessica watched as the young woman walked away, making mental notes—long, blonde hair, about five-foot-eight, thin frame, fair complexion, light blue backpack, tattoo of flying birds on the exterior of her right wrist. It was a habit Jessica had developed over the years, cataloguing people's physical attributes. She might want to find this student again, and it wouldn't be that hard. The computer science department was small, and females were very much a minority. The bird tattoo narrowed the group even more.

"We caught a break," she said to Byron as she got back in the car. "Go to this place first. Hopefully, Levi will be there."

While Byron drove, Jessica relayed what the student had said—that Levi was so broke he moved into a converted garage. It added weight to her theory that money—or the idea of earning a boatload of money—might be a motive behind what happened to Martina. They arrived at the address a few minutes later, a small house tucked among several apartment buildings. It was walking distance from the campus, on a street where many Wexford students rented. Even though he was driving an unmarked police vehicle, Byron parked some distance from the house. He didn't want to alert Levi or the homeowner to their arrival.

Whether it was fear of crime or a dislike of being bothered, many people ignored unsolicited knocks at their door. Byron and Jessica agreed it would be less threatening if she approached the front door alone, while Byron hung back near the sidewalk. He watched as she climbed the porch steps and rang the doorbell. Eventually, the screen door opened a crack, and an older woman's face showed in the crevice. Jessica, with a business card ready, slipped it through to her, and only then did Byron make long strides up the driveway and onto the porch. It was unlikely this woman would slam the door on two detectives from SVPD.

A few minutes later, Jessica and Byron stood in the rear yard, knocking on the side door of the garage. The homeowner, Mrs. Fuentes, told them Levi was inside; she'd seen him return just a half hour earlier after being gone for several days.

After his talk with Eliza that morning, Levi had resigned himself to talking to the cops, and he responded to Byron's forceful pounding. It had been more than a week since Martina's death, and Levi knew he couldn't avoid this conversation indefinitely. He stepped into the yard and did his best to appear cooperative.

Jessica dug in on questions about money and shot them off in rapid succession: "What's your bank account going to show? Why'd you move into the garage? Do you have other sources of income? Funds from student loans? A car? A motorcycle? A trust fund?"

Levi visibly straightened at the onslaught. "Whoa, I'm out of cash," he said. "Down to my last few bucks. Is that a crime?"

"Answer her questions," Byron prodded, "and tell us why you're sleeping in a dank garage. I'm guessing this place isn't even permitted as a rental unit."

"Like I said, I'm *broke*. The prosthetic project sucked up every dollar—you obviously know about that—and I'm maxed out on credit cards. I'm waiting for my parents to send something so I can pay Mrs. Fuentes the rent."

"Where were you last Tuesday morning, Levi?" Byron asked.

"I was here, sleeping. I woke up when I heard the police cars and helicopters," he responded, his tone flat and matter of fact.

"Can anyone verify that? Were you sleeping alone? Anybody sharing the bed?"

Levi showed a half-grin. "As a comment on my sorry situation, I was definitely alone," he said. "I talked to Mrs. Fuentes in the yard around noon because all the helicopters were making such a racket. Maybe she can verify that my car was parked in front of the house that whole morning. I don't know if she noticed it."

"Do you mind if we take a look inside your room?" Byron asked.

"Do you have a warrant?" Levi retorted.

The two detectives exchanged a look. "Let's go for a ride downtown, Levi. We have more questions, and we need a sample of your DNA," Byron said.

"Do I need a lawyer?" he asked. "Are you arresting me?"

Byron, growing impatient, said, "Mr. Newcomb, We're asking you to accompany us to the department so we can collect a DNA sample. The choice is yours. If you elect not to come, my partner and I will question that decision and wonder why a purportedly innocent person would not want to help with our inquiry."

"You can't take the sample here? The swab thing is pretty simple."

"We don't have a kit with us," Jessica admitted. "Look, Levi. It's your call. We want your DNA, and we're gonna get it. So why drag this out? Grab your shoes and your phone and maybe a sweatshirt. You may need to wait awhile, and the air conditioning is always on full blast in our building. C'mon. Let's go."

Levi weighed the situation, and he saw there was little to gain from being difficult. Within a few minutes, he had brushed his teeth and found his shoes. He also sent a text to his attorney that he was headed to SVPD headquarters voluntarily, but he might need a lawyer before the day was out.

∼

Kennedy Thompson had enjoyed the last twenty-four hours. All the praise coming his way for finding the missing backpack was energizing. At last, his star was rising on the campus police force, as it should be. Mama always said he was meant for great things. She had buoyed him against the teachers and coaches who didn't see how clever and talented he was. He was sorry she wasn't there to enjoy his moment of fame. Two years had passed since the sneaky and unrelenting ovarian cancer had defeated her.

She would be pleased that he was headed to a meeting with Professor Noto-Fox. Mama had always liked the art history professor and used to tell Kennedy that Noto-Fox was one of the good ones. In her job as a waitress at Wexford's faculty club, Marjorie Thompson had spent twenty years attending to faculty, and she had developed an infallible system for cataloguing them. There were the egotistical ones, the egg-heady ones, the crazy ones, the ambitious ones, and the good ones. Kennedy planned to tell Professor Noto-Fox how much Marjorie had appreciated the professor's small kindnesses and attention to making sure the staff at Wexford felt cared for.

At 4:30 p.m. exactly, Kennedy stepped into Francesca's office. He reflexively responded to her friendly smile, then seemed surprised there was a second person sitting at the desk wedged against the window.

"Come in. Come in," Francesca greeted. "Have a seat," pointing to a chair in front of her desk. "Can I offer you water or a soda?"

"No thank you, ma'am. I'm fine. I didn't know you were sharing this space now," he said, motioning toward her officemate.

"It's only temporary. This is a graduate student who's been helping me," Francesca explained, without introducing the woman.

Not to appear rude, Eliza waved half-heartedly and turned slightly toward Kennedy in a modest greeting.

"Go Dodgers," he said in response. "I bet you're headed to the game tonight."

"For sure," Eliza replied. "Gotta leave in a few."

"Kennedy," Francesca said, trying to draw his attention away from the disguised Eliza. "How are you doing? I don't think I've talked to you since the memorial service for your mother. Was that a year ago now?"

"Almost two years, ma'am. I've been keeping busy. A lot's been going on here at the campus."

"Wow, two years already," Francesca said, pacing her words to show proper respect. "Well, thanks for making a trip to my office. I wanted to let you know how much our family appreciates what you did. Locating Martina's backpack was so important. How did you find it?"

"It was no big deal, just part of the job. Did anyone tell you it was in the dumpster behind the cafeteria?"

"No. I didn't know that. What made you look there?" Francesca asked. "Did you get a tip?"

"No, nothing like that. Maybe you've heard about the cooks and the dishwashers. They go back there and get stoned after the lunch rush, and Campus PD has been trying to stop that. I was doing my regular patrol behind the cafeteria," Kennedy explained.

"Were the restaurant workers there when you found it?"

"No, nobody was around. I went to throw away some trash, and there it was, a black backpack in the dumpster."

"Well, I know everyone in campus leadership appreciates your hard work, Kennedy. So many problems this year. I only recently heard that Martina's belongings had also been stolen earlier this year while she was at yoga. From the wellness center. I guess she wasn't the only one whose things were taken that day."

"Yeah, a bunch of lowlifes have been coming onto campus and causing trouble. I've been working on those thefts at the wellness center too," Kennedy said pridefully. He then grew solemn and looked to the floor. "Sorry for your loss, ma'am. I knew your niece. I met her when she reported her stuff stolen from the lockers at the wellness center."

"Thank you, Kennedy, although she wasn't my niece, but my young cousin. How well did you know her?" Francesca asked.

"Not well. She seemed a bit lonely here, so far from her parents and friends. But she was out of my league."

Francesca's phone pinged just then, and she glanced at it nonchalantly. It was a text from Eliza. Francesca then asked Kennedy, "What do you mean 'out of your league'? I'm sure she would have been happy to spend time with you. Did you do that? Spend time with Martina?"

Eliza, perched at the other desk, was doing all she could to stay quiet. The last thing she wanted was for Kennedy to think he'd been set up. Texting questions to Francesca on the fly wasn't ideal, but it was better than passing her mother a crumpled paper note.

Kennedy turned toward Eliza with an odd look. Was he suspicious, she wondered? "There's going to be lots of traffic getting to the game tonight. I heard it's a sellout," he said.

"You're right," Eliza said. "I should get going. My friends will be mad if I'm late. Just enough time for a restroom stop before I head out."

While she didn't want to leave her mother alone with Kennedy, Eliza's presence in the office was chilling the conversation. Francesca's last question about whether Kennedy spent time with Martina was still in the air, unanswered. He wasn't going to speak freely with some unknown graduate student within earshot.

Grabbing her purse and phone, she left the office and walked part of the way to the bathroom with exaggerated footsteps. Eliza then doubled back on tiptoe to the doorway of Francesca's office, stopping just outside the threshold. Eliza stood to the side out of sight. Thankfully she could still hear her mother's voice inside the office. Francesca must have filled in with some small talk as Eliza stepped to the restroom. Now, her mother was taking a second pass at her earlier question.

"A wonderful man like you, Kennedy?" she flattered. "Martina would have enjoyed spending time with you. Did you spend time with her? With Martina?"

Eliza smiled inwardly at her mother's smooth approach.

"A little," he stammered. "I helped her with her insurance claim one day. I... brought some papers to her apartment."

"I'm sure she appreciated that." Francesca started to say more and then stopped. She saw that Kennedy was caught up in his own thoughts.

"I remember her that morning," he said quietly. "She had her hair tied back with a beautiful scarf. The colors reminded me of the beach. Who looks like that at 9 a.m.?"

"What day was that?" Francesca prodded gently, but Kennedy stood up without answering. Their meeting was over. Francesca grabbed a bottle of chianti from her desk drawer and stood up, extending the wine toward him. "Thank you for coming by today, Kennedy. Please take this wine as a gift from our family."

"I have to go," he said as he took the bottle.

Eliza took this as her cue to reenter the office, nearly brushing shoulders with Kennedy as he left. He ignored her, leaving without further comment or eye contact, a vacant expression on his face. "Go Dodgers," Eliza said in his direction, her voice at half her normal volume.

Eliza noted the abrupt change in his demeanor. He seemed disconnected, as if he'd mentally left planet Earth. In her college psych classes, Eliza remembered reading about dissociative disorders, people who lost continuity between their thoughts or actions when they couldn't cope with something traumatic. Eliza had never seen anyone in this state, but she wondered if Francesca's questions had triggered an emotional response in him.

"Oh, dear," Francesca said. "He was fine until I got him talking about Martina. He told me about being at her condo one morning, even remembering details about what she was wearing. Then he got... I don't know... sort of fuzzy. He left so abruptly. I don't think he thanked me for the wine. What do you make of that, Eliza?"

Stepping to Francesca, Eliza enveloped her mother in a tight embrace. "Mama, although I can't prove it yet," she said softly, "he knows what happened to Martina. I believe he's our killer."

∿

It was 5:15 p.m. and Levi was getting worried. Detective Fonseca seemed hellbent on keeping him at the station. Twenty minutes had passed since someone had collected his DNA sample, but he was still sitting alone in a room. Levi was feeling exposed. He had reached the office assistant for his attorney and learned that his lawyer was hiking in Canada and unreachable for the next week. Levi then did the next best thing and messaged Eliza. A few minutes later, she texted contact info for her buddy Abigail Chao, a criminal defense attorney. She let Levi know that Abigail would be in touch shortly.

To his relief, an hour later Abigail walked into the small room at SVPD headquarters where Levi still sat waiting. She handed him a retainer agreement and said, "I'm here to represent you. Or you can wait until you're charged and ask for a public defender."

"What's the price?" he asked, fearing the worst.

Abigail pointed to a section of the retainer agreement where the hourly rate said $0 per hour. The paragraph explained that Levi would be responsible for Abigail's out-of-pocket expenses. "Because you're a friend of Eliza's, and I owe her a big favor, I'm willing to cut you a deal. I'll represent you for the next couple of days at no charge. If you're still in need of a lawyer after the weekend, we can amend our agreement and revisit the hourly rate. Of course, you'd be free to switch lawyers at that point."

Levi didn't need to think twice. He signed the agreement. With the paperwork done, Abigail went in search of the detectives. Byron finally appeared. "You're free to go," he told Levi. "But stay in the immediate area. That means you're sleeping in that garage where we can easily find you."

"Okay," Levi said. Even though he felt that SVPD owed him a ride home, he didn't dare ask the cops for a lift. Abigail, headed to dinner on Los Angeles's westside, begged off giving him a ride. Fortunately, Willie's disability didn't prevent him from operating a motor vehicle. Levi made the call, and Willie arrived twenty minutes later to pick him up.

CHAPTER NINETEEN

Thursday, May 16—Morning

*L*i-Ann valued her spot on the Wexford swim team and didn't want to piss off her coach by being late. She walked along the southern edge of the gym at a fast pace, her bag of gear slung over her shoulder. She was due in the pool in twelve minutes and still needed to slip into her swimsuit. It was only 6:15 a.m. and the campus was quiet. Although getting to practice so early every morning was rough, seeing the sunrise was Li-Ann's favorite part of the day.

She hastily made the last right turn at the southwest corner of the building that housed the gym and the outdoor campus pool and stepped into the shadows of the exterior foyer. As she reached out to open the door, a human presence soundlessly came up behind her, hovering over Li-Ann's five-foot-three-inch body. She caught a whiff of sweat. Her instinct was to step away to get some distance, but she didn't react fast enough. There was a crushing blow to her head just before she saw the starbursts. Li-Ann folded to the ground, inches from the threshold that led inside.

∽

Chief Mendoza was at his desk when the call came. It was the 911 dispatcher letting him know that paramedics were en route to campus, responding to reports of an unconscious student at the gym.

"That would explain the sirens," he said.

Chief Mendoza looked out into the squad room to see who had arrived for the early shift. Most of the campus safety officers didn't start work until 7:30 a.m. or later. A rookie named Dakota Mayer was at her desk, and Kennedy was just walking in. He called them both into his office with instructions. They were to secure the area around the building and report back on what they'd found. He would locate the rest of the squad and send more officers, depending on what had happened.

"Have you ever worked a developing situation?" Kennedy asked Dakota, as they climbed into a campus golf cart.

"Nope, this is my first response call. Everything till now has been paperwork or following up with witnesses after the fact."

"Okay, then," Kennedy said. "Follow my lead, and most important—don't move anything, and don't touch anything with your bare hands. Use a glove."

"Roger that," Dakota said.

The Wexford campus was so small, it only took about five minutes to drive from the campus police station to the gym. The golf cart rolled to a stop just as the paramedics were loading the victim into the ambulance. "Who's down?" Kennedy yelled. "What's their status?"

A female paramedic leaned out from the back of the ambulance. "Young woman, maybe twenty years old. Member of the swim team. Serious wound to the head. She was collapsed by the door. Breathing, but in and out of consciousness. We need to get her to the ER. STAT."

Minutes later, the sirens again reverberated around the campus as the paramedic van drove over Wexford's manicured lawn and made its way to the road that circled the campus. Li-Ann was being transported full speed toward the nearest emergency room.

As Kennedy and Dakota stood near the exterior wall along the western edge of the pool, he listed the top priorities for the rookie: figure out the victim's name and locate the person or persons who found the body.

"Do we think she was attacked inside the pool area?" Dakota

asked. "Maybe she fell on the pool deck and then made it to the door before she went down."

"Good point," he said. "Why don't you find the swim coach? It will probably be Coach Griffin. See what she knows." With gloved hands, Kennedy started digging through the gym bag at the scene for a student ID. He located a keycard for student Li-Ann Wong. He shot off a text to Chief Mendoza with the victim's name and status. Then Kennedy began to secure the area.

∿

Just after 7 a.m., Byron and Jessica were each in their own cars driving toward downtown San Vicente. They were supposed to meet at headquarters with the full investigative team for a briefing on the Noto case—that was until Chief Mendoza messaged them about an incident that had just taken place at the campus pool. Although he didn't have many details, the chief was concerned since it involved Li-Ann Wong, who was tangentially connected to the Noto case.

Jessica called Byron, and they quickly regrouped. She turned toward the hospital where Li-Ann was being transported, while Byron made his way to Wexford.

∿

By 9 a.m., Eliza had returned home after dropping Lucas at school and picking up a few groceries. She had already heard from Laura, who'd left a voicemail early that morning. Laura relayed that David was referring her and Roberto to a patent attorney who would help them, should Martina's work with Levi generate future earnings. Laura confirmed what Levi said about the patent being a transferable asset.

With the patent question resolved, Eliza sat down with a copy of the *LA Post* as a breakfast companion. It looked like Vanessa Delaware had been good to her word. A long article about Martina began on the paper's front page, along with several photos of her cousin, a few that depicted her as an adorable little girl.

The article's tone was perfect. Vanessa had covered Martina's life in a respectful way, underlining that a talented young person had been struck down, and the community had suffered a loss. There were poignant quotes from her childhood friend Ana Maggio, former boyfriend Jason Chang, and Professor Guzman at Wexford's business school. Toward the end of the article, Vanessa's approach turned more critical as she painted Detectives Comstock and Fonseca as borderline incompetent. Lastly, the reporter addressed safety concerns that parents were expressing. Eliza was particularly pleased with the article's closing paragraph:

> Come August, will incoming freshmen feel safe at Wexford? It's an open question as long as the perpetrator of this crime walks freely in San Vicente.

She laughed quietly to herself. "You go, Vanessa. Hit them right in the budget." Eliza knew the last thing the school wanted was for the freshman class to start dwindling because of safety concerns at Wexford. If enough incoming students changed their plans, it would put the campus on its back foot, leaving the admissions office scrambling to fill the vacancies.

The article would do its intended work, Eliza was certain. The police and the campus would be under increased pressure from parents and civic leaders to put more resources toward the investigation. The detectives would be under a microscope until they figured out what had happened at Carter House.

As she picked up her phone to send a thank you text to Vanessa, a call from Francesca rang through. "Hi, Mama," Eliza said. "Did you see the article in the *Post*?"

"Not yet, dear. That's not why I'm calling. I just heard from Chief Mendoza. There's been another attack on campus. A girl on the swim team. She was attacked early this morning and is in very serious condition. I don't know much more."

"On the swim team?" Eliza asked. "Are they saying it was a rape? Some type of sexual attack?"

"I don't think so. It sounded like a physical assault, like an attack with a knife or something. But I don't really know."

Eliza needed time to digest what her mother had said. "Let me make some calls and get back to you," she told Francesca. "I'll find out what's going on."

∿

When Byron got to the campus, he found Kennedy and another officer, a young woman who looked to be fourteen years old, deep in conversation with two very tall students. Both dressed in sweats branded with the Wexford logo, they were obviously members of the men's swim team. Byron eavesdropped long enough to find out that the two athletes had discovered Li-Ann lying in the building entrance. At that point, he stopped the conversation and pulled Kennedy aside. "Thanks for your work so far. This is an SVPD case now, Officer," he said.

"Why?" Kennedy demanded. "We were first on the scene. It clearly happened on campus property. The victim could have cracked her head open for a bunch of reasons. Maybe it was a slip and fall. What makes you think this incident is linked to something you're working on?"

Byron found it difficult to hide how annoying he found Kennedy. "Sorry, son," he said. "I'm not explaining myself to you. You and your rookie partner need to step aside. Now. If you want to help, keep those gawking students over there at least fifty yards from the area so they don't contaminate it."

As Kennedy and Dakota reluctantly withdrew, Dakota nodded toward Byron and asked, "Who's that?" To which Kennedy loudly responded, "That's a dickhead."

Amused by Kennedy's reaction, Byron allowed himself a small smile and then apologized to the two swimmers for the confusion. He quickly learned that they'd arrived early for the men's swim team practice and found Li-Ann in a heap at the entrance to the gym. It was lucky they discovered her when they did. Receiving first-aid at the scene and getting to the ER quickly would give Li-Ann a fighting chance. *You gotta love swimmers*, Byron thought. *They all earn extra cash as lifeguards, which means they all know first-aid.*

As Byron worked the scene on campus, Jessica was five miles away at the hospital. She'd talked to the paramedics who'd brought Li-Ann in. The young woman had sustained a large wound near the crown of her head, likely from something solid like a crowbar, which ruled out that it was a slip-and-fall injury. With the absence of defensive wounds, the girl was most likely attacked from behind and had been caught by surprise. She texted Byron and alerted him to look for possible weapons, a heavy tool or even a golf club. She also had Li-Ann's clothes bagged to be sent to the lab for analysis. If Li-Ann survived, it would be hours, or days, before she could answer questions. In the meantime, her clothes might offer some clues. Lastly, she called for a liaison officer to interface with the Wong family and wait at the hospital for news.

Jessica then set out to find Chelsea Miller. Chelsea, who had no alibi for the events at Carter House, was back in Jessica's sights. Two female students at Wexford had been struck down now: one was dead and one was in critical condition. And Chelsea was connected to both victims. What did that add up to? Jessica was working to put the pieces in place.

∽

After talking to her mother, Eliza looked at the sports teams on Wexford's website to see the members of the women's swim team. Only one name was vaguely familiar—Li-Ann Wong. She opened her laptop and saw in her case notes that Li-Ann Wong was on the list of possible witnesses, along with her buddies Chelsea Miller and Dahlia Moreno. Kendra had told Eliza that these sorority sisters had been less than friendly to Martina. If Li-Ann was, in fact, the victim of this morning's attack, Eliza had no doubt that her assault was connected to Martina's death. Everyone was too intertwined for it to be a coincidence.

She next called Vanessa Delaware, relieved when the reporter answered in a sunny voice.

"Hi Eliza. Did you see the story?" the reporter chirped.

Dialing up the charm, she thanked Vanessa several times, remarking on how great the article was and how quickly it came together. Eliza then pivoted and asked if Vanessa had any intel on that morning's incident at Wexford.

"I'm at the campus now," Vanessa said. "We're waiting for Chief Mendoza to make a statement."

"Vanessa, I know this is a developing story, but do you know the name of the victim—unofficially?" Eliza pressed.

"My source tells me her name is Li-Ann Wong. She's on the swim team. Do you know her, Eliza?"

"No. Never heard of her," she replied, with no misgivings about her lie. Eliza's relationship with the reporter was transactional. Vanessa was as trustworthy as a hacker mining for the password to your bank account. "Good luck with the story today," Eliza said, ending the call.

The knot in Eliza's stomach was growing. She was certain the attack on Li-Ann was an escalation, and Kennedy Thompson was involved. While Eliza still lacked the evidence she needed, things were stacking up. She had a bruise on her arm from Kennedy's forceful grab two days earlier, and he had acted so strangely in Francesca's office the day before, precisely when her mother asked if he spent time with Martina. Eliza's intuition said that Kennedy was growing desperate. He needed to be stopped. Now.

∿

Jessica was fixating on the toxic relationship Chelsea Miller had with Martina. Now Li-Ann, who was part of the same circle of friends, had been attacked. Only a fool would think that the two incidents were unrelated. But where was the connective tissue? On a hunch, Jessica called Gil Mendoza and asked him to pull Chelsea's class schedule for the day. Somehow, Jessica wasn't surprised to learn that Chelsea had had a 7 a.m. Pilates class in Dance Studio B, which began thirty minutes after Li-Ann was due at the pool. Consulting the campus map, Jessica figured out that the dance studios were inside the theatre arts building, situated near the gym that housed the pool. Based on the evidence from the paramedics, the attack on Li-Ann was not a random incident but looked to be pre-meditated. The attacker would have known that the swimmers arrived at practice before 6:30 a.m. each morning. Chelsea certainly knew this as one of Li-Ann's close friends. Chelsea could have been strategic, Jessica figured, and planned the attack for a moment when Chelsea was on her way to class. If the timing was very tight, it would cast doubt that Chelsea was involved.

Jessica plotted the steps Chelsea might have taken:

- ☐ Before sunrise, go to an area outside of the pool, wearing a hoodie or similar clothing so she wouldn't be recognized
- ☐ Hide somewhere where she could see people approaching the pool
- ☐ Wait until Li-Ann was approaching, then move into position in the foyer of the building entrance; the early morning shadows would add more cover
- ☐ Wait until Li-Ann passed by, then take a swing at her from behind
- ☐ Duck into the nearest bathroom to change clothes.
- ☐ Clean and dispose of the weapon
- ☐ Go to Pilates class

It could definitely work, Jessica thought. And if Li-Ann happened to walk up at the same time as another teammate, the plan could easily be abandoned. Even if someone saw Chelsea crouching by the entrance and spoke to her, she could have a story ready about losing something, like an earring. In either case, Chelsea could go to her

Pilates class as if nothing was amiss. Presumably Chelsea would have a gym bag with her, where, if the plan was aborted, the weapon would remain concealed.

Satisfied with her developing theory, Jessica called Byron and asked him to meet her at the theatre arts building in forty-five minutes. She hoped to get a few facts from the Pilates teacher to fill in some gaps.

~

Since arriving at campus that morning, Byron's phone had rung non-stop, and it was getting annoying. He considered turning it off so he could get some basic facts without interruption, but that wasn't a real option—not with the situation on campus still unfolding.

First Gil Mendoza had called. Contrary to Officer Thompson's annoyance at having SVPD intervene, the chief was happy to let Byron take the lead. He was no fool. Why would he want to have a spotlight on his small squad of campus police? Everyone on the Wexford campus was already nervous; this morning's events would dial up the tension even more. People were going to start imagining monsters in the bushes.

Vanessa Delaware's article had added considerably to the community's anxiety level. Within the past hour, Byron had received numerous texts and voicemails from his superiors at SVPD and from community and campus leaders who all wanted to know the status of the investigation. Even his mother-in-law had called to ask if it was safe for her to go to the supermarket. While he hadn't turned off his phone, Byron had put it on silent, and he was largely ignoring these calls for now.

He had talked to Jessica, of course. She'd called from the hospital with a list of things they needed to do, including search all the bathrooms close to the gym for anything suspicious, like a tool that could have been used as a weapon, and meet at the theatre arts building at 10:30 a.m., which meant he needed to leave the gym in the next ten minutes. Fortunately, the forensics team was in place and working the scene.

It was the last call that had intrigued him. It was from Eliza Fox. Byron had met Eliza the day the Noto family had come to the police station. Now, she was calling to request a meeting with him ASAP. Eliza wanted to discuss her ideas about the investigation. While Byron was skeptical of people who wanted to play cop, he also took seriously his duty to follow leads that could solve a case. The odd thing was that Eliza had asked to meet him without Jessica. Somehow, his partner, who was usually so good with people, had taken a misstep with the Noto family.

Given Eliza's request that they talk right away, he agreed to meet her at noon. Byron figured he needed to stop for twenty minutes to eat and could talk to Eliza then. The only question was whether he'd tell Jessica about it. While he didn't know anything about Eliza Fox, his instincts told him that putting Jessica and Eliza together could be like putting a spark to an explosive. Since Byron preferred the path of least resistance, it was likely he'd avoid the fireworks and keep Jessica in the dark about his lunch meeting.

He walked the short distance to the theatre arts building, still not sure why Jessica wanted to meet there. As he approached, he could see that she was pacing—indicating that she was amped up. Byron knew to tread carefully when Jessica Fonseca was both energized and walking nowhere. At a certain point in a case, she became intensely focused, going for long periods without food or sleep.

Fundamentally, Byron understood that she wanted—needed—the case to be over. They were all drained... too much work, too much pressure, too much dealing with puzzle pieces that didn't fit. While Jessica radiated stress-driven kinetic energy, Byron carried the tension across his shoulders starting with a tightness in his neck. After the case was wrapped up, he and Jessica would talk, as they always did, about the craziness of their job. They'd order some expensive bourbon and sit in a quiet bar for an hour. Before that, he would do his best to support her and find the answers the community needed.

"You first," Byron said, when he got close enough that he didn't need to shout. "Bring me up to speed."

"Okay," Jessica began. "Our latest victim is in surgery. It'll be a while before we can talk to her, assuming that she makes it out of the operating room. So, while we wait for her to be verbal, I'd like to look again at Chelsea Miller."

Jessica told Byron what she'd learned about the timing and location of Chelsea's Pilates class and her theory that, while it was tight, Chelsea could be in the frame for the attack at the pool. Rather than interrupt, Byron held back and let Jessica roll.

With Byron briefed, they stepped inside to find the dance studios. Fortunately, the instructor who'd taught the 7 a.m. Pilates class that morning was still in the building. She confirmed that Chelsea had made it to class, arriving about five minutes late. Jessica asked how Chelsea had seemed.

"Fine. Why? What's this about?" the instructor asked.

"Is Chelsea often late for class?" Jessica responded, answering with another question.

Indeed, Chelsea was late sometimes, the instructor offered, along with several others in the class—nothing out of the ordinary for a 7 a.m. start time. Satisfied, Jessica turned to go when the instructor called after the detectives. "Chelsea was in a hurry to leave today," she told them. "She packed up and was gone before we finished our cool down."

∿

As Byron and Jessica walked out of the dance studio, their phones pinged in quick succession. Campus PD had received the list from the IT department that showed which keycards were used to enter Carter House on the morning of May 7, with the exact times they were swiped. The list wasn't terribly long. Five staff members and fourteen students had used keycards to access Carter House between 8 a.m. when the facility opened and when Kendra swiped in at 11:27 a.m. This group included Martina.

SVPD had already talked to the students who had waited to be interviewed on the day of Martina's attack, which was most of the list. Three of the names were new, however. These were students who had swiped in after Martina had but who were not in the building—and were not interviewed—directly following the police's arrival. These three students were a priority now, and Byron recruited two other detectives from SVPD that he trusted to find them and talk to them.

"Did you notice who's missing from this list?" he asked Jessica.

"I did," she said. "Levi and Chelsea are both missing. And for a full accounting, Tim O'Keefe is also absent from the list. None of them used their keycards to enter Carter House that morning. But you and I both know we can't fully rely on this data."

"I get it," Byron said. "People innocently go into secure buildings all the time without the proper credentials. One person holds the door open for someone else, or someone lends their keycard to their roommate because that kid left his own card in the dorm."

"Exactly," Jessica said. "This list is a snapshot of the keycards used that morning, but that's all it is. What is more interesting to me is this: the only suspect so far who has a solid alibi for that morning is O'Keefe, whose house cleaner confirmed that he was home. Neither Levi nor Chelsea can produce anyone to verify their whereabouts. Levi says he was home, but the landlady doesn't see him until the helicopters start circling. Chelsea says she was studying on campus somewhere, but she has no receipt for a coffee, no interactions with other students, nothing."

"And then there's the incident today outside the pool," Byron added. "Chelsea was in class this morning around seven, but we don't know her exact movements before then. And to complicate it more, we also don't know where Levi was this morning when Li-Ann was attacked."

"No, we do not," Jessica concurred. "And as long as we're discussing holes in the evidence, I'm also curious to hear the stories from the three people on this swipe list who were not on our radar until now."

"Right," Byron said.

Both feeling the weight of the work ahead of them, the two detectives decided to spend the rest of the day on separate tasks. Jessica would stay on campus and focus on the morning's attack. She wanted to retrace the path Chelsea would have likely taken from her dorm to Pilates class, allowing for a detour to the pool. She also wanted the area between the pool and the theatre arts building to be searched for anything that could be connected to Li-Ann's attack. The plan was for Campus PD, working under Jessica's direction, to scour that section of the campus. She'd also continue to monitor the updates from the hospital.

Byron would take the lead on Carter House. He had a nagging worry that they'd missed something there. As he drove away from Wexford, he felt a little guilty about his sin of omission with Jessica. He assumed that nothing would come of talking to the victim's cousin, so why complicate things more. He would likely spend a few minutes listening to Eliza rant about the need for the police to leave no stone unturned, and then he'd get back to work. Byron had heard it from family members before, and he was a good listener.

Less than ten minutes after leaving campus, he pulled into the parking lot at Lulu's, and Eliza waved as he stepped out of the car. She was sitting at a secluded table in the patio. The spring air was warm and inviting. It was one of those perfect days that made people move to Southern California. San Vicente's persistently overcast skies had cleared that morning, and people seemed more upbeat. Byron felt the happy anticipation of the months ahead—beach trips, pool parties, summer camp, and family vacations in Tahoe or Yosemite.

He approached Eliza's table and sat across from her. "I got here a little early and ordered something," she said, pushing an extra glass of water toward him. "Do you want to go in and get some food? Or I can offer you half my turkey sandwich when it gets here. The portions are huge at this place."

"I'm good," Byron said, considering the fifteen pounds he should lose before putting on a pair of swim trunks. "Tell me what's on your mind."

Eliza started by expressing her family's appreciation for all that he and his partner had done. She knew they were working long hours.

"That's nice of you to say. Maybe you could call my bosses and tell them. The *LA Post* story made us look like bozos."

Eliza, having brokered Vanessa Delaware's story, ignored the comment and continued, "Can you tell me what's going at Wexford this morning? I know Gil Mendoza just held a press briefing. Anything you can share that hasn't been released? Any connection to what happened at Carter House?"

"Look," Byron said. "It's all ongoing. I can neither confirm nor deny whether the two things are linked. You know I'm limited in what I can share, even to the victim's family."

"Okay, I get it," Eliza said. "Look, I know you're busy. Here's what I wanted to say: I believe that Kennedy Thompson, who works for Chief Mendoza, is somehow connected to my cousin's death. I don't have proof, and I need your help to put the whole picture together."

Byron worked to conceal his reaction. It was true that he found Kennedy bothersome, but he didn't want his distaste for the man to cloud his thinking. "Tell me what you know," he said quietly.

Eliza explained her background as a PI and admitted that she'd been working on behalf of Martina's parents, conducting her own investigation. She knew Byron and Jessica wouldn't be pleased about it, but there was no going back now. She'd asked to meet with Byron alone because Jessica appeared to be fixated on Levi, based on what Eliza had heard from Levi himself. Eliza then explained about the patent and why Levi lacked any real motive to get rid of Martina. In reality, Levi was in a worse place without Martina as a collaborator. Eliza filled in what she had learned from Willie Ducane and the strides they'd made toward fine-tuning their device.

"Levi and Martina were close to achieving a working prototype to show potential investors," she said. "During this last phase, I assume that he would have needed my cousin's technical expertise, but it was more than that. He would have needed her charm and beauty, her ability to dazzle investors. I've thought a lot about this," Eliza said. "It's true that Levi is edgy and broke and hyper-worried about intellectual property theft. But I don't see how taking Martina out of the equation helps him get over his financial hurdles. It actually puts him in a less favorable position."

Byron took this in. Clearly, Eliza was deep in her own investigation. "Tell me why you're focused on Kennedy," he said.

Eliza started with Kennedy's role in investigating the theft at the wellness center, which gave him proximity to Martina; then there was his visit to Martina's condo on a weekend morning to bring her paperwork, which seemed beyond what most police officers would do. Eliza also found it curious that Kennedy was conveniently all alone when he found Martina's backpack behind the cafeteria. It raised the question of whether he had planted it there and pretended to find it. Lastly, she cited his weird behavior on at least two occasions—outside of Carter House, when he'd grabbed Eliza's arm, and in Francesca's office, when he seemed to go into a trance while talking about Martina.

Eliza knew that her evidence was thin, but it amounted to something. "It was time to consult with the cops" she told Byron. "Maybe we could work together—unofficially—to build the rest of the case."

He took a minute to respond. Although he wasn't ready to admit it to Eliza, Byron also had some uneasiness about Kennedy. He agreed with Eliza that the discovery of the backpack was more than a lucky find. It didn't add up. It was weird that Kennedy had left the backpack unattended in a dumpster while he went to find a clean trash bag. Byron could understand an overexcited rookie making that mistake, but Kennedy wasn't a rookie. He could have called someone to help him transport the evidence. Byron had to consider the possibility that Kennedy had placed the backpack in the dumpster himself and then gotten tripped up in creating a fake cover story about how he found it. Something definitely seemed off.

"Okay," Byron said. "You got my attention. Let me think about the best way for us to work together. We can talk later tonight or in the morning. What other angles are you looking into?"

"I'd rather not say just yet," Eliza replied. "I'm hoping that something else comes together related to Kennedy, but I need to follow up with some sources."

Byron smiled. "It's not a competition. Seriously, who are you talking to?"

"Hmm.... Again, I don't want to say right now," she repeated. "It's not that I don't trust you, but it may be nothing. And if it's nothing, I don't want people needlessly dragged into this mess and then badgered by SVPD or campus police. Sorry, that's the truth."

"Okay, fine." Byron said. "But promise me one thing: You'll stick to the crime at Carter House and not dig into what happened on campus this morning. Let me and Detective Fonseca work that angle."

"Interesting. I was going to track down another Wexford student, Dahlia Moreno, this afternoon. Which crime does she relate to? Carter House? The one on campus this morning? Or both?" Eliza goaded.

"Ahhh," Byron said forcefully. "Stay clear of Dahlia. Given how close she is to Li-Ann, that poor girl must be freaking out right now, and we'll need to approach her carefully. Let my partner talk to her. Promise me you won't contact her."

"Okay, I promise," Eliza said, "now that you've confirmed Dahlia is a witness and you'll be talking to her. I have plenty of other things to do."

Byron walked back to his car wondering how well this new alliance would work. One thing was clear, he wouldn't be able to stop Eliza Fox from doing what she'd set her mind to. Hopefully, by collaborating with her, Byron would know what she was up to. He was also worried that if Eliza got too close and spooked the killer, she could become a victim herself. That was something he needed to prevent.

Byron headed next to Carter House. Armed with the list of keycards used that Tuesday morning, he approached Jeanne Voisin, the director of Carter House. He was curious if she knew any of the people on the keycard list, especially the three students who were never interviewed.

He was also interested in the staff and student workers at Carter, a group the police had not paid much attention to so far.

Byron first met Jeanne years ago when he was a rookie campus cop working for Chief Mendoza. She brought a French sensibility to Carter House that Byron found intriguing when he was younger. Heck, he still did. Her fashionable clothes and chic haircuts set her apart from most campus staff, who dressed in sloppy campus wear. Although he wasn't yet born in 1971 when the film *The French Connection* was released, the gritty police drama was one of his favorite movies. He had asked Jeanne about her life in the 1970s when she was growing up in Paris. He still remembered her answer: "cold, gray, and wonderfully vibrant." With her background in design, Jeanne had an artist's eye and observed people and her surroundings intently. Given all that had transpired with the investigation, he'd neglected to talk to her. Now, more than a week after the deadly incident at Carter House, that seemed like a huge misstep, and he decided to pay her a call.

"Hello Byron. It's been too long," Jeanne said, still holding on to remnants of her French accent. "How's your life as a detective with SVPD?"

They spent a few minutes on small talk, but they both knew his visit wasn't a social one. He took out his computer tablet and showed her the keycard list. "What can you tell me about any of the people I underlined?" Byron asked. "That includes the staff and student workers. Anything you remember from that morning, or even something that struck you as odd at a different time. Obviously we're looking for connections to the deceased, Ms. Noto."

She considered the list and handed the tablet back to him. "Nothing comes to mind about any of them. Sorry, I wish I could help you."

"Did you know Martina? Did she say anything to you that might be a clue?" he asked.

"No. I knew who she was," Jeanne replied. "She would come into the building and then head to the basement. We didn't have any real conversations. She stood out as a European. I noticed that."

"How so?"

"It's subtle—the clothes, the shoes, the handbag. She sometimes wore an expensive looking French scarf. I noticed it that morning when she came in—that last day."

"Martina was wearing a scarf that day when she came into Carter House? Are you sure?"

"Yes, very sure. She had on a blue dress, and a silk scarf wrapped loosely around her neck."

"Can you describe what the scarf looked like?"

Jeanne closed her eyes. "It was a combination of blues and greens, maybe with whites too. I remember thinking that the scarf worked well with the shade of blue in her dress. It was a passing thought."

"Thank you, that's very helpful. Here's my card," Byron said. "Please reach out if you think of anything else."

"Of course," she said. "Such a tragedy, and I understand we had another incident on campus this morning."

With a need to keep tight control on information, Byron defaulted to being reassuring. "We're doing everything we can to figure this out, Jeanne. Take care," he said.

"I know you're all working very hard," she said, "including everyone on Gil Mendoza's squad. It's a lot for them. Campus police aren't used to dealing with crimes of that magnitude. I talked to Officer Thompson a day or two after it happened. He seemed very stressed."

The mention of Kennedy caught his attention. "What do you mean stressed? How so?"

"I don't know, maybe more amped up than he normally is. I assumed it was because he happened to be here at Carter House that morning. Maybe the trauma of that had put him on edge. I know he's been missing his mom."

Byron looked again at the list of names, those who had swiped in with keycards on the morning of May 7. Kennedy Thompson's name was not listed.

"Sorry, I don't understand. Are you saying that Officer Thompson was here at Carter House before the body was found? I don't show him as using his card to enter."

"That's because I opened the door for him," Jeanne said. "Kennedy told me he'd left his keycard in his work locker. Since we're on the edge of campus, sometimes campus police forget about us. I'm always grateful when they stop by and have a look around. Now that I think about it, it's very unsettling that even when the campus police were on the premises, something terrible happened."

Byron's brain was whirling, electricity bouncing around in his nervous system. "Jeanne, I didn't get here until later that morning. Do you remember Kennedy being involved as a first responder that day? Was he here when the paramedics arrived?"

She ran a hand through her gray curls, her index finger grabbing a lock of hair. Jeanne spoke deliberately, recounting each scene as she recalled it. "I remember letting him in the front door. It must have been before 10 a.m. I believe he looked at some of the new art we'd hung in the lobby, and then he went downstairs. I went back to my office. The next thing I remember was maybe an hour later hearing screaming and commotion from the practice rooms."

"This is important, Jeanne. Did you see Kennedy again that morning after he went down to the lower level?"

She shook her head. "It's hard to know for sure, there was so much excitement. I don't have another clear memory of him from that day. I believe the next time I saw him again was when I talked to him a couple of days later. I saw him in the gardens behind Carter. Maybe Thursday or Friday. He said he was doing extra patrols. I thanked him, of course."

Byron knew there was no functioning CCTV on the basement level of Carter House to show Kennedy's whereabouts. As for the exterior cameras, Byron would need to check on the status of those videos. Would Kennedy show up on those recordings?

"Byron, what's going on?" Jeanne asked, concern in her voice.

He took Jeanne's hand in both of his and looked directly at her. "I need you to keep this conversation to yourself. It's important that you don't tell anyone what we just discussed. If Kennedy comes here for any reason, act as you typically would, but you need to call or text me immediately. Can you do that?"

Jeanne agreed and didn't ask anything else. Byron walked out of Carter House and found a quiet spot where he wouldn't be overheard. He called Sonia Cadena, the coroner's investigator who had responded to the crime scene at Carter House. Sonia confirmed that there was no silk scarf in the practice room, either on the victim's body or among her things. Sonia also had no record of interacting with a campus police officer named Kennedy Thompson that day.

Byron texted Jessica next. "I've been busy," he said. "When can you meet?"

∿

After leaving Lulu's, Eliza collected Lucas from his after-school play group, and they went home. She was exhausted. She had no real plan to talk to Dahlia Moreno or to anyone—at least not today. The low-grade headache she felt was a sign that she needed a night off. Even as she lay on the couch, it was almost impossible to turn off her brain. This case was a puzzle, and Eliza found herself sorting and resorting the information she knew, hoping to realign it into a clearer picture. Although she was well short of enough evidence to have Kennedy arrested, Byron was now onboard, and that alone was a positive step. Hopefully, she'd given him enough tidbits that he would pick up the trail. Tomorrow, she'd follow up with Jay. Maybe one of the merchants had captured some useful surveillance video.

As for the pressure campaign to keep the money and resources flowing, Vanessa Delaware had come through big time. *You gotta admire that woman's work ethic*, Eliza thought. Worry and fear were percolating like primordial soup on the campus and in the community, and that state of mind would continue to draw police resources to the case. The attack earlier that morning involving a Wexford student athlete was also going to stir up hysteria. Even though Eliza couldn't have foreseen the latest assault, she felt badly that the investigation had not wrapped up before anyone else was injured. People were justifiably scared. Hell, she was getting scared. She didn't have a clue if Kennedy was responsible for the second attack or if it was someone else's work. The whole thing was overwhelming.

Eliza knew she needed to recharge if she was going to have the stamina to make it to the end of the case. But before she checked out for the evening and switched exclusively to mother-son time, she called Kendra. Eliza wanted to know about the atmosphere on campus.

Kendra's voice sounded fraught. She was edgy and on the cusp of tears. President Gardener had sent out a message urging students to remain calm. Classes were canceled for the remainder of the week, and many students were heading home or on mini vacations. Kendra confirmed that the latest victim was Li-Ann Wong. Li-Ann's family and friends had formed a prayer group in the hospital chapel. Everyone was waiting to see how Li-Ann would do. She was currently in a medically induced coma.

"Kendra, have you heard anything about Li-Ann's closest friends? About Chelsea or Dahlia? Their whereabouts? What they're saying?" Eliza asked.

Kendra didn't know much. She'd heard that Dahlia talked to the police, and then retreated to her parents' house. Chelsea was a question mark. Chelsea wasn't on Kendra's radar, given how she'd treated Martina.

Finally, Eliza asked Kendra if she had any ideas about who attacked Li-Ann. Who knew her swim practice schedule? Who would want to harm Li-Ann and why? Kendra was quiet before sharing something she'd heard from Li-Ann.

"I feel stupid now that I didn't say this to anyone sooner," Kendra almost whispered into the phone, "but I talked to Li-Ann a few days ago. I saw her in the library, and I asked how things were going. She seemed nervous... preoccupied. She's usually upbeat, but she wasn't her normal self. I thought maybe she was fighting with Chelsea or

Dahlia. Anyway, Li-Ann said she had a weird feeling that she was being watched or followed."

"What?" Eliza said.

"Yeah, I know. It's something, right? Li-Ann said it happened sometimes while she was at work in the library. When she was alone re-shelving books in the stacks. Or sometimes when she walked across campus. She said she felt she was being watched."

"So someone was stalking Li-Ann? Is that what she said?"

"Not in those words. Li-Ann said that lately she had an eerie feeling another person was standing near her when she was in the stacks, but she'd look around and no one would be there. Or she felt like eyes were on her when she walked across campus. But when she turned around, she wouldn't see anyone. She said sometimes when she was crossing campus, she'd see one of the campus cops on their bike and feel relieved because they were patrolling."

"Kendra, I need you to write down everything that Li-Ann said to you about this, including the date and time of your conversation. Then email it to me. We need to tell Detective Comstock about this right away."

Kendra agreed and they hung up. "Oh, my God," Eliza said to herself. She then went to the kitchen and poured a generous glass of wine. She and Lucas had plans to construct a castle that evening, and Eliza was more than ready to escape. "Kiddo," she called. "Let's get started. I need a fantastic palace with a big moat and a drawbridge. I want brave knights. I want singing minstrels with their guitars, and I want court jesters in those funny outfits. Can we build a castle like that, please?"

"Sure, Mama. We can build it, and then we can go to sleep and dream about it," he said with an awareness well beyond his four-year-old psyche.

CHAPTER TWENTY

Friday, May 17—Morning

Jessica Fonseca awoke predawn, thinking. The previous night, Byron had filled her in on Eliza's theories about Levi, explaining his lack of motive to go after Martina. And Jessica could see the point. Besides, there was no direct evidence that he was in Carter House that morning. Aside from Levi's lack of alibi, nothing linked the graduate student to the scene in the practice room. They were still waiting for his DNA results, but Jessica was starting to doubt that he was culpable. Given all of the people who used that specific practice room at Carter House and touched the piano keys, the bench, the door, and the windows, DNA evidence wasn't serving them well in this case. The victim's body and clothing had carried cells, hair, and fibers from males and females. It turns out that Carter's practice rooms were as dirty as the sofas at the public library.

Byron had also laid out his thoughts about Kennedy Thompson, and Jessica was still mulling it all over. She agreed that the evidence stacking up against Kennedy was worthy of their attention. This was especially true considering the new eyewitness account that Kennedy was physically present inside Carter House before Kendra arrived there to find Martina. Byron had arranged to take an official statement from Jeanne Voisin later that morning. But even if Jeanne could place Kennedy in Carter House at a crucial time, the evidence was still circumstantial and could be explained away. They had to consider that Jeanne could be mistaken about the timing of when she opened the door for Kennedy. A lot had gone on at Carter House that morning. Or, if Jeanne was correct, maybe Kennedy had innocently come and gone from Carter that morning. They would need more evidence to build a murder case against the campus police officer.

As Jessica lingered under the covers, she considered the new second-hand information from Kendra. Li-Ann had told Kendra she felt as if she were being watched or followed, and somehow a campus cop might have been linked to this. It was yet another piece that needed attention, although it sounded too vague to Jessica to have much weight. With Li-Ann in a coma and presently nonverbal, Jessica had called Kendra late last night to verify the story. While her detective sensibilities wanted to hear about these odd experiences from Li-Ann herself, Jessica didn't get the impression that Kendra was lying or misremembering. Based on Kendra's account, it sounded like Li-Ann had a very real sense that she was being stalked, and it had scared her.

Frustration was the keyword for the morning. More than twenty-four hours after Li-Ann was found by the pool entrance, the search of the campus bathrooms hadn't yielded anything—no weapon, no discarded clothing, nothing. Campus surveillance footage also wasn't worth much. The video showed that around 5 a.m. on Thursday morning, a dark figure wearing a hoodie had walked toward the gym. It was impossible to make out who the person was. The figure then walked behind a tall hedge that ran parallel to a portion of the front of the gym. Unfortunately, the shrubbery blocked the camera's view. That was it, no other useful video.

Piecing together bits of information, Jessica learned that only one door to the gym was open during early-morning swim practice. All the swimmers knew to enter through a door on the far right. Clearly Li-Ann's attacker knew this too. Jessica reasoned that this person would have been careful to avoid being seen by the other swimmers. She again thought about how the crime might have been carried out against Li-Ann, with the attacker moving close to the door and lying in wait for her in the shadows. But who had done this? And why? One thing was clear, this assailant knew where the surveillance cameras were pointed and how to evade them.

As part of their field operations at Wexford yesterday, Jessica had coordinated with Chief Mendoza to deploy some of the campus police force to build a profile of Li-Ann. Jessica wanted to know who her friends were, how she spent her days, and if she had a romantic partner. She wanted to know Li-Ann's social media activity, whether she was on a scholarship, what her major was, and whether she was a star student, on academic probation, or somewhere in the middle. Gil Mendoza was supervising his officers as they put this information together. The only caveat was that the campus police limit their inquiry to the event at the pool and let Detective Comstock work the Noto case at Carter House.

With the sun starting to show, Jessica pulled herself from bed and went to the kitchen to make coffee. As she performed the familiar task, her mind turned to the Chelsea question again. Jessica had been surprised to find out that after her early morning Pilates class, Chelsea had boarded a flight to San Francisco. She'd gone to the Bay Area for a meeting about a summer internship. Jessica had verified this with both the airline and the San Francisco company where Chelsea wanted to intern.

It was maddening that Chelsea wasn't available for Jessica to question her face to face. On the other hand, Chelsea had no obligation to stay tethered to San Vicente. It was unlikely the DA would press charges in Chelsea's cyberbullying case. Ironically, the fact that the victim of the fake Tinder profile was now deceased had worked in Chelsea's favor. Martina wouldn't be able to give testimony about how the bullying had affected her. LA County was also a very big jurisdiction. It made sense that the DA wouldn't pursue misdemeanor charges against a Wexford student, especially one whose father was a well-connected lawyer.

That Chelsea had left on a flight for San Francisco late Thursday morning also made Jessica question her own theory that Chelsea had attacked Li-Ann outside the gym. To make the timing work, Chelsea would have needed to commit the attack just before 6:30 a.m., get rid of the weapon, and arrive at Pilates class close to 7 a.m. as if nothing had happened. After that she would have had to hurry to catch a 10:30 a.m. flight from Burbank Airport. While the timing was possible, it was tight. Another factor was whether Chelsea had the emotional wherewithal to pull it off. Jessica remembered Chelsea hyperventilating before being transported to police headquarters for questioning. While Chelsea appeared to be a cool customer, Jessica suspected it was all an act. More likely, Chelsea was an anxiety-ridden mess on the inside.

Jessica showered and found some comfortable clothes for the day. She knew it'd be a long one.

∼

"Mom! Squirrels!" Lucas yelled through the house as Eliza groggily arose from sleep Friday morning. Squirrels were jumping about in the back garden, and he was eager to share this wonder with her. She pulled herself from the blankets and went with him to the window. They watched as two squirrels ran along the top of the fence and jumped in and out of their neighbor's avocado tree. Eliza wondered if they were watching a mating ritual, or if the two small animals were simply ecstatic over finding so much fruit. It was undeniably spring in Southern California. Farmer's markets were full of asparagus and strawberries, and her friends were deep into summer vacation planning. She sighed, thinking of the last vacation she and David took as a family. They'd rented a beach house in La Jolla. Lucas had loved the tide pools and delighted in pointing out the sea anemones and hermit crabs.

"Lucas, would you like to go on a mini vacation to the beach soon? Maybe for Fourth of July, where we can see the fireworks. I'll invite *Nonna* to come with us."

His wide grin lifted her spirits. An hour later, she had dropped

Lucas at school and was back home at her desk. Eliza planned to spend the morning looking at the surveillance video that Samay from Snack & Go had downloaded for her. Then she'd check in with Jay to see if any other merchants had come through with video. It had only been forty-eight hours since she'd talked to him, but she felt a pressing sense of urgency.

~

By 9 a.m. Jessica was parked on campus near the Wexford police station, but she found herself lingering in the driver's seat and scrolling through her phone. Her personal life needed attention. Her sister had sent a text asking about their mom, and there were several unanswered messages and voicemails from close friends. As she was about to call her sister, a new text from Gil Mendoza flashed on her screen. His team was ready to report out the background information they learned about Li-Ann.

Be there in 10, she replied. Jessica summoned her energy. She'd have to catch up with family and friends later. She could rest when the case was over. With any luck, it would be on the deck of a mountain cabin with an escapist novel and a glass of cabernet.

Minutes later, Jessica was seated at one end of a long conference table. She assessed the small team of uniformed officers assembled in front of her. After spending a full day on campus yesterday, she was starting to know them. She had identified the hard workers and the shirkers, the leaders and the ones who lacked initiative. Gil had ceded control of the meeting to Jessica, and she began by calling on Officer Luis Alvarez, an amiable young man, who was also fluent in Spanish. Jessica was considering him as a potential recruit for SVPD's training program.

"Tell me what you learned, Alvarez," she ordered.

"Ma'am, I partnered with Officer Denton on this assignment. Our focus was on the victim's family. We went to the hospital and spoke with her parents and relatives. Nothing stood out to us as unusual. The victim is of Chinese descent. She grew up in the city of Cerritos, which is about twenty-five miles south of San Vicente. Her father works for a food company that imports items from Taiwan; her mother is a lab tech at a hospital. She is the middle child, with an older sister and a younger brother. The family had always expected her to be a high achiever, which appears to be the case. Do you want me to continue?"

"No, that's good. Thank you, that was very helpful. Let's move on. Officer Thompson, what did you learn about the victim?"

"Okay, I worked with Dakota. I mean, Officer Mayer. Our assignment was to look into the victim's campus life. She lives on campus on the third floor of Stinson Hall. She is on the swim team and also works in the library. She's on a scholarship. She belongs to a sorority, the same one that Chelsea Miller belongs to. She's been on the dean's list every semester she's been at Wexford."

"Tell me why you mentioned Chelsea Miller?" Jessica asked.

"Sure. I know from the Noto investigation that there has been an interest in Ms. Miller. Dakota and I talked to some of the sorority sisters and we believe there's been a falling out between Ms. Miller and Ms. Wong, our victim from the pool incident. We would need more time to figure out why this falling out occurred."

"I see," Jessica said. "Officer Mayer, what led you to think there was a problem between Li-Ann Wong and Chelsea Miller?"

Dakota looked a little stunned that she was asked to speak. "It's what the sorority girls said—that Li-Ann had been sad lately and keeping more to herself. She wasn't as tight with Chelsea as she used to be. We tried to confirm this with Chelsea but we couldn't locate her."

Jessica looked at Gil to see his reaction. "Thank you," he said to the group. "We need to pause this briefing for now. Kennedy, could you step into my office please? Dakota, you can go to your desk for a minute."

Jessica cornered Dakota before she walked away. "Who made the decision to look for Chelsea? Did Kennedy say anything about Chelsea being off limits from your assignment yesterday?"

"No, ma'am. He never said that we should stay clear of Ms. Miller. I just followed his lead. Like I said, we weren't successful. I mean, we didn't talk to Chelsea. We couldn't find her," Dakota emphasized. "She skipped her afternoon classes."

"Okay, thank you," Jessica said, and then she stepped into Gil's office. His voice was elevated: "Why do this, Kennedy? Yesterday I told you in clear terms to stay away from any links to the Noto investigation. You knew last week that Chelsea is caught up in the Noto matter. I expect you to follow my directives when you're in the field, even more so when you're training a new recruit."

"Sir, with all due respect, given that we learned about a possible conflict between Ms. Miller and Ms. Wong, I felt it was important to locate Chelsea Miller ASAP. It's very possible that Ms. Miller is the person who committed the attack at the pool. At a minimum, we need to know why there was tension between our victim and Chelsea Miller. It's odd for sorority sisters who were so close to suddenly become so distant. Maybe something triggered Chelsea to go after Li-Ann."

Gil and Jessica again exchanged looks. "When were you going to loop us in about what you heard?" Jessica asked. "Rather than going after Chelsea yourself, you should have called one of us immediately after talking to the sorority girls. Why did you wait until this morning's briefing to bring it up?"

Gil didn't wait for Kennedy to explain further. "Kennedy, I'm pulling you from the Wong case. You can focus on the break-ins at the wellness center. That case is still open. Partner with Dakota. Maybe the two of you can figure out who broke into those lockers. Have you checked with LAPD and the sheriff's office to see if they have any leads about people moving stolen computers? What about neighboring cities, like Burbank or Arcadia? I want a briefing in one hour on the status of that investigation."

Kennedy muttered, "Yes, sir," and left the room, leaving a heavy silence in the small office. Jessica saw how troubled Gil looked. "You talked to Byron, didn't you?"

"I did. Early this morning," Gil confirmed. "Byron is convinced that Kennedy is wrapped up in the Noto thing."

"What's your read on it, Gil? You know Kennedy better than almost anyone," Jessica asked.

"I don't know what to think," Gil told her. "I have my blind spots with Kennedy. I know that. The employees who've worked on this campus for a long time are a family, and I was fond of Kennedy's mother. I try to keep an eye on him now that she's gone. Until these cases are figured out, I'll keep him away from you and Byron."

"For what it's worth, Gil, I also don't know what to think. I don't like it when cops get caught up in bad acts. I want to be very sure we are not falsely accusing Kennedy. I won't let that happen."

Gil nodded his appreciation. "You can have Alvarez as your campus contact while you work this thing, Jessica. Just promise me that you won't recruit him for SVPD—at least not for another year. I'm going to need Alvarez for a while as the campus recovers from so much turmoil. Students and their parents will be skittish long after these crimes have dropped out of the news."

"Okay, Gil. I won't steal Alvarez, at least not yet."

∼

Thankfully, Eliza was able to speed up the video she'd received from Samay and still get a clear picture. After two hours of viewing, she hadn't found any images of Martina during the first week of May, including the morning of May 7. It was likely that her cousin had walked a street parallel to Whitmore Road as she climbed the hill to Carter House. Just to be doubly sure, Eliza isolated the video from the morning of May 7 and watched it more closely. Still not seeing any images of Martina between 8 a.m. and 9:30 a.m., Eliza left her desk to stretch her legs and make a cup of tea.

Back at her desk, she was about to close the video viewer on her laptop, when something on the screen drew her attention. She backed the video up and watched the brief segment again, this time at a slower speed. It was a bicyclist heading south on Whitmore Road in the opposite direction of Carter House. Eliza zoomed in on the image and froze it. The timestamp was 10:34 a.m.

Her heart was pounding. The picture was grainy, but she could make out a man wearing a Wexford police uniform. He was riding the type of bike used by the campus cops. While it was impossible to say for sure, the cyclist resembled Kennedy Thompson. His face was obscured because he was wearing a bike helmet, but he certainly had Kennedy's bulky frame. The part that electrified Eliza was the dark-colored backpack resting on his back, one that looked a lot like the backpack Kendra had described as belonging to Martina.

She closed the video and carefully saved several copies of it— onto her laptop, in the cloud, and on a flash drive. This was a big development, if two things were true: they could verify that it was Kennedy on the video and that he was carrying Martina's backpack— the one he purportedly found in a campus dumpster. If those things were provable, Samay's surveillance film was a big piece of evidence.

Eliza went to take a shower. She wanted to feel the warm water and catch her breath. She also saw that she needed to get moving. She was on a roll, and she wanted to see if Jay had uncovered any more useful surveillance footage.

CHAPTER TWENTY-ONE

Friday, May 17—Afternoon and Evening

Around 1:30 p.m., Francesca checked her email as she did each afternoon. The small habit marked the end of her self-imposed daily break from technology. The ninety minutes between noon and 1:30 p.m. was her private time. Often, she ate a small meal and took a walk. If the weather in San Vicente was rainy or too hot to go outside, she used the time to listen to Italian opera and look at art books. Once in a while, when life was overwhelming, she closed her eyes and rested. Francesca found that by following this routine, she could almost always face whatever the afternoon demanded of her.

Today, she was hoping for a message from Carole Gardener amid the batch of post-lunch emails, and she was excited to see it in her inbox. Francesca opened it and smiled at Carole's one word response: *Approved*. Francesca had spent many hours that week working on expedited approval for a new Wexford scholarship. It was to be named in honor of Martina and awarded to a computer science major. Francesca was poised to contribute the scholarship's initial seed money, and she would work with the donor relations office on future fundraising. With luck, the scholarship would soon become self-sustaining.

Ironically, Wexford's computer science department, in disarray after the fall of Tim O'Keefe, had threatened to slow roll the process. It was a department without leadership, and its faculty worried that the announcement of a new scholarship would also bring negative publicity about O'Keefe and his unprofessional relationship with Martina. But Francesca was a force of her own, and she saw no advantages to putting the scholarship on hold. She turned to Professor Guzman in the entrepreneurial program for help. Given that Martina had charmed Fernando Guzman, he was enthusiastically supportive of a tribute in her memory. The business school agreed to host the scholarship and have a role in selecting the recipient each year.

With the campus approvals in hand, Francesca thought about when and how she'd tell Roberto and Laura about the scholarship. Based on what Eliza had said about her conversations with Detective Comstock, SVPD was close to apprehending someone and closing the investigation. Her family would be leaving soon, and Francesca wanted to be ready to share her news.

∼

Eliza was standing in front of a pizza restaurant about a half block from the Snack & Go, waiting for Jay to walk over from his store. He had notified Eliza about some video that was recorded on the restaurant's surveillance cameras. Jay, who had not seen the video himself, had offered to go with Eliza to talk to the restaurant's manager. As she stood on the sidewalk outside the restaurant, she took in the scene. The smell of baking pizza was seductive. The small café with its affordable prices and offers of pizza by the slice drew in Wexford students. The restaurant had pushed onto the sidewalk and set up several tables for al fresco dining. With the day's perfect weather, customers were now arriving for lunch and filling the patio tables.

Soon Jay arrived and went inside to talk to the manager, leaving Eliza still standing in front. She found herself chewing on a thumbnail, an old habit that returned when she was stressed. To pass the time, she checked the local headlines on her phone. She saw stories about San Vicente's schools and parks, but no reports of further criminal activity on the Wexford campus, which she viewed as a positive. Jay eventually motioned for her to go inside, and they were directed to a miniscule office next to the kitchen. The restaurant manager, a woman named Sofia, cued up the video on a desktop computer and then stepped out of the office to give them space. Eliza sat down at the keyboard and Jay leaned in behind her. Before pressing play, she noted that the video was from Sunday, May 5, just before 2 p.m., two days before the events at Carter House.

"Ready?" Jay asked her.

"No. Not really," Eliza said. "Do you know what we're about to watch?"

"No, I'm not sure, only that Sofia thought it was important."

"Okay," Eliza said. "Waiting won't make this any easier."

The black-and-white footage had no sound. Based on what the video showed, the camera was mounted above the restaurant's front door and looked down and out toward the street. In the first minutes of the video, the front patio tables were empty, so Eliza felt a small jolt when an image of Martina appeared. Her cousin walked to a table and sat down. Because Sofia had set the video to play at twice normal speed, the scenes were unfolding in overdrive. Soon a bottle of mineral water was on the table and Martina's laptop was open. She appeared to be continuously typing, giving the impression that Martina was working rather than casually browsing the web.

"Is that your cousin?" Jay asked. Eliza nodded, finding it hard to talk. Seeing Martina, even on the silent, black-and-white video, made her emotional.

The restaurant looked quiet for a Sunday. Because the date was *Cinco de Mayo*, Eliza figured that people had opted for tacos instead of pizza, given how popular the Mexican holiday had become in Southern California.

They watched for another thirty seconds or so, and Eliza started to wonder if the video would reveal anything beyond her cousin's whereabouts that afternoon. Mindful of Jay's time, she reached toward the keyboard to advance the video when he grabbed her hand.

A man had appeared in the frame standing at Martina's table. Eliza immediately recognized Kennedy, even though he was dressed in dark slacks and a polo shirt rather than his police uniform.

"So not on official business then," Eliza quipped, stopping the video and restarting it to play at normal speed.

Within a few seconds of arriving, Kennedy had pulled out a chair and sat down opposite Martina, and this seemed to trigger a visible reaction from her. She shook her head back and forth, seeming to say no, and pointed to her laptop. Martina then drank some water, looked at her phone, and pointed again to her laptop. But Kennedy continued to sit. Eliza thought he appeared calm; his movements were infrequent and controlled. Nothing in his body language showed he was agitated or upset. It was Martina who was unnerved. She waved her arms expressively, just as Eliza's mother did when she got excited.

She and Jay continued to watch. About five minutes after Kennedy had arrived, Martina stood up and began to pack her things. She then went into the restaurant and emerged a few moments later carrying a pizza box. Martina walked off as Kennedy continued to sit looking after her. He then stood and walked in the opposite direction as the video clip ended.

"*Dio mio*," Eliza exclaimed. "It's proof that he was harassing her and probably stalking her. I'll bury that bastard. Jay, what did you think?"

"I don't know who that man is," he said. "But she didn't want him at her table. That much was obvious."

Eliza thanked Jay profusely as they went to look for Sofia in the dining room. Eliza needed a copy of the video and the restaurant's work schedule for Sunday, May 5. Someone would need to speak with the staff who worked that day to see if anyone had overheard or observed what had transpired between Martina and Kennedy.

Eliza also expressed her gratitude to Sofia. Before leaving the restaurant, she ordered a couple of large pizzas to show further appreciation. She would surprise her family with dinner.

~

On most Friday nights, Byron, his wife, and daughter had a family classic movie night. He would pick up kabobs with rice and hummus from their favorite Armenian restaurant, and they would settle in for a screwball comedy or a noir thriller. Not this Friday. Tonight, he had sent them off to enjoy a mother-daughter dinner and a trip to the mall.

He'd connected with Eliza a few hours earlier. She'd been busy since their meeting the day before, and his respect for her was growing. He had just watched the two videos she sent. Eliza believed they further incriminated Kennedy Thompson, and Byron had to admit that she wasn't wrong. The video of a campus cop heading away from Carter House on the morning of May 7 was troubling. It was impossible to say for sure that the image was Kennedy, but it was a strong possibility. He hoped that the IT team could enhance the video more.

Byron also had an important piece of information that Eliza wasn't aware of: Jeanne Voisin was willing to testify that she saw Kennedy inside Carter House shortly before the body was found. While the evidence against Kennedy didn't yet reach the standard of "beyond a reasonable doubt," anyone could see that things were stacking up against him. The restaurant video was also intriguing. It showed Kennedy being a pest and intruding on Martina's space. This raised the question of whether he had been stalking her, which dovetailed with Kendra's tidbit that Li-Ann felt she was being watched or followed.

Byron was collecting his thoughts before calling Jessica. He wanted to know if she'd found any evidence that took Kennedy out of the frame for the attack outside the gym. Had Kennedy been at work and physically in the office at 6:30 a.m. when Li-Ann arrived for practice? That would be a very good alibi, full stop. If not, did he have a motive to go after the swimmer? Finally, they needed to make some decisions about Levi. Was Levi culpable for one or both of the crimes they were investigating, or was he ruled out?

Just as Byron picked up his phone to call Jessica, she called him. "Hey partner," he said. "Excellent timing."

"Big news. The tech guys got past the encryption on Martina's laptop. They're still combing through her files, but they found something you need to see. She was keeping a bit of a journal, and I'm sending it to you now. There's not that many entries. Read the most recent one first. It was written two days before she died. Then call me back."

MARTINA'S JOURNAL

May 5

Mad. Angry. Annoyed. Furious.

That's all the English words I can think of to say *arrabbiata*. Why do men think they can follow me, or sit at my table uninvited, or interrupt my work? Why do they expect me to be polite and not say how I feel? Why wouldn't that crazy cop leave when I said I have to work?

RESPECT MY SPACE.

RESPECT MY DESIRE TO ACHIEVE SOMETHING.

RESPECT ME.

After speed-reading the journal entries, Byron sent the video links to Jessica, telling her to watch them before they talked. Then they spent an hour on the phone hashing out what they knew. Jessica brought Byron up to speed on her meeting a few hours earlier with Dahlia, who had moved back to her parents' house for the tail end of the semester. Nail biting and tearful, Dahlia had no real information about Li-Ann's attacker. Dahlia confirmed that in recent days Li-Ann sensed she was being watched, most often when she was working in the library. Dahlia also told Jessica that she and Li-Ann were no longer friends with Chelsea. Although Dahlia wouldn't say why they had a falling out, Jessica suspected it was over the cyberstalking incident. When school pranks turn into police matters, even the closest friendships fall apart. Jessica had seen it happen more than once.

Jessica also confirmed that Kennedy couldn't use work as an alibi for the attack at the pool. According to Gil, Kennedy walked into the campus police offices around 7 a.m., at least thirty minutes after Li-Ann was due at practice. Kennedy would have had enough time to get from the pool to work.

"That's all I have," Jessica concluded. "What about you?"

For Byron's part, he reported that the interview with Jeanne Voisin had gone as expected, no further surprises. He had confirmed with their bosses about overtime and staffing. Everyone was onboard to work through the weekend. He'd requested that the IT team work on enhancing the videos Eliza had discovered. He also requested that another pair of detectives—those who were tracking down the remaining students on the Carter House keycard list—get statements from the staff at the pizza restaurant. Jessica could relax knowing that trusted colleagues were pitching in.

As their conversation moved into theories and motives, Byron and Jessica agreed that Levi was looking less culpable. Byron had come around to Eliza's perspective that it made no sense for Levi to get rid of Martina simply because he didn't want to share any profits. While there was evidence from Martina's journal that she was worried Levi would cut her out financially, nothing suggested it was more than a worry. Business deals were full of risk. That didn't mean Levi had slipped into Carter House and killed her. It was the same reasoning with Chelsea. Chelsea was never friendly with Martina, and she had fallen out with Li-Ann and Dahlia, but those facts alone didn't add up to violence in either case. For now, Byron and Jessica agreed to focus on Kennedy for the Noto crime, while keeping an eye on Levi and Chelsea as suspects. They figured that if they could prove the first crime, the evidence around the assault of Li-Ann Wong would fall into place.

In the morning they would meet Gil Mendoza at SVPD headquarters for a strategy session. It was also time to update their bosses on the recent developments in their investigation. With overtime approved, Byron sent an unmarked car to Kennedy's house for a night of surveillance. He wanted to be sure Kennedy was home and not involved in any illicit acts. While no one at Wexford wanted it to be true, it was starting to look like Officer Thompson had taken his pledge to protect the campus and turned it on its head.

CHAPTER TWENTY-TWO

Saturday, May 18—Early Morning

At daybreak, Byron called the officer parked near Kennedy's house for the night and sent him home to sleep. Even in an unmarked car, it was a risk that Kennedy would notice the vehicle and recognize it as out of place. Byron didn't want to trigger an unwanted response from him.

Byron, Jessica, and Gil now sat around a large conference table at SVPD headquarters, as the small city awoke to its Saturday routine. Ten days had passed since the murder at Carter House, and the whole community seemed focused on this fact. At least that's how it felt. Jessica had the foresight to stop at her local *panaderia* to pick up *pan dulce*. She knew that Byron and Gil would want food and be happy to chew on the sweet pastries as they analyzed and planned. Even though all three of them worked well together, it had been a rough several days for the campus and the community. As Jessica's mother often said, "Small comforts go a long way in terrible times."

To get the meeting started, Byron laid out the most important facts. Martina's journal and the restaurant video confirmed that Kennedy Thompson was pursuing her in some way. The statement from Jeanne Voisin, a reliable witness, placed Kennedy at Carter House on the morning of Martina's murder. Byron also shared another detail Jeanne had provided: Martina's scarf was missing from the crime scene. The coroner's investigator had not itemized it as part of the victim's belongings, but Jeanne was certain she saw Martina wearing it. Kennedy had retrieved the missing backpack and laptop from a campus dumpster, but he had not produced a scarf.

Gil interrupted with a question that had been troubling him since his last conversation with Byron: "If what you're suggesting is true, and Kennedy took the victim's backpack from the practice room, why would he knowingly put her computer back into police hands, especially if he didn't know what was on it? Why not return the backpack and destroy the laptop?"

"A couple of reasons," Byron said. "My guess is that Kennedy didn't envision that she was writing a diary on it. He probably assumed the laptop contained schoolwork but not much more. Maybe he saw it was encrypted and figured no one could get into it, so why destroy it."

"That was a bad call on his part," Jessica said. "But I get it. As police officers, we would be more excited about the retrieval of a working laptop, than one that's been crushed with a hammer. If he's looking for praise, finding a shiny computer is better than a dead computer."

"Right," Byron said. "For whatever reason, he left the victim's phone at the crime scene. But he had a lot to gain from staging the recovery of her missing stuff. In Kennedy's mind, no one would suspect him of committing the crime if he was working to solve it. I agree that it was a risk to pull her backpack out of a dumpster, but it was a calculated risk."

"I see," Gil said. "I did give Kennedy lots of praise for that discovery. He wouldn't be the first one to commit a crime and then be involved in investigating it as a way to deflect guilt. You two are probably too young to remember the fire chief from this area; the guy was eventually convicted of arson. He would start a fire, which no one suspected him of because he was the fricking fire chief, and then he'd be part of the team to investigate the same fire he had set. He even burned down a large hardware store."

"Wow! That's some nerve," Jessica said. "I wonder if Kennedy knows that story."

"He might," Gil replied. "He just might."

"Okay," Byron said. "Let's focus." He was ready to talk about a plan to close in on Kennedy. He'd spent most of the night thinking about it.

~

Lucas was due at the park at 8 a.m. His T-ball team had an important game that morning, at least in the minds of their coach and some of the parents. Since Lucas's team was composed of four- and five-year-old kids, Eliza didn't understand how, on a grand scale, this particular game was so important. Whatever. David would be at the game to cheer Lucas on, which was a new thing. Even though her ex was remarried with a pregnant wife, it still made Eliza anxious to be at public events with him. She didn't know how to act. Should they sit together and support Lucas as a parental unit? Or would that be weird? She found herself obsessing over protocols, which was not how she usually spent a weekend morning.

She was also at loose ends with the investigation. After sharing the latest evidence with Byron, she'd run out of obvious tasks to push the investigation forward. She had no legal authority to arrest people, so SVPD had to be involved. But Eliza still felt uneasy. Kennedy was out there and that alone posed a threat.

Adding to her disquiet, once the T-ball game was over, Eliza would spend the day without Lucas. He was going home with his dad and wouldn't be back with her until after dinner. Waiting for the game to start, she came up with a plan to make herself useful during her free afternoon. With Kennedy continuing to be a source of worry, she decided to spend a few hours being proactive, either conducting surveillance on him or talking to his neighbors and possibly learning something the detectives could use. The case wasn't over yet, and she wasn't ready to stop.

~

By noon, Byron had a search warrant for the Thompson house and Kennedy's personal vehicle. With the Dodgers on the road that weekend, Gil reasoned that Kennedy would be settled in front of the TV for the afternoon. Gil described Kennedy as a dedicated Dodger fan who never intentionally missed a game. He also wasn't the type to go to sports bars or watch with his buddies. Odds were high that he'd be home in front of the TV for the first pitch.

It was an advantage to have Gil's input. Kennedy lived in the house he'd grown up in, which was situated in the hills above San Vicente. Gil had been there a few times for barbecues. It had stunning views, Gil remembered. Marjorie, Kennedy's mom, had hosted many Fourth of July parties and fireworks were visible across the night sky from the home's deck.

With some prodding from Byron, Gil provided background on the Thompsons. Marjorie and her husband bought the house when they were first married. Kennedy was just a baby at the time. Then his dad had died in a car accident when he was young. Marjorie never remarried and had raised Kennedy on her own. He had been a quiet child, socially awkward, and Marjorie had worried about the boy's future. It was Gil who had encouraged Kennedy to study criminal justice in college and later to join the Wexford campus police force.

The campus police at Wexford didn't carry firearms, but Kennedy was the registered owner of a couple of guns. Byron would advise the team from SVPD to stay sharp. Given the curvy roads in Kennedy's neighborhood, Byron wondered if Kennedy would be able to see the police cruisers from his deck as they drove up the canyon. No one wanted Kennedy to get spooked and try to escape.

Gil also briefed Byron and Jessica on the interior and exterior grounds of the Thompson house. Typical of many hillside homes, the structure was built into the hillside and extended down into the canyon below. Its front entrance and garage were at street level, but the bedrooms and a family room were on a lower level beneath the main floor. With any luck when SVPD arrived, Kennedy would be downstairs in the TV room and not focused on what was happening on the street outside his door.

Eliza had packed a couple bottles of water, snacks, and a good book. She hoped they would sustain her for a few hours as she sat in her car and surveilled Kennedy's house. She also took along a camera, her good Nikon with the telephoto lens. If needed, she'd be ready to take photos of Kennedy from a distance. The camera could also serve as a prop if a nosy neighbor approached her. She'd used the birdwatching excuse when she'd encountered Kennedy behind Carter House, and she was prepared to repeat it. Didn't birders need to document their sightings? "That's right. I'm a birdwatcher," she told herself. "I'm looking for a yellow oriole," which was the only oddball bird Eliza could think of as she looked toward Kennedy's childhood home.

It had been easy to find his address in the database she used for her job, the same database she'd tapped into with less success when she was trying to locate Levi Newcomb. Kennedy happened to live in a neighborhood Eliza knew well. One of her best friends growing up had lived on a nearby street and as kids, they'd spent many afternoons exploring the area's canyons and ravines.

She had parked the Volvo on Kennedy's street just west of his house, where she could see if he drove off. At the same time, she hoped she was far enough away not to draw attention. Kennedy was home. She had watched him step outside and set down a bowl of food for a stray cat. For now, Eliza was content to read her novel and observe. She decided to hold off on interviewing his neighbors, realizing the idea could backfire. No matter how carefully she framed her questions, a neighbor might figure out that Kennedy was in trouble. Why risk tipping anyone off?

Twenty-five minutes passed as Eliza watched, paying half attention. She was getting sleepy in the warm car and was close to dozing off when she observed a man resembling Chief Mendoza approach on foot. He was walking up the hill toward Kennedy's house. She closed and opened her eyes a few times and then squinted into the sunlight. As far as Eliza could see, he had a six-pack of beer and some takeout in a plastic bag. She watched as he knocked on Kennedy's front door. Within a few seconds, the screen door opened, and the chief stepped inside. *Where is his car,* she wondered.

~

Byron had wanted Gil to go in with more sophisticated communications equipment, but Gil had stubbornly declined. Gil was old school and disdained fancy listening devices. As a compromise, before approaching the house, he had called Byron's cell. Gil then muted his phone and slipped it into his pocket while the call was still active. While the quality wasn't great, Byron could at least overhear Gil and Kennedy talking. Byron worried that the spotty cell coverage in the canyon would cause the call to drop. But it was all Gil would agree to. They would have to make do.

Based on what Byron could discern as he eavesdropped, Kennedy sounded happy about Gil's surprise visit and agreed to watch the Dodger game with him. The two men had gone downstairs to where the TV was. Byron and a couple of other patrol cars were waiting around the curved road just east of Kennedy's home. With Kennedy and Gil on the house's lower level, Byron moved his team into place. Jessica was parked at the bottom of the hill ready to move in any direction in case Kennedy decided to flee. "So far, so good," Byron told her by radio. "We're moving."

~

From Eliza's perspective, with Chief Mendoza inside Kennedy's house, supplied with food and beer, she felt she could abort her surveillance mission. Kennedy had another person to talk to, and all the better it was the chief, whose demeanor was steady and father-like.

Before driving away, she lingered in the tranquil neighborhood a few minutes longer, just to verify that Gil was settling in for a visit.

If so, she'd leave knowing Kennedy was in good company. To pass the remaining time, Eliza shelled pistachios and looked up from her novel every few lines, not expecting to see anything. She froze, her hand midway to her mouth, when three SVPD police vehicles slowly rolled into view and strategically stopped in front of Kennedy's garage. "Oh my! It's on," Eliza whispered to the empty car. She watched as Byron and a uniformed SVPD officer approached Kennedy's door and knocked forcefully.

∿

With their ersatz listening device still engaged, Byron heard the annoyance in Kennedy's voice through his phone's earpiece: "No one ever comes to the door at this house, not even the UPS guy," Kennedy said.

"Why don't you go up and open it?" Gil prodded. "Nothing's happening in this inning."

Byron then heard footsteps climb the stairs and approach the front door. Kennedy opened it a few inches, then wider. "Why are you here, Detective? Was there an incident in the neighborhood?" he asked, puzzled.

"No, Mr. Thompson. We have a warrant to search this property and your vehicle," Byron explained calmly, stepping over the threshold. "Why don't you sit with Gil downstairs while we do our work."

Byron signaled to the search team that they could enter while Gil motioned from the bottom of the stairs for Kennedy to return to the TV. When Kennedy realized what SVPD intended to do, he was no longer compliant. His space was being invaded, and that was something he couldn't agree to. He began to pace around the upstairs rooms yelling, "NO, NO, NO!"

Byron and Gil had discussed their strategy in advance. Unless Kennedy was under arrest, Gil had asked Byron to go easy, and Byron had agreed. Even as the confusion inside mounted, Byron was able to direct his officers to various parts of the house. At the same time, he tried to assist Gil with controlling Kennedy. The three men were now in the kitchen, where Gil was offering Kennedy a glass of water to calm him. The atmosphere was increasingly chaotic as the police spread to the downstairs. Byron still felt things were loosely under control—until the moment Kennedy made a connection that pushed him into action. Catching both Byron and Gil unawares, he moved with surprising speed to the adjacent laundry room and closed the door behind him. Byron could hear Kennedy placing something under the doorknob to prevent them from opening it.

"Kennedy!" Byron yelled, pressing his shoulder to the door. "Don't do this. We need you to stay calm."

Once in the laundry room, Kennedy opened a cupboard and grabbed the item he was after. Then he continued past an old sink and the washing machine to another door that opened into the garage. He pressed a button on the wall, and the wide garage door started its slow upward climb. Kennedy's first plan was to drive away, but two empty police vehicles stood in the driveway, blocking his car's exit. Instead, he grabbed his mountain bike and pedaled out of the garage. Before Byron and Gil had reached the front porch, Kennedy was riding up the road and out of their reach at a decent speed.

Eliza, mesmerized by the unfolding scene, watched as a mountain bike swerved out of the garage and approached in her direction. Instinctively, she grabbed her camera, which now doubled as binoculars. She pointed the long lens toward the bike and looked into the viewfinder. It was Kennedy. Eliza shot several frames while sitting in the driver's seat. Then without consciously considering her next move, she got out of the car and planted her feet in the middle of the road. She fired photo after photo of the bike heading toward her.

Everything felt like it was happening at warp speed. As the bike got closer, Eliza could see that Kennedy was clutching something in his hand. A piece of fabric, it looked like a banner or maybe a flag.

As Eliza stared at Kennedy through the camera lens, it looked for an instant as if he turned the bike's wheel to his right, intent on climbing up a vacant lot and escaping into the chaparral above the neighborhood. But then he corrected his course and homed in on Eliza.

She stood squarely in the road, watching Kennedy as he pedaled closer. Then the pieces clicked, and she recognized the blue-and-green cloth entwined in his fist. It was a silk scarf, and it was Martina's. Eliza had seen her cousin wear it a few times.

The bike's tires screeched to a stop a few feet in front of her. Sweaty and red-faced, Kennedy jumped off and threw the bike to the street. He still had the scarf in his right hand, and with his left, he grabbed for the elongated camera lens. The camera strap was around Eliza's neck. She held tightly to the camera's body and turned away from him.

"It doesn't matter!" Eliza yelled. "The photos go straight to the cloud. You can't undo it. Breaking my camera won't change anything. Just stop!"

Maybe it was Eliza's tone, as if she were yelling at an unruly child, but at that moment, Kennedy understood he was beaten. With a free hand, Eliza reached for Martina's scarf. Kennedy continued to grasp the other end of the silk, and they both folded to their knees. She untangled the strap from around her neck and set the heavy camera down on the street away from Kennedy's immediate grasp. Sobbing and breathing unevenly, he crouched over, his head close to his knees with Eliza at his side, her hand clutching his shoulder, as if to anchor him. At that point, Byron and then Gil reached them, both panting from the half-block run.

At the same time, Jessica pulled up just behind where Eliza and Kennedy sat in the road. She jumped out of the police vehicle, weapon raised. By this point Byron had his large hands firmly behind Kennedy's head while Gil gently unfolded the fingers entwined in the silk. With the scarf in police custody, Byron pulled Kennedy's arms back and secured the handcuffs.

"Kennedy Thompson. You're under arrest for the murder of Martina Noto," Byron said, calmly and clearly, and then read him his Miranda rights.

∾

Eliza arrived home the next morning. She called David after they apprehended Kennedy, and he had agreed to keep Lucas for the night. She'd spent hours at SVPD headquarters, where she'd given a statement and handed over her camera's sim card as evidence. Roberto and Laura had also been there to confirm that the scarf in Kennedy's possession had been their daughter's. They still needed Jeanne Voisin to verify that Martina had worn it to Carter House that day, but that wouldn't be a problem.

Vanessa Delaware was outside the police station at 10 p.m. when Eliza finally emerged. The reporter had pressed her for an interview, and Eliza felt obligated to say a few words. Eliza was convinced that Vanessa's piece on Martina, which presented her cousin as a fully-drawn young adult, had made the story more real and kept the pressure on the police to apprehend someone. Eliza was grateful for that.

Eventually, they had all gone back to Francesca's house to unwind. Her mother had produced a bottle of brandy to calm everyone's nerves. As they raised a toast to Martina, Francesca brought Roberto and Laura up to speed on her latest project, the launch of the Martina Noto Memorial Scholarship for Excellence in Computer Science at Wexford College. In the past week, Francesca had not only secured approval for the scholarship at Wexford, she had also reached out to the University of Bologna, where Martina was simultaneously enrolled during her year abroad. Francesca was in touch with administrators on the Bologna campus about establishing a second scholarship there.

Laura and Roberta couldn't find words to express their thanks to both Eliza and Francesca. And that was fine with them because nothing needed to be said.

After two shots of the strong brandy, coupled with the excitement of the day, Eliza had dropped off to sleep on the sofa in Francesca's living room. She'd gone home to shower around 8 a.m. and now stood in her kitchen with an espresso in hand. She grabbed her ringing phone. It was Byron.

"Did I thank you yesterday?" he said.

"Yes, multiple times," she replied. "What's up?"

"I wanted to let you know that Kennedy made a full confession this morning. He took responsibility for the attack on Li-Ann too."

"Why?" Eliza asked. "What did Li-Ann do to him?"

"I shouldn't share this information, but you earned the right to know. Kennedy learned that Chelsea Miller was involved in some kind of cyberbullying related to Martina. He had also somehow figured out that Chelsea and her friends had a falling out over it. After things with Martina had spiraled out of control at Carter House, and he left her dead in the practice room, Kennedy needed to deflect attention away from himself. He was obsessed with putting the blame on someone else. He zeroed in on Chelsea as someone who hated Martina, and who could plausibly want to hurt her. His plan was for us to think Chelsea had killed Martina at Carter House and then attacked Li-Ann to silence her.

"Sounds like Kennedy was getting desperate," Eliza said. "How is Li-Ann doing?"

"Better. We got a message from her family that she is out of the coma. She still has a long recovery ahead. It's not good when someone hits you on the head with a garden trowel."

"Was that the weapon?" Eliza asked. "A little shovel for planting flowers?"

"Yep. Kennedy wiped it clean and put it back in the tool shed at his house. It was hiding in plain sight."

"Was Kennedy always kind of off? Or did he decline after he lost his mom?"

"I don't know," Byron said. "For what it's worth, Eliza, I don't think he intended to hurt Martina. He wanted to be her boyfriend. Except when he approached her in Carter House, she wasn't having it. He told us that he sat next to her on the piano bench and tried to hug her or grab her breast or both, and she pushed him away. They struggled, and she fell and hit her head on the stone foundation in that room, which caused the blunt force trauma. Then he panicked when he saw she was non-responsive."

"What about DNA? Didn't you find his DNA on her?"

"That was a problem. She was in a public space where students touched everything—the piano, the keys, the bench, and all the rest. Maybe now forensics can go back and look more closely for Kennedy's DNA. But I doubt that will happen, since he's confessed. By the way, we did not find any of Levi's DNA, just to put that theory to rest."

"I knew Levi wasn't the guy," she said. "What did Kennedy do after it happened? I mean how did he get out of Carter House?"

"First he opened the window in the room Martina was in, but then he decided not to go out that way. I'm not sure why. Maybe he saw people hanging out near there, or he was worried about leaving footprints in the dirt. So, he grabbed her backpack and hid for a bit in another vacant practice room, where he had a minute to think. Then he slipped out of the window in *that* room at the back of the building. After that, he jumped on his bike and rode down Whitmore Road where your friends at the Snack & Go picked him up on CCTV at 10:34 a.m."

"I don't understand. Why take the backpack? And what about the scarf?" Eliza asked, still missing pieces.

"He knew a theft ring was operating on campus. Kennedy was investigating it. If Martina's backpack was stolen a second time, Kennedy figured it would look like someone brazenly walked into her practice room to grab her stuff while she sat at the piano. Once your cousin's head hit that stone foundation, Kennedy was in a panic and casting about for options. It was only later that he got the idea to frame Chelsea."

"Okay, but what about the scarf?"

"It was in the backpack. She must have worn it into Carter House that morning and then stuffed it into the backpack when she sat down to practice. He didn't discover it until later. He kept it as a remembrance. It was in a drawer in the laundry room at his house, which is why he went nuts when he figured we might find it in the search."

"That souvenir sealed the deal against him," Eliza said. "Thank God he was sentimental."

"Okay, a question for you, Eliza. When Kennedy was heading toward you full speed on his bike, you never flinched. I expected you to turn and run, but you stood there. Explain that to me."

"Ya know, I'm not sure how to explain it. Instinct took over. I was so focused on getting evidence against him that I wasn't thinking he could hurt me. I wanted to take him down. Maybe it was stupid and I should have been scared, but I wasn't. Besides, you and Gil were only a short distance away. How much damage could he have done?"

"Well, your idea to shoot photos of him was a big help. The camera drew Kennedy toward you and stopped him from fleeing into the hills. We would have captured him sooner or later, but everyone was relieved that nobody got hurt that day. Gil was so worried that Kennedy would end up dead. He's very glad that didn't happen."

"I just acted... or reacted," Eliza said. "There wasn't any intention behind it. Maybe my camera created a false sense of protection or distance. I don't know for sure."

"Let me know if you want a job as a cop," Byron said. "The department's hiring."

"Ohhh. That would be a big change for me," Eliza said. "For now, I'll do my own thing."

"It never hurts to ask. You'd make a good detective, Eliza Fox. And we know I'm not easily impressed," Byron said, ending the call.

Eliza knew she'd done well. Laura and Roberto were relieved and could rest now that Kennedy was in custody. That's what mattered most.

She assessed her own well-being. Although she was sleep-deprived, she felt lighter, unburdened after the pressures of the last two weeks. Tomorrow she'd go back to her regular job, and she and Lucas would return to their routine. She was ready for normality—

with an extra focus on fun, like the Fourth of July trip she'd promised him to see the tidepools. Hopefully, Francesca would join them.

Lucas was due home shortly, and Eliza was eager to wrap him in a big hug. She set about making waffles, her son's favorite. "*Sì, la famiglia è tutto*," she said, turning up the music on her phone. She wanted the house to have good smells and happy sounds when her boy arrived.

EPILOGUE

December 12

*E*liza, Lucas, and Francesca had settled into their seats and were waiting for the plane to take off. It was a long flight to Rome, and Eliza hoped that Lucas would calm down enough that he'd sleep through most of it.

Roberto and Laura had returned home about a week after the police had wrapped up their case. The coroner finally released Martina's body, and they'd carried her ashes with them back to Rome. Now six months later, they were all anxious to see one another. Roberto and Laura had become an extra set of grandparents to Lucas, and Eliza was so grateful for that connection. She was also looking forward to being in Rome for Christmas. She wanted Lucas to see the larger world, even though he was only a kid.

Sometime that summer, Eliza and Francesca had decided to be with Roberto and Laura for their first Christmas without their daughter, so they started making plans for this trip months earlier. They would attend Christmas mass at the neighborhood church near where the Notos lived and visit with other cousins and family friends. Eliza also hoped to sneak off to Florence for a few days of alone time to visit the museums and do some shopping.

It had been a rough year, but she was optimistic that the next year would be better. She was ready to move on from Fowler & Haverford. She'd worked long enough as a paralegal. She liked research and investigative work, but the firm only used her in that role sporadically.

She was thinking of her options: Start her own PI practice? Take a different investigator job? Apply to law school? She might even go work for SVPD. There were lots of possibilities.

Although investigating Martina's case had been emotionally taxing since it involved her family, Eliza was also energized by it. In the end, she was proud of herself for chasing leads and thinking of creative ways to find information. She had uncovered important evidence the police never would have found. She had a knack for investigative work, and she pictured where her career might take her.

With Lucas watching cartoons on one side of her, and her mother reading a book on the other, Eliza got more comfortable in her seat and scrolled through the movie offerings. She smiled at herself when she settled on an international spy thriller. *There's no harm in dreaming big,* she thought, ready to get lost in the action and intrigue.

ACKNOWLEDGEMENTS

Books don't write themselves. Authors depend on others to listen, to read, to critique, and to encourage.

My husband Dennis allowed me the time and space to write, which was a true gift. My mother, Mary Lou Watkins, a poet and life-long reader, reviewed early drafts and encouraged me when I was befuddled. My fellow author Nancy Boyarsky, a mentor and friend for decades, provided inspiration and invaluable advice that helped this story get lift.

Finally, many thanks to the family and friends who read the manuscript and provided feedback. Your careful edits and thoughtful comments were much appreciated.

To the team at Torchflame Books, it's a pleasure to work with you. Thank you!

ABOUT THE AUTHOR

Cathleen Watkins is the author of the debut mystery, Deadly Quiet, the first book in the Eliza Fox Files mystery series.

Like the protagonist she created, Cathleen is a licensed private investigator in California. In this career, she has talked with countless people about their experiences and perspectives. Cathleen has been involved with both criminal and civil cases, focusing on matters stemming from the #metoo movement, on civil rights claims, and on student cases involving sexual assault. She has mentored new investigators and developed training programs on conducting interviews and finding evidence.

Cathleen has always enjoyed writing and editing, and her experiences as an investigator have helped to shape her voice as a writer. Blending her career with her creative side, she has worked to create characters and settings that feel genuine.

After studying journalism in college, Cathleen worked as an editor before becoming a P.I. Her other interests include photography and cooking. Ask her about the ribbons she won at the Los Angeles County Fair for her homemade jams.

Cathleen grew up in Los Angeles and continues to live in Southern California with her husband, Dennis, and their Cardigan Welsh Corgi, Henry. Their older son and daughter-in-law, and their younger son all live nearby.

For more information about Cathleen, visit her website at:
www.cathleenwatkins.com